SCHOOL SPIRIT

Books by Tom McHale

PRINCIPATO
FARRAGAN'S RETREAT
ALINSKY'S DIAMOND
SCHOOL SPIRIT

SCHOOL SPIRIT

a novel by

TOM McHALE

DOUBLEDAY & COMPANY, INC., GARDEN CITY, NEW YORK
1976

The author gratefully acknowledges the aid
of the John Simon Guggenheim Foundation during
the writing of this novel.

DESIGNED BY LAURENCE ALEXANDER

ISBN: 0-385-01466-x
Library of Congress Catalog Card Number: 75-14830
Copyright © 1976 by Tom McHale

To Sara the Riveter

CONTENTS

PART I The Case for Sterling Lloyd   1

CHAPTER 1 Rookie in Barstow   3
CHAPTER 2 To the Eagle's Nest   15
CHAPTER 3 Call Me Azrael   33
CHAPTER 4 At the Center of the Nation   51
CHAPTER 5 An Astonishing Paternity   71
CHAPTER 6 Chez Vauchon   85
CHAPTER 7 The Drunkard of Notre Dame   105
CHAPTER 8 A Little Town in New Jersey   125
CHAPTER 9 More of the Enemy   147
CHAPTER 10 Some Allies   157
CHAPTER 11 Feast of Lupercal   Feast of Mars   169
CHAPTER 12 Alma Mater   181
CHAPTER 13 Unfortunate Rejection   201
CHAPTER 14 Sterling Lloyd's Mother and the Sun
            Queen   211
CHAPTER 15 The Killington Affair   223
CHAPTER 16 Limbo   241
CHAPTER 17 The Trial   255
CHAPTER 18 The Punishment   267

PART II Sterling Lloyd's Justice   273

CHAPTER 19 First Crack in the Wall   275
CHAPTER 20 Second Crack in the Wall   283
CHAPTER 21 All Fall Down   293

SCHOOL SPIRIT

SCHOOLCRAFT

PART I

THE CASE FOR
STERLING LLOYD

CHAPTER 1

Rookie in Barstow

When they were finished with burying his wife, Magruder was driven home from the cemetery by his neighbor Hobbs.

"It's a blessing she's gone, Egil," Hobbs told him as they pulled into the Desert Flower Mobile Home Park. "She suffered terrible this last year with the asthma. It pained me to see her trying so to get a breath."

"Yes, it was a blessing, Albert," Magruder answered, thinking there was really nothing else to say, and that he had heard the word "blessing" too many times already in the three days since Florence had died. They pulled up before Magruder's trailer and both men were silent for a long moment, staring at the green swath of Magruder's well-tended grass, the row of cactus plants that scratched against the trailer's cinder-block foundation in the gusts of wind that blew westward and chill in late November out of the Mohave.

"I think I'll transplant some of the cactus to her grave before I leave," Magruder spoke after a time. "She loved the cactus flowers when they first bloomed in spring."

"Are you sure you have to leave, Egil?" Hobbs begged. "You've been here four years now in Barstow. You've got good friends here at Desert Flower. You could join the club after your mourning is done and raise a little hell with the rest of us. She'd want you to, Egil. Florence would want you to after all the years you took such good care of her. Just next week me and the gang are going into L.A. for a couple of days. . . ."

Magruder smiled, acknowledging the invitation, wondering at the same time how long after his wife's dying it would take to become as lonely as his fellow widower Hobbs. Hobbs, the orgy of his late-night crying put behind him, had blossomed forth into a dude, donned a jet-black wig to cover the near complete baldness of his sixty-fifth year, sported flashy mod jackets and flare bottom pants and roared up and down the desert highways in the lime-green Chrysler convertible with a built-in custom bar. He owned forty pairs of varicolored shoes (too pointed-looking for Magruder's taste) that he changed as often as five times a day, and tooled about Desert Flower in a blasting, full stereo-equipped, electric golf cart seeking members for the club he himself had founded.

The club, a gaggle of Desert Flower singles—widows, widowers and the divorced—traveled together like a wolf pack, crossing over into Nevada to pump quarters into the one-arm bandits in Las Vegas for a weekend, going into Los Angeles to see the films that never made it out to Barstow, or to sample the hot foods of Mexican restaurants that always gave Magruder a heartburn that refused to subside for days. They went to dances and played shuffleboard and bingo in a hall in downtown Barstow, held cookouts on the identical slivers of turf before each others' trailers, played the old card games—rummy and casino—and traveled regularly to a nudist camp near San Bernardino in the warmer months. Magruder, responding to the promptings of Florence, aflame with curiosity but too inhibited to attend herself, had gone along with them once, sat naked and wheezing with embarrassed laughter at the sight of Hobbs and Ethel Sandstone, another Desert Flower regular, who had danced together naked for hours on the volley ball court, lewdly suggesting the function of organs that Magruder surmised were years past being inspired again.

Returning home, he had told Florence that mass nudity, if anything, was boring, and that people of Hobbs's age ought to know well enough when to call it a day. . . .

"What do you say, Egil? Want to go along with us?" Hobbs asked again, breaking into his recall.

"Thank you no, Albert, but I've got a bit of unfinished business to take care of back East. I'd better attend to it pretty soon. In the next couple of days, as a matter of fact."

"Will you come back to Desert Flower, Egil, when your business is finished?"

"No, Albert, I don't think so. Thought I'd like to try Florida for a bit. I never did like this desert except that it was easier on Florence's asthma condition."

"Well, don't leave without saying good-by, Egil."

Magruder patted Hobbs's arm as he left the car. "Don't worry. I'll make the rounds and see everyone before I go."

Hobbs drove off up the small incline of a hill toward his trailer and Magruder went inside his own, picked up a Bourbon bottle and a glass, covered his shoulders with a woolen blanket, and came outside again to sit in a deck chair in the weak sunlight. He poured himself half a glass of the liquid and sipped at it, watching two lizards who scampered along the rock border of the lawn that Magruder had four years before painted white if for no other reason that every other rock border in Desert Flower was the same color.

What caprice of God had sent him here to bury Florence? he asked, his eyes traveling the forest of TV antennas and aluminum flag poles that reached skyward above the flat expanse of trailer roofs.

From upstate New York, where people had roots and it seemed to him at least one near or distant relative locked away in the madhouse, to this dry furnace of a place that gathered in transients from everywhere. Hobbs was from Arkansas, his lady friend Mrs. Sandstone from Washington state. Years before when he and Florence had lived in Troy beside the upper Hudson and Magruder was football coach at St. Anselm's School for Boys, he had never known a person from Arkansas. Never cared if he met one, either. But his life had been uprooted (cruelly, Magruder thought), and carted off to Barstow by Florence, her asthma, and her doctor, forced to leave behind the comfortable old Victorian pile they had lived in for years near the St. Anselm campus, a sprawling house with spreading lawns and winter fir trees, summer weeping willows, and the three cavorting little colored jockeys Florence had bought at an antique shop in Saratoga Springs that had played in their flower beds for perhaps twenty years until, two years before Magruder's retirement, the school's first hired black faculty member had protested their existence at a party on Magruder's lawn, and Magruder, then sixty-two and confused at the apparent giving of unintended insult, had been compelled by the headmaster to remove them.

Arriving in Barstow, Magruder had actually climbed into his car on the second day, gone off to the desert away from Florence and wept. Neon and dust, the brittle rattle of undernourished palms, the sight of junk cars that refused to disintegrate, the neat rows of look-alike trailers, the nagging sense of impermanence about the whole place had undermined his spirits, demoralized him in a way he had not thought possible.

They had taken a trailer through the enticement of an ebulliantly friendly realtor who did not recognize them the next time he encountered them after the closing date of the sale. Surprisingly, to Magruder's bafflement, Florence loved the long tin tube, the ease of cleaning it, the way the plumbing and almost new appliances worked effortlessly after the tentativeness of everything in their Troy house.

Then they settled in in earnest to wait for Florence's dying. Disjointed, he had been at first apprehensive of their new neighbors, their strange accents and the possibility of their automatic disapproval. He had lived cautiously among them, testing for the existence of other Catholics like themselves with whom he would feel more comfortable, and tried at the same time to imitate the coda of the place. He used his apportioned share of water on the tiny lawn and bought two plaster flamingos and a bird bath for its center not unlike everyone else's. Back home in Troy they had hung the American flag stripes downward from two hooks on the front porch for holidays. In Barstow he purchased an aluminum pole, put it up with Hobbs, then ran up the flag, flying it from dawn to dusk of every day, taking it down in the selfsame ritualistic way as his neighbors greeted the darkness: the creak of pulleys, the slap of rope against the aluminum shaft. The flag folded, put away safely for the night, it was time for the universal hour of cocktails at Desert Flower Mobile Home Park, where Magruder learned to like Bourbon whiskey.

In the beginning Florence's asthma grew better. She seemed to thrive in Barstow when Magruder thought instead of languishing. Slack with nothing to do, he threw himself into organizing a football team in conjunction with a young priest, also a rookie in Barstow. The team, composed mostly of Chicano kids, the sons of migrant farm workers, ebbed and flowed in strength like the pulsing of tides with the seasons of planting and harvest in far-off northern California or Idaho, leaving Magruder at times with barely a first string so that games were frequently forfeited, and at the end of the first season they were disqualified from the league they had sought so avidly to join.

After that Magruder had taken ill, lain in bed with a nameless disease that the doctor, a wry desiccated man only a few years younger than Magruder, called "a withdrawal from a life of workoholism. . . ."

The new life, at the doctor's suggestion, began in the Barstow public library. Magruder spent hours of the air-conditioned day and evening there, his bowels whirling with the unaccustomed pleasure, reading his way through a list of titles the young priest had provided: surveys of literature that leapt conveniently across twenty centuries, European and American novels, Shakespeare and the Romantics. He wondered to himself and out loud to Florence how he had gotten through sixty-four years of a life on the barely recalled forced readings of his college days, followed by almost forty years of subscription to the *Reader's Digest* and the *National Geographic*. Ever tense, ever full of pre-game adrenaline even when there was no game, he had not been able to wait out the pages of a book. Even a newspaper was too long, except for the sports pages that he had devoured ravenously, battening his soul on the intense rivalries of local high schools and private schools, his inner world more turbulent than that of the Medici with alternate hatings and gloatings that now seemed very far away and silly besides.

Then he took a giant step: He agreed to begin reading moral philosophy at the behest of the young priest who was equally starved and lonely in Barstow. The head librarian, delighted, and keeper of a rarely assaulted purchase fund, readily ordered the books out of Los Angeles, joining Magruder and the priest evenings for discussion in the cleric's house over flaming snorts of tequila and quarts of cooling Mexican beer.

But in time, alas, the cant of the moralists brought Magruder grudgingly back to the central problem of his life that he had sublimated for ages now, buried beneath the passage of years and the notion of futility because he had no clear idea how to solve the quandary. In their third year in Barstow he had opened the coffin of the thing with Florence: In retrospect it seemed her real dying began there.

"Oh, Egil," she begged, her voice gasping, "can't you leave it alone? Just let it die and we'll have a little peace in our old age. Keep reading and don't think so much. Those boys are grown men by now. They have wives and families. If you were going to do something you should have done it way back then. It's pointless now."

But Magruder was plunged into the power swell of all the literature he had devoured in Barstow: "Would Emile Zola or Sherwood Anderson have left it alone, Florence? Would that Russian fellow who wrote *Cancer Ward* have left it alone? What about Harriet Beecher Stowe? Look at the effect *Uncle Tom's Cabin* had on this country. . . ."

She had not answered, only fell by degrees back into the decline Magruder had recovered from, watching him tack up the wall map of the United States, set the marker flags in place for the ones he was certain of, telephone back to the alumni office at St. Anselm's for news of the ones he was not certain of, until he knew where they all were and there were eleven flags on the map. Then he contacted local information and got all their telephone numbers, agreeably surprised that not one of them, even McFadden, who was reputedly a millionaire, or Vauchon, who had been born one, had an unlisted number.

In the week before she died, Florence had struggled out of bed, drawn a line with one emaciated finger across the six flags that clustered somewhat proportionately about interstates 15 and 80 that traveled east from California to New Jersey and said simply, "When you go back to close the case, Egil, here's the easiest way to go."

"Yes," he agreed with her.

In five days she was gone. Three days after that she was to be buried by the young priest in the local Catholic cemetery. Magruder chose a Spanish-style grave marker—the traditional mission belfry with a cross set in the bell tower—and gave the cemetery attendant extra money to seed the plot and tend it well. Then he made arrangements with the priest for his own burial beside Florence. He wrote his sister in Queens, New York, entrusting her with the responsibility of shipping his body to Barstow.

Now, the funeral done and sitting before the trailer, he considered the remaining things to do before he left to close the case, as Florence had called it. The car was gassed and readied, his traveler's checks obtained; he would call the poorly memoried realtor and instruct him to sell the trailer for the best possible price and forward the money to Queens. He had packed his bags that morning.

He went inside, phoned the realtor, then California Bell and the utility company. He thought too of phoning the priest and the librarian to say good-by, but instead penned each of them a short note of thanks and gave a forwarding address.

Then he sat down resolutely before the phone to begin the costly toll calls to inform them that he was about to set out eastward to Red Bank, New Jersey, at dawn on the morrow. He phoned the nearest of them first, McFadden, who presided over a real estate and bail-bond empire 150 miles away in Las Vegas. McFadden, finally reached through what seemed to Magruder an army of scrutinizing receptionists, came on exuberant and playful, no less a

11

child than he had ever been for being forty years of age: "Coachie! Coachie! Where the hell are you? In Vegas?"

"No, I'm in Barstow, Martin. Mrs. Magruder was buried this afternoon. I'll be in Las Vegas tomorrow in the late afternoon if all goes well. I'd like to stay over with you and the wife, if possible."

"Of course, coachie. Of course. I'm so sorry about Mrs. Magruder, coach."

"It was a blessing, Martin. Her asthma was an agony for her. I wonder, Martin, if I might ask you to have a couple of cans of gas available for me. With this energy crisis, I'd hate to run dry out in the desert somewhere."

"No problem, coach. I just took over a hotel supply outfit. We've got loads of gas down there for the trucks. How long can you stay? A week? Two weeks maybe?"

"Just a night, Martin. I'm heading out for Provo, Utah, the next morning."

"That's where Jack Welsh lives . . ." McFadden's voice was reflective when he said it. There was a pause and Magruder heard a long sigh, then McFadden came back, his tone apprehensive now: "Coach, where are you on your way to? I mean what's your final destination?"

"Red Bank, New Jersey, Martin."

"Oh, coach, for Christ's sake, it's been twenty-three years!"

"It's time, Martin."

"Coach, those three guys are married and have children. Have a heart."

"We made a pact, Martin. We swore on it, remember?"

"Coachie, things change. We were teen-agers then. Reality intervenes, you know, families, trying to keep it all together and make a living. I mean, God Almighty, Vincent Adnizzio's daughter is being married there in Jersey next Saturday. Carlotta and I just sent a present to her. You're liable to show up to collect that debt on the wedding day. We agreed on twenty years, coach. Twenty-three have passed. When we didn't hear anything back in '70, we thought the thing was a dead duck."

"I was sick then, Martin. I'm a well man now, my mind is alert and I have one thing left in life to do."

"Coachie, your own wife, Mrs. Magruder, she didn't want you to do it either. She told me that herself at one of the reunions."

"It's time, Martin. I'll hang up now and see you in the evening tomorrow with luck."

"Ah, coach . . . coach, think what you're doing. Come and visit us, but let sleeping dogs lie, coach."

"In the evening tomorrow, Martin."

Magruder softly replaced the receiver in its cradle. He decided not to waste his money phoning the others: With McFadden and wife working two lines, they would all know within the hour he was coming their way.

CHAPTER 2

To the Eagle's Nest

Magruder woke late the next morning, his head hurting dully from the Bourbon he had drunk, to find the phone and electricity already disconnected. He dressed quickly, loaded his bags into the Buick, locked the trailer and left Desert Flower, neglecting to say good-by to Hobbs, Mrs. Sandstone and the gang. He drove first to the cemetery, to the fresh crumbly earth of Florence's grave, where he transplanted some of the cactus he had dug up from around the trailer's foundation.

In time he left the cemetery, curiously devoid of any feeling about Florence, and instead found himself easily imagining what had transpired the night before after his call to McFadden: abject terror, reasoned logic, threats and vilification racing every which way along the wires. They kept in touch with each other, Magruder knew, the surviving first stringers of St. Anselm's rock-bottom 1950 football team, dead, murdered Sterling Lloyd Kasprzak the uncanny glue that held them all together. Kasprzak was the recurring nightmare, a pox of conscience that returned eternally to haunt them, refusing to leave, infesting their minds with a dread speculation as to when Magruder, the agent of retribution for the crime against

Kasprzak might explode a bomb in the midst of their adult lives. In 1970, the year the reckoning was actually due, the year that Magruder was sick unto death with depression, he took some small sustaining consolation in the notion that the remaining nine were sweating it out the entire 365 days. And beyond that: For on the last day, on New Year's Eve, when they had actually gathered in New Jersey at Adnizzio's home to celebrate a kind of bacchanalia of triumph, and then, two minutes into 1971, they called him, roaring drunk, to wish him a happy new year, Magruder had wordlessly returned the phone to its cradle, letting them know by his accusing silence that their debt was not yet paid.

But now it was time. Nosing the Buick eastward through glittering Barstow toward the interstate highway, he half consciously flipped down the sun visor as he had done so many times in the past whether it was needed or not to confront the sad, bloated face of Sterling Lloyd Kasprzak. His black-bordered Mass card, given out by his mother on the day of his funeral in 1950, was taped to the visor between the car registration, a St. Christopher medal and Florence's plastic image of the anguished Virgin of Coahuila, who wept tears of blood.

Beneath the picture was printed *S. L. Kasprzak, 1933–1950 Requiescat in Pace.* But alas, he did not rest in peace, or Magruder would not let him: He was never able to tell the difference. Satiated at the sight of dead Kasprzak, he turned the visor upward again: Christ, how ugly he had been, Magruder thought involuntarily, as he did each time he lowered the visor.

He eased the Buick onto the interstate that sliced

through the desert, keeping fifty miles an hour, glad for the ponderous weight of the old car that hardly budged in the air stream of trucks roaring past.

In Las Vegas, four hours later, the sun had begun to set in a brilliant band behind Magruder. The neon had all come on, and Magruder, battling distractions that advertised Elvis Presley and Andy Williams, followed McFadden's instructions to a downtown office building, parked the car in front and informed the doorman he was expected by McFadden.

Minutes later the elevator doors opened and Martin McFadden, who, despite his fanatic absorption with running his empire, had doubtless been watching from above for his arrival, raced the length of the chrome-walled building at Magruder. Two of McFadden's goons, whom McFadden called "associates," followed behind.

"Coachie! Coachie! Jesus, coachie, you look good!"

McFadden was a kisser and Magruder went limp with the resignation that McFadden, a huge and powerful man, would lift him up, dangle him about and plant a big wet kiss on his forehead. He did, swinging Magruder about twice in a dizzying circle, Magruder overwhelmed in the smells of McFadden's colognes before he came to rest again.

"Anything he wants! Give him anything he wants!" he ordered the two associates. "Vegas belongs to coachie for as long as he stays!"

"I'm leaving in the morning, Martin," Magruder told him. "That is, if you'll be so kind as to supply that gas."

"A thousand gallons if you need it, coachie. But give it a few days. You haven't been to Vegas in ages."

"Tomorrow, Martin," Magruder said stonily.

"OK, coachie, whatever you say. You're the boss," McFadden said meekly. "Come on, coachie, we'll go to the apartment in my car. Take coachie's car and put it in the garage downstairs," he told the two associates.

Outside the building, McFadden stopped suddenly at the sight of the old Buick: "Coach, you're going to cross the country in that? That car has to be twenty years old."

"Eighteen to be exact, Martin. It's a '55, but it's in fine shape."

"Coach, I just won a two-year-old Caddy in a poker game about a week ago. It's yours if you want it. Air conditioning, the whole megillah. It's got less than ten thousand miles on it."

"Thank you, no, Martin, it won't be necessary. My car and I understand each other very well."

"You must get tired driving that thing, coachie."

"It's not so bad. Besides, today I picked up a young man on his way to Boulder City, and he drove quite a distance while I napped. I'll pick up others, I suppose."

"Who was he, coach? One of those hippie kids?"

"I guess so, Martin. He had long hair and wore earrings."

"I wouldn't pick up any more of that riff raff, coach. I wouldn't fall asleep either, if I did. We try to keep them the hell out of Vegas. Spoils the image of the town for the tourists, if you know what I mean."

"Yes," Magruder assured him. Four years of living in a house trailer with pink flamingos strutting on the front lawns had taken the edge off Magruder's snobbery and he could not defend castigating McFadden as vehemently as he wished. But, Lord, the one-time St. Anselm's right tackle was an ass. In McFadden's Lincoln, with a bar in the rear like Hobbs's convertible, they glided through the look-alike files of expensive cars, past the blaring neon of more hotels and casinos that McFadden and his minions kept clean of longhairs. They halted for a light. McFadden ogled two porcelain-looking young women with identically tinted hair as they passed before the car.

"Carlotta's really been looking forward to your coming, coachie," McFadden said. "She's been working all day on her stuffed lobster. Had them flown in fresh from Maine just this morning."

"I'll enjoy seeing Carlotta, Martin," Magruder said. They both knew full well that Carlotta McFadden despised him: A jealous woman, Mexican-born and rich, she had taken McFadden, a dumb Mick from the Bronx whose politician father had stolen enough to put him through expensive St. Anselm's, and molded his clay into McFadden of Las Vegas. She hated Magruder's hold upon her husband. Also she cooked nothing: A secret Chinaman lived in their penthouse kitchen, slaved away all day at his chopping and spicing, served up feasts that Carlotta passed off as her own, even to the coy, willing dispensing of her recipes once she had coerced them from the Chinaman, authenticating them as pure Carlotta by presenting them part in English and part in Spanish. Among outsiders, only Magruder knew her secret, he decided. Once, after dinner, when he could stand them no longer, he left the penthouse and went for relief to the sleeziest bar he could find. There the Chinaman swilled beer, intending to get falling down drunk, and cursed the

19

name of Carlotta McFadden and her progeny to all eternity.

They rode up in the elevator of the building McFadden owned to the unmarked penthouse. There the door opened into a fortress alcove with a real sheet-steel door. McFadden sounded the door buzzer twice and a black maid opened an inner door, then the outer steel door and admitted them to Carlotta's bastion against Las Vegas.

The maid took their coats and exchanged pleasantries with Magruder, then disappeared abruptly at the sudden appearance of Carlotta. Magruder was surprised at her early entrance. Usually she lingered at her dressing table, while McFadden plied their guests with drinks, then swept in in a vivacious, unexpected surge that usually caused someone to spill a drink. Forewarned, she clearly had the mission to New Jersey on her mind.

"Coach Magruder, how wonderful to see you."

She came up to him, kissing his cheek, and Magruder smiled inanely in spite of himself. It came to him on the instant that he loved parts of Carlotta if such a thing were possible: her eyes, the dark sleekness of her hair that she wore always tied back, never fluffed or sprayed like so many other women in California and Nevada. Her accent was sultry and perfect like that of Katie Jurado, whom Magruder had seen often in his fantasies when the thrill of Florence had died. Among life's ironies, this one indeed was hopeless: McFadden, dumbest and clumsiest first stringer of that rock-bottom year, had somehow been snared by the most beautiful wife.

"Come out onto the terrace, coach," she invited. "We'll

have a drink and see the abomination of Las Vegas glowing at our feet before it becomes too chill."

They passed along the dimly lit hallway from the entry toward the terrace, where the glow of the city beneath them rose upward. Carlotta had redecorated the passage since Magruder had last been there. Two altarpieces, a wormwood saint and a jeweled monstrance on a marble pedestal lit by a hidden spotlight, graced their way. McFadden's duplex apartment was a Spanish treasure house. McFadden, who may never have heard of the artist before Carlotta assessed his dumbness and found him perfect, owned a genuine Goya ink sketch. According to the story, Carlotta's father, old Gomez-Acerbo, First Secretary at the Mexican Embassy in Madrid during the thirties, had taken advantage of the confusion of the Civil War to reverse the historic direction of the treasure ships: he had ripped off everything the loyalists had not nailed down, returned it to his house or the vaults and warehouses of his brothers, the bankers and merchants in Guadalajara. One version of the tale had it that Carlotta's father was assassinated by leftists and that she fled to the United States with a tenth of the loot to invest in McFadden and Las Vegas.

But there were variations that Magruder loved to hear. Alternatives to the simple fact that she had had the stuff shipped out of Mexico and into the United States by cargo boat via the port of San Diego. Most of them were elaborate lies that usually begot her a kind of punishment for the original crime of her father. When she became the other Carlotta, drunk on margaritas and confessional, she often told of squadrons of creaky old booty-filled Dakotas sneaking under border radar into the States. Sometimes of a single plane, with one failed engine, flown by Carlotta herself, her feet sandaled with the rubber of discarded tires. At such times she alluded darkly to the Indian blood in her veins, her shoeless childhood, the endless diet of tamales. Then McFadden was given a chance to earn his keep; furious with embarrassment, he would beat the hell out of her. She loved it. Black and blue, trembling with a temporary humility, she actually would cook McFadden's breakfast the next morning. Magruder was sure she would earn herself a beating this night.

On the terrace, there was no chance of it growing too chill. Above them, beneath the canopy that ran about the penthouse, heater elements glowed red in the soft darkness. Magruder stood beneath one of them, warming himself, while Carlotta went to the portable bar and mixed a batch of margaritas. McFadden looked far down on the crawling traffic; the tight smile of his face told he did not think Las Vegas to be an abomination.

Carlotta handed them the margaritas, and touched glasses lightly with Magruder, speaking softly:

"I'm so sorry about Mrs. Magruder, coach."

"As I told Martin, Carlotta, it was a blessing God took her. She suffered badly this last year."

"You buried her in Barstow, am I right, coach?"

"Yes, Carlotta. She liked the desert very much."

"It's too bad you don't like it as much, coach, then you'd have the good sense not to be heading East in your sixty-eighth year to fulfill that stupid vow a bunch of teen-agers running around in jockstraps made to their coach more than twenty years ago."

She was already in gear, early and unexpected. For support, Magruder backed uneasily into the wall behind him.

"It wasn't a stupid vow. A young man was murdered, Carlotta. His murderers have never been brought to justice."

"I've got all the information on it, coach. We wives have been talking to each other about it for years. This thing is going to backfire on you. It wasn't premeditated murder. At best it was involuntary manslaughter. Twenty-three years later it isn't going to wash." She said this harshly, narrowing her dark eyes, draining the margarita in a single gulp. She went back to the bar for another.

"Carlotta, I don't want you to drink too much," McFadden told her.

"Shut up, stupid. Let me worry about how much I can drink." She came out from behind the bar like a she-lynx and Magruder thought for a moment she might hurl the drink in his face. But suddenly she demurred, smiling past him, and Magruder sensed with certainty that her children were there.

"Coach, you remember Manuel and Teresa?" she lilted. They came forth, dark-eyed, handsome children, well groomed and perfectly postured in an age of indiscriminate long hair and slouching.

"I remember them well," Magruder said. "Isn't it almost time for you two to begin high school?"

"Next year, coach," Manuel answered, shaking hands.

"Manuel is going to Choate," Carlotta said after a moment.

23

"You shouldn't tell people that, Carlotta," McFadden interrupted. "He might not get in."

"He'll get in," Carlotta said flatly.

"And you, Teresa?" Magruder asked. "Will you go to a New England school also?"

"Teresa will not be going to school in America. She's already enrolled in convent school in Salamanca, in Spain."

"Ah, Salamanca . . ." Magruder returned, smiling at Teresa in what he hoped passed for approval. Actually he pitied her, anticipating the endpoint of Carlotta's fanaticism: Goodness, purity and the rest of it were not to be found in the American Southwest apparently and certainly not in Las Vegas. Manuel to crusty New England then, Teresa to the dictator's Spain . . .

"Kiss mother good night, dears," Carlotta begged. Her children advanced, each smothering a half of her face with kisses before they went off to eat dinner together. They did not kiss their father. Each shook a polite good-by with Magruder.

"Your children are quite fine and well mannered, Carlotta," Magruder told her, thinking to assuage her anger about Kasprzak.

"Aren't they though, coach? Martin and I have spared nothing. Just think what would happen to them if Martin were one of the desperadoes instead of the three in New Jersey. Or to me, coach. . . . Think of their wives and children. Adnizzio's daughter is being married on Saturday. . . ."

Ah: Magruder saw it now. Carlotta cared nothing about the dead Kasprzak or the guilty ones. It was the institution of the family she was defending, Carlotta's own special place where she reigned supreme over a compliant husband and adoring children. Magruder was her natural enemy. An interloper.

She wolfed down another drink. "You're doing a terrible thing, coach."

"Carlotta, I have asked you not to drink too much," McFadden said.

"And you can shut up, McFadden! How can you treat him with any respect? A stupid old widower with nothing else to do, so he decides he's the divine avenger all over again. The vow was for twenty years. It's been twenty-three already. Your claim is getting invalid, coach."

"Señora, the dinner is prepared."

"Thank you, Maria," she spoke to a Mexican woman who also wore a maid's uniform. Magruder recalled the black maid was not permitted to serve meals. "Martin, light the candles, will you? I didn't mean what I said, coach," she purred. "We Latins are so excitable."

They sat at the table on the terrace overlooking Las Vegas and the woman Maria ladled out gazpacho. McFadden poured wine, then smiled approvingly at Carlotta. "Your soup is great, Carlotta. Carlotta makes it herself, coach. It's an old family recipe."

"It is quite good," Magruder lied in turn, thinking of the bleary-eyed Chinese. "I've learned to like gazpacho since I've come to California."

"Coach . . . Carlotta is right, you know. All the years, they distort this sort of thing. Those guys are all married, they all have kids. I've talked to Matty Vauchon out in Chicago about this lots of times. You know he's a big-time lawyer for the Daley bunch, don't you? Well, he says it won't go. There isn't a county prosecutor alive would touch this thing after so many years. It's looking for trouble."

"Man's justice is frail, Martin. There's a higher ideal. What about God's own justice?"

"Fuck God's own justice!" Carlotta screeched. "He isn't down here in Las Vegas trying to keep body and soul above the poverty line. You don't know what you're in for, coach. It's you I'm thinking of. Adnizzio's family are thick as thieves. We've met them all. He's got four brothers and they all carry guns. They weren't preppies either. They were goons before the family cornered the olive oil trade and got respectable enough for St. Anselm's. They'd put you in a tub of cement and take you to sea off Asbury Park somewhere. . . ."

"You're wrong, Carlotta, Vincent Adnizzio would never permit that to happen to me. My boys would never do that to their old coach. You know them. You've met them at the reunions. I know some of them have been here to visit with you."

"I think you'd be surprised to learn that your boys aren't boys any more, coach," Carlotta said. "And I know them. They've lost much of that sweet purity that went into that silly vow years ago. Jack Welsh up in Provo smokes marijuana and is married to some hippie girl about half his age. And Carruthers at Notre Dame . . . God! He came here to dry out last year and you've never seen such a contemptible spectacle! And my children had to watch it! Oh, this is useless . . . !" She stopped briefly, searching for a means, then picked up her bowl of gaz-

26

pacho and hurled it against a wall, splattering the contents across a flung arc.

"Goddamn you, Carlotta! I'm going to beat you for that!" McFadden raged.

"Good! It's been almost a month and I'm in the mood for it tonight. Don't stay too long over coffee and have a few shots of cognac so you'll be extra nasty."

She got up abruptly and left the table, walking angrily away from the terrace. Magruder stood and began wiping at the wall with a napkin. McFadden drained his wine in one gulp and poured another.

"The hell with that, coachie. Maria can clean it up later. Why don't you finish your soup? We have that nice lobster I was telling you about."

"I don't think I'm very hungry, Martin. I had no idea Carlotta would react so strongly."

"She'll be all right in the morning, coach. I'll give her what she wants tonight."

"Be gentle, Martin. She's a beautiful woman."

"I know, coach, and I love her. That's why I won't touch her face. Don't worry about that." McFadden got up to leave. "You sure you don't want any lobster, coach?"

"Thank you, no, Martin. I'll put it off this time. I'm tired and want to rest. Carlotta will make us a big breakfast, I take it?"

"For sure. I think I'll have Maria do up the lobster anyhow and shell them. Carlotta makes a wicked lobster omelet."

"That sounds quite appetizing."

"Yes," McFadden agreed. He walked to the bar and, as

Magruder watched, disbelieving, threw down three co-gnacs in quick succession, his eyes growing distended and more wrathful-looking with each belt. Then he saluted Magruder and staggered along the hallway bouncing against the art treasures. Magruder heard a sob from Carlotta as the bedroom door was opened, then a plaintive whine: "Not my face, Martin . . . not my face . . ."

He heard the sharp crack of McFadden's artistry and the low moan of Carlotta's appreciation. The maid Maria came through the hallway, closing the doors to the terrace behind her. She smiled with embarrassment at Magruder and shrugged her shoulders. Then she went to the wall and began sponging off the gazpacho. Magruder smiled sympathetically, poured himself more wine and sat looking over Las Vegas while Maria cleared the table. In time, the beating evidently completed, she reopened the doors and turned off the lights of the terrace after Magruder assured her it was all right. He sat sipping wine, silent in the darkness.

Minutes later McFadden came down the hallway and into the living room. He dialed a long-distance number. Through an open sliding door Magruder heard him say, "He's on his way. He won't listen. Carlotta talked to him too." Then silence. "What? Are you crazy? He's the coach. No way! You handle it at your end. I've got a wife and family to think about too. Besides, I didn't lock the poor son of a bitch in the freezer. You guys did. *Ciao*, baby."

In a moment, McFadden walked onto the terrace and Magruder heard the sharp intake of his breath as McFad-den realized he was still sitting there.

"Coachie. I thought you had gone to bed. You heard me call?"

"Yes, Martin. Do you really think they'd kill me?"

"Why wouldn't they? They just asked me to do it. Carlotta wasn't kidding about that Adnizzio bunch either. Vincent may be smooth, but those brothers of his are rough. If you'd been around Vegas enough, you would know the type. Look, coach, why not cancel out and go home? Kasprzak was a dumb asshole of a kid. God knows he's probably better off dead. Where would he go in life with a puss like that?"

"Kasprzak was the saddest, loneliest boy ever to pass through St. Anselm's in all the years I was there. It broke my heart to see the way you guys treated him. He had a God-given life and a soul. He was not expendable for being less well formed or intelligent, Martin. If your children had been born distorted, would you wish them dead by way of mercy?"

"All right, coachie, you win. But be careful. If you need help, call me, OK?"

"Thank you for the consideration, Martin, but my boys would never harm me. I know that."

McFadden, despite his drunkenness, looked at Magruder pityingly, Magruder thought. He tried to change the subject. "Carlotta is feeling better I take it, Martin?"

"She's sleeping it off now."

"Manuel and Teresa are very fine children, Martin."

"Shit. They're like plastic, coach," McFadden snorted, tossing off another cognac. "All thanks to Carlotta baby. If Manuel doesn't get into Choate, it would be the best thing for him. I hope he runs off and joins the Navy or something. What the fuck was I thinking when I first ran into her?"

"I can't say, Martin."

"No, I guess you can't. She just plain overwhelmed me. There was no chance to escape. Say, coach, did you ever hit Mrs. Magruder?"

"I have never hit a woman in my life."

"You don't know what you've missed, coachie."

"You shouldn't drink any more, Martin. Training rules, you know."

"Training rules! Ah, coachie, if only there were something to be in training for again." McFadden was nearly sobbing, slapping his paunch. "I'm bored out of my ass with everything. I've got so much money I don't know what to do with it. Every day of the rest of my life looks exactly the same as the one before."

Magruder nodded quietly, patting McFadden's shoulder. His sadness became bottomless when McFadden began crying softly. Finally, Magruder stood up, said good night quietly, while McFadden wept behind two fists held to the sockets of his eyes, and took himself off to bed.

In the morning, when McFadden was gray with a hangover, a humbly smiling Carlotta, with mean-looking bruises on her arms, prepared lobster omelets in the kitchen, imploring her husband to try just one little bite until he appeased her more by throwing his omelet across the room where it spattered against a range of refrigerators. Quietly sniffling, she cleaned up the mess on her hands and knees while Magruder ate his omelet and McFadden made himself a pitcher of recuperative bloody marys.

Then it was time for Magruder to go. He shook hands gravely with Carlotta, who did not wish him a good trip; he then descended in the elevator with McFadden. Beneath the building portico, the old Buick sat astride four new tires. The two in the rear were snow grips.

"How much do I owe you for the tires, Martin?"

"Nothing, coachie. These are new radials. You're going to need them where you're going. It's almost winter, you know. I also had the motor tuned up. It should run pretty well."

"Thank you, Martin. I'll say good-by now. One thing, though, have you ever been to that town in New Jersey, Red Bank, where Adnizzio, McFarland and Matland live? Will I have a hard time finding them?"

"I doubt it, coachie. They live in three identical houses around a cul de sac in one of those developments that Adnizzio's family put up. The only three houses there as a matter of fact. They've been waiting for you to drive into that little turnabout for over fifteen years now. Be careful, coachie. Be careful, please."

CHAPTER 3

Call Me Azrael

As he headed toward the Arizona line, Magruder suspected he might see the snow that McFadden had prophesied in the high country of western Wyoming or Nebraska. As he reached the Wasatch Mountains in Utah, heading toward Provo, where Jack Welsh lived, he first saw the snow at sunset, pinkish tints ringing the mountain peaks in an otherwise cloudless sky. The beauty of the scene was dazzling, a promise of forthcoming relief from the desolate landscape through which he had traveled all day that had yielded up not a single hitch-hiker for conversation and left him constantly scanning the band of the faint-voiced car radio that crackled with incessant static.

Inexplicably, when he began the real crossing of the Wasatch range, he thought of Kasprzak's frozen body in the big walk-in food locker in the basement of the St. Anselm's kitchens. Kasprzak, fat and eternally frightened, with tiny eyes that sought everywhere to ferret out the next potential attack of schoolboy cruelty before it became an agonizing reality, had died beautifully, if it could be called that, arms crossed on his breast like the image on the lid of a king's tomb, a smile—incredibly!—like a

33

welcome to Death on his face. Tears, heedless of the salt they were supposed to contain, had frozen beneath his eyes, and when Magruder and the ancient security guard at the school had crept into the locker, trying to keep their terrible secret from the rest of St. Anselm's, they had both cried openly at the sight of Kasprzak's tears. The guard had taken a quick belt from a pocket flask, raged briefly about the great lie of accidental death they were in the process of creating, then, while Magruder watched, had plucked the tears from Kasprzak's smiling frosted face, put them onto a sheet of paper and deposited them overhead on a shelf. Magruder, mystified at the act, had stolen back into the locker the evening of the day of Kasprzak's funeral that was attended by every member of his class. Somehow, not surprisingly, the tears were gone and Magruder suspected the old man had taken them, managing somehow to convey them home to a refrigerator freezer where they were stored like a ceremonial slice of wedding cake: The notion had struck him as so bizarre, yet profound at the same time, that he had never dared to ask the man about it.

Near Provo, in blue night, Magruder stopped at the lighted phone booth outside a closed gas station and phoned Welsh as per instruction. The air was chill. Inside the booth, clouds of breath smoke frosted the panes of glass. Welsh, when he lifted the receiver, knew who was calling.

"How did you know I was here, Jack?" Magruder asked bemusedly. "Have they got sentinels this far west?"

Around Magruder were hills covered in pine forests, smelling pungent and clean after Las Vegas: The silent

34

darkness of the firs made Magruder think of assassination by a high-powered rifle.

"Look up into the hills to your left, coach. The lights you see are my chalet. I'll drive down and lead you up here in a few minutes."

Magruder hung up and waited beside the Buick, listening in the stillness to the whir of a small car's gears descending the road from the house, seeing the headlights cutting through the trees every so often. In another minute Welsh in a Volkswagen was there, tall and trim in classical ski-country turtleneck and sweater, a kind of badge of expectancy, Magruder thought, for someone who lived evidently for the coming of the snows. At forty-one he was not much heavier than when he had been St. Anselm's quarterback. But something had changed: The old entrepreneur's aggressiveness was gone, replaced by an almost whimsical sort of calm.

"How have you been, coach? I really didn't expect you until sometime tomorrow."

"Sorry if I've disturbed your plans, Jack. I was making good time and there didn't seem anything to be gained by spending the night at some motel in the desert. You look very well, I must say. I've just seen McFadden in Las Vegas. He doesn't look nearly so well for once having been an athlete of sorts."

"Marty drinks too much, coach. But who wouldn't with that wife of his. Is he still beating her up?"

"Evidently. They had one last night."

"Well, at least he's getting some exercise. Come on up, coach, and meet the little woman."

"That would be fine, Jack. Her name is Janet, I believe?"

"That was the last little woman, coach. The new one's name is Astrid."

"Ah, Astrid, a pretty name," Magruder told him, not knowing what else to say. Unless he had lost count, Astrid was wife number two. Welsh stared at him a long moment, impishly, testing him for disapproval perhaps, then motioned him to follow the Volkswagen.

Magruder trailed him in the Buick, up the range of curves, which must be treacherous when the real snows came, until they reached the chalet, a simple two-story building surrounded by decks that looked out in every direction on the dark silhouettes of the mountains. There was a warm glow of lights from inside, a fire burning in an immense fieldstone fireplace. A woman—very young and lovely, wearing a beaded Indian dress, twin curtains of straight dark hair framing her face—came outside to greet them. A German shepherd was with her, a huge black beauty who seemed joyous at the return of Welsh but barely interested in Magruder.

Inwardly, Magruder smiled at the threesome, fondly remembering Welsh, first among equals, when Magruder had hauled them across the line to Vermont in January for their yearly two weeks of ski camp: A gutsy kid who disdained style, he skied like hell down anything. To Magruder it was somehow inevitable that Welsh would end up in Utah, building up a small resort that he sold for a neat profit, content (unlike McFadden or the forthcoming Vauchons) to live in the forest in this unassuming house. Magruder recalled the photos in a recent issue of the *Alumni Review* of Welsh's classmates. They were mostly prosperous with correct-looking children, and generally spreading with weight. Among them Jack Welsh skied godlike and rebellious into the rays of a blazing sun. . . .

"Coach, this is Astrid, my wife. Astrid, Coach Magruder."

"Welcome to this house, Azrael," she said, taking his head in her two hands and kissing the forehead. She smiled at him, somewhat mockingly, Magruder thought, as though she considered him and his mission a unique but curious kind of self-indulgence rather than a real threat to anything, as did Carlotta McFadden.

"Who was Azrael, Astrid?" Welsh asked.

"The angel of vengeance."

"Ah, perfect. Yes, perfect." Magruder watched Welsh stroke his wife's sleek hair, obviously pleased that she knew things that he did not. Love takes different forms, evidently, Magruder considered. McFadden still played the offensive lineman in the midst of his marriage, the bruised Carlotta on the opposing line, their life an endless march and countermarch up and down the marital playing field; Welsh, the natural athlete, loved the softness of women, was even delighted by them: The mention of Azrael had touched an untroubled part of himself.

They went inside to a decor that was not unexpected. Rough, comfortable furniture, Indian weavings on the wall, two bearskin rugs on the floor. The fire leapt in a curious assortment of mirrors about the room. There was a baby, too, over which the German shepherd resumed guard. He lay asleep on a fur rug and Welsh introduced him to Magruder: "This is our Jason. He's Astrid's baby from the first marriage. He's named after his father."

"His father was a junkie who O.D.," Astrid said suddenly.

"He seems quite well made," Magruder compensated, recalling something he had read about the possibility of heroin use causing distortions in the fetus. "Perhaps he'll be a championship skier like his new father."

"He'll never know I'm not his father and you're right, he probably will be a championship skier."

"Have you got any kids, coach?" Astrid asked.

"Unfortunately no. Mrs. Magruder's health was too frail. She miscarried the first time, and the doctors warned us that we must never try again."

"Too bad," Astrid said sympathetically. "We were lucky. It was a wonderful coming together of all things. Jason got a great father and Jack got a son. Jack is sterile."

"Oh, I'm sorry, Jack," Magruder said. He could not think of anything else to say.

Welsh shrugged. "*C'est la vie*, coach. The planter still works, the seed just doesn't grow. Say, you must be tired after all your driving. Dinner will be ready in about forty minutes so you'll have time to freshen up."

"I think I'd like a cocktail, Jack. I'm feeling a bit shaky after all that distance."

"We can give you some wine, coach, but that's all. We don't drink."

"Why don't you have some pot with us, coach?" Astrid invited. "We always have some before dinner. It makes the food taste so much better."

"Is that marijuana, Astrid?"

"Yes."

"A young man I picked up hitching offered me some, but I declined."

"You were wise not to smoke while you were driving, coach," Welsh said.

"How will it affect me?" He had already decided he would try it: With Florence gone and he on his second start in life toward the end, he was eager for experience and wanted to try everything the old life, with its relentless quest for financial security, its studied emulation of other peoples' notions of propriety, had caused him to fear.

"The quiet speak with the gift of tongues, coach. The voluble are blessedly silent."

"If I talk too much, just tell me to shut up, Jack."

"All right, coach." He walked to a wall cabinet. A humidor turned on its side was filled with rolled cigarettes. There seemed to be hundreds of them. Welsh removed three and passed them around.

"Smoke it like a regular cigarette, coach. Draw the smoke deep into your lungs."

Magruder took a seat before the fire beside Astrid and took a deep puff on the cigarette. The acrid smoke made him cough repeatedly. Welsh and Astrid giggled at his novitiate. Magruder held up the joint, looking at it speculatively: "I don't think it's working, Jack. Is it possible that it doesn't work for some people?"

"It works for everybody, coach. Just enjoy."

Magruder took a second puff. "McFadden and Carlotta send you their regards, Jack. Martin said they might be

going up to Salt Lake one of these days and would make
a point to stop in and see you."

"I hope the fuck they can't find us," Welsh said annoyedly. "God Almighty, they've got to be the worst people in the whole world."

"Unbelievable," Astrid concurred. "We went down to
Vegas to see them about two months after we got married
because Carlotta was on the phone every night, just dying
to see what a dear young new wife darling Jack was married to. Anyhow, coach, was that ever a zoo. I wore my
buckskin dress and Hopi jewelry into McFadden's palace,
and when Carlotta finally made her grand entry after
making us wait an hour or so, she was wearing this incredible gown that the last Queen of Spain was buried in
or something like that. I mean Carlotta really looked
dead, coach. You should have seen all the paste and shit
she had on her face."

"Our next mistake was not accepting a drink," Welsh
chimed in. "When we lit up a joint Carlotta went rigid
with fucking indignation. Do you remember back in
school how we used to have to eat a square meal like the
West Point guys if we were bad boys? Well, Carlotta did
that routine for ten margaritas, then she toppled over and
passed out right on the floor."

"Christ Jesus!" Magruder howled, stomping his foot on
the fieldstone of the fireplace, overcome with mirth at the
notion.

"Their kids smoke grass, coach," Astrid said reflectively.

"You're kidding?" Magruder demanded, not really car-ing, trying to feign disbelief behind the tears that streamed down his face.

"Yep. Their father's driver, who takes them back and forth to that incubator of a school they go to, turned them on a couple of years ago. He gets them their stuff."

"How did you find out?"

"A continuation of the zoo story, coach," Astrid said. "We ate dinner with McFadden alone, then went to our room to smoke another joint in bed. And while McFadden was beating the shit out of Carlotta, Manuel and Teresa sneaked in to share a couple of joints and then ended up staying the night, all four of us in the same rack. . . ."

"Oh God!" Welsh exclaimed, slapping his head. "If that big Mick father of theirs ever walked into the bedroom, we'd all be dead for sure by now!"

Now the bottled-up irreverence went mad inside him: Magruder alternately howled with laughter and puffed greedily on the cigarette.

"That kid Manuel really had a beautiful body," Astrid said. "Almost as nice as Jack's. And God was he horny! I made him keep his underwear on, but he had these little skivvy boxer shorts his mother buys for him, and his thing kept coming through the hole in the front, so I made him put on a pair of Jack's Jockey shorts, but that didn't help much either."

"Did you finally ball him?" Welsh asked, sounding almost disinterested.

"About five in the morning, I think," Astrid said. "Otherwise it was going to happen all over my stomach. Boy, if his mother doesn't let him off the leash pretty soon, his next playmate is going to be his own sister."

"Did you ball Teresa, Jack?" Magruder asked, intrigued to know it all.

"No, I fell asleep pretty early on. Besides, it wouldn't go. Her mother has her checked out every month or so to make sure the old hymen is still stretched tight."

"Teresa didn't sleep a wink all night, though," Astrid said. "She just did this tracing number on Jack's face with her finger all night long. It was weird. Anyhow, with any luck those kids will turn out OK. At least they get a chance to go away to school next year and get away from their parents."

"Are you in contact with any of the other guys, Jack?" Magruder asked, suddenly intrigued with the idea of testing them when he felt so ragingly comic about everything. "I mean do you hear from Deutsch in Nebraska or Vauchon or the three in New Jersey?"

"We see Carruthers a lot. He comes out here sometimes to dry out. He's got a favorite ledge on a hill out there where he likes to sit bare-ass and guzzle beer to come down off the hard stuff. We've never heard so much from the three from New Jersey as this week, coach. They called about two days ago to make sure we lived in the mountains. They suggested a humane way for us to help them with their little problem with you would be to cut a small slit in your brake lines before you left here."

"Thoughtful of them to give me a fighting chance with the emergency brake," Magruder quipped, smiling inanely, lost in the fantasy of himself careening expertly down the sides of mountains on his new radial tires and rushing out onto the flatland of desert where the old Buick, its momentum gone, simply halted before a host of approving spectators of every race and nation on the earth who cheered the certainty that Azrael still lived, then split their ranks apart to permit him to continue on to New Jersey. . . .

Abruptly, the phone rang and Welsh rose to answer it, pausing with an impish glow on his face to ask them, "Any bets?"

"Carlotta," Astrid guessed.

"Adnizzio, McFarland and Matland," Magruder said bemusedly, knowing with certainty, telepathically perhaps, that the three were on the wire.

"Hello. Oh, hello, Vincent." Welsh grinned.

"Yes, he's here, Vincent. Well, right now he's getting stoned with us before dinner." A pause: "Yes. That's right, Vincent, marijuana."

There was a silence while Magruder guffawed, staring into the flames.

"No, Vincent, it doesn't prove he's a moral degenerate and therefore it's a better idea that I should file a slit in his brake lines. Bullshit, Vincent, I'll bet your own kids smoke the shit, too. Here, Vincent, I'll let you talk to him."

Welsh carried the phone to Magruder, who took it, still mesmerized by the fire.

He waited a long moment, then heard a voice: "Coach . . . ? Coach, this is Vincent. How are you feeling, coach?"

"Rather well at the moment, Vincent. I'm trying pot for the first time in my life. And you yourself?"

"A little apprehensive, coach, as you might expect. You're on your way East, I guess, huh?"

"Yes, Vincent, it's time . . . past time as a matter of fact."

From the other end of the line Magruder heard sighs and then varied expletives that told the three were together and probably listening on some telecom system. The whispering came back over crackling wires and then Adnizzio asked, "Are you getting set to hook up with Interstate 80 there in Utah, coach, then come east through Wyoming and Nebraska that way?"

"Exactly, Vincent. Are you planning to have me ambushed on the way?"

Adnizzio giggled, uneasily. "Coach, I wouldn't do that to you. Besides, there are no Italians in Wyoming or Nebraska as far as anyone knows, so who would I trust to do the job?"

"But there are plenty of Italians further east, beginning around Chicago, Vincent," Magruder suggested.

"Coach . . ." Adnizzio protested. "Coach, the real reason I called was to invite you to my daughter Aurelia's wedding. It's this coming Saturday. The way I figure it, with stops to see Deutsch in Nebraska and Vauchon in Chicago, you should be here in Red Bank by Saturday morning in time for the festivities."

"That's the stuff, Vinnie," someone said in the background. "Tell him he doesn't have to bring a present either."

"I thank you for the invitation and will proudly attend the wedding, Vincent, since I should arrive by Saturday.

But you've missed one stop. I'm going to see Carruthers in South Bend, Indiana."

"Carruthers? That goddamn lush? Is he still teaching at Notre Dame?"

"Yes, Vincent. He teaches moral theology there. Which is probably why he drinks so much in this day and age. And I need one more consultation with a moral theologian before I descend upon you three. . . ."

"That's the one to lean on!" someone—either McFarland or Matland—exclaimed excitedly behind Adnizzio. It astounded Magruder that they failed to understand he could hear them. "I'll bet a thousand bucks that drunk would tell the old bastard anything we wanted him to. . . ."

"Vincent . . ."

"Yes, coach?"

"Tell them I can hear them plainly, will you? And save your money. Carruthers is too far gone. He'd take your money from you and tell me the truth anyhow. Now I'll say good night since it seems we're about to sit down to dinner out here."

"Why don't you two shut the fuck up and stop talking so loud?" Adnizzio shouted at his companions. They were the last words Magruder heard: The line went dead in the next second. Adnizzio had evidently slammed down the receiver in disgust.

Magruder returned the phone to Welsh. Behind the sofa, the baby slept effortlessly on his rug, heedless of the furies that charged the air. Welsh and Astrid merely shook their heads in disbelief.

"How sentimental are you, coach?" Astrid asked.

45

"About as much as the next man, I suppose. Why? Are you afraid I'll crack at his daughter's wedding?"

"You might. If they can't stop you one way they're sure to try another."

Magruder smiled, too old to dare predict this far in advance any one sure outcome to the problem. Besides, he felt inside himself a growing hunger, more ravenous than any he could remember in his life. "Is dinner far off, Astrid?"

She pulled him to his feet. "I guess you're ready, coach."

They went into the kitchen where their places were already set at a rough-hewn plank table and ate a meatless meal of recognizable brown rice, plus mounds of unusual natural foods that Magruder washed down with glasses of chilled chablis. Finally satiated after three helpings of a dessert of pumpkin bread (he had always despised the taste of pumpkin), Magruder asked, "How is it that you two aren't haranguing me like the others of our little group not to continue on to New Jersey?"

"Frankly, coach, I don't give a shit," Welsh told him. "I'm curious, don't get me wrong. I'd like to know the outcome and if those three guys don't kill you, I'd appreciate a phone call."

"You were always good to Kasprzak, Jack. You had no cruelty in you. Wouldn't you see his death avenged?"

"No, coach, that's not what I'd like to see avenged. I've thought a lot about it over the years. His dying was merciful, I think. He wouldn't have lived this long anyhow. If he hadn't killed himself by now, then his glandular disease would've done it for him. No, what I'd like to see vindicated are those few guys around old St. Anselm's that I always admired but never had the guts to join up with, who were always being kicked out for realizing long before their fortieth year of traditional disillusionment what a mealy bunch of middle-class assholes we were all being programed to be."

"I won't be the one to avenge that, Jack. I didn't know I was programing assholes, as you call it. I tried to teach the value of honesty, to mold good character in our boys. If the fruits of those teachings are not validated in the next few weeks, then I've failed tragically."

"They won't be validated at all, coach. I'll guarantee it. Those qualities you refer to are abstractions. When it comes right down to the line with the threat of breaking up those guys' families, of destroying the fortunes they've spent twenty years abuilding, you're going to be facing three snarling tigers with their backs to the wall. Beware."

"Thanks for your concern, Jack, but I think I'll sleep on it. The pot seems to have made me very tired. I'll have to leave early in the morning. With any luck I might make Cheyenne or Laramie, Wyoming, by nightfall."

"I'll have you up at six, coach. I've got that gas for you, too. Also, would you mind taking along a present for Vincent's daughter? That is, if it's not too much trouble . . . ?"

"It's not too much trouble, Jack. The entire back seat is empty. Good night, now."

"Good night, coach," they called in unison. He left them, their faces played over by the flickering candles, and headed toward his room, walking past the baby on the rug, awake now, and eying him somehow speculatively, if such a thing were possible for babies. He thought of kneeling to tickle the child, but decided against it when he saw the black shepherd alertly watching him from beside the fire.

He wondered suddenly (the pot still treading gauzily through his brain) if there were not a whole pack of salivating shepherds and Dobermans awaiting his arrival in a certain suburb of Red Bank, New Jersey.

In the morning he awoke feeling more refreshed than he had in ages. Outside, his breath smoking in the weak early sunlight, Welsh was pouring gas from jerry cans into the Buick, which was covered with frost.

In the kitchen, while he breakfasted, Astrid packed the wedding-gift box for Aurelia Adnizzio. Magruder watched as she put in a beaded Hopi dress, a necklace of pounded silver and then, inexplicably, the rolled skin of an enormous diamondback rattler, perhaps seven feet long, that she held up for Magruder to admire. The sound of the rattle stiffened the shepherd into a growling crouch.

"Why that, Astrid?" he asked, bemused at the notion of such a bizarre gift making its way eastward to a wedding that would doubtless be posh and suffocating under the weight of fine china, silver bowls and crystal vases that the guests would certainly heap upon the bride and groom.

"For courage. The Hopi consider the rattler a symbol of courage. It will help young Aurelia Adnizzio Modesti sustain herself through a lifetime of servitude as a suburban New Jersey *Hausfrau*."

"She may want exactly that, Astrid. Some find it a comfort, you know," Magruder said, finding himself unexpectedly vexed by the superiority Welsh and his wife felt to any other kind of life-style than their own: Snobbery comes in many forms, Magruder thought.

Within fifteen minutes he left them, Welsh waving slowly, unsmiling, his eyes and thoughts on Magruder hidden behind the dark shelter of sun glasses. Astrid, the baby Jason papoose style on her back, did not smile either, and watched Magruder's departure with arms tightly crossed in front of her against the chill. The shepherd followed after him as Magruder negotiated the downward trail through the pines, his brakes evidently not tampered with. Then the dog began short-cutting through the trees, appearing before the car on the bottom curve of each switchback until he waited beside the highway at the bottom of the trail, watching with steadfast gaze as Magruder turned northward onto the asphalt toward Salt Lake City and the Wyoming line.

CHAPTER 4

At the Center
of the Nation

The blizzard started in western Nebraska near Ogollala about noon on the second day.

Magruder first heard of it the previous night as he watched the late news coverage before retiring in a room at a motel near Laramie. But then the impending storm had been dismissed as snow flurries and Magruder concurred with the laughing meteorologist. It was too early in the year for a full-fledged storm and, it seemed to him, the sky threatened nothing. All day across Wyoming, where he had the companionship of two hitch-hikers, it was inordinately blue and cloudless. The next morning it was identically the same in Wyoming and in Nebraska.

But by two o'clock in the afternoon, Magruder could barely see for the wind-driven whiteness. He drove slowly eastward along Interstate 80, clinging to the glowing taillights of a behemoth of a truck, hoping somehow that its driver intended going right past Albert Deutsch's farm near Omaha, where he was due that afternoon.

But the truck veered off, heading south toward Auburn, and Magruder pushed on, guiding his way along the interstate with the help of the reflective sign posts beside it, faintly reassured that, since this was flat Nebraska rather than hill-ridden Utah or Wyoming, the worst he might do would be to run off into the stubble of somebody's wheat field.

Instead, about eight o'clock, he toppled into a deep ditch along the rutted dirt road that led to Albert Deutsch's farm when he moved over too far in the snow-blown darkness to allow for the passage of a plow going the opposite way. The plow driver did not see the accident happen and continued on. The Buick settled into the ditch with a soft clunk at about a forty-five-degree angle. The wheels of the driver's side suspended in the air. The motor still ran, the transmission was in drive and the air-borne rear wheel turned at the speed of a slow idle.

Magruder sat still a long minute, piled in a heap against the downward-side passenger door, thinking with a faint bemusement despite his problem that he was doing a better job putting an end to his avenging angel's trip to the East than the three who wanted him stopped could possibly do.

He reached across the steering wheel to cut off the ignition and decided to leave on the lights lest the snow plow return and bury the doors shut. Then after he listened a moment to the howling of the wind that somehow blew snow through the rubber flashing of the fully closed windows, he climbed up the incline of the front seat, pushed open the door and pulled himself out onto the snow at the top of the ditch. By now there was an accumulation of at least fifteen inches and even as Magruder watched, the wind began filling in the cleared swath the plow had made. Far off to his right were the lights of a house. He wondered whether he should stay with the car or try to walk the distance to ascertain whether or not it was Deutsch's house. Yet he remembered blizzard stories about people walking around in circles despite their good sense of direction and decided to stay put. Perhaps the plow would return. In minutes more he saw the lights of a truck bouncing along the road toward him. The truck, a high four-wheel-drive pickup, stopped beside him. It was Albert Deutsch and his wife, Marta.

"Coach, are you hurt?" Deutsch asked, leaping from the truck.

"No, Albert, I'm fine. I pulled over to make room for a snow plow and the car slipped into the ditch."

"Come into the truck with us, coach. Dinner's been waitin' for hours now. You must be starved."

"I am. But what about the car, Albert?"

"Leave it, coach. And we'll leave the parking lights on too. I'll send some of the hands over to get it first thing in the morning and they can charge up the battery for you."

Deutsch scrambled down to the car, retrieving Magruder's suitcase, and put it in the truck behind the seat. Magruder climbed in and acknowledged the troubled smile of Marta Deutsch. Behind her, Albert's gun lay across a rack.

"Hello, Marta, it's good to see you again."

"Hello, Coach Magruder. It doesn't seem like Nebraska's been too hospitable to you so far."

"No, Marta, but I'm sure you'll make up for it."

"I've made you sauerbraten, coach, with sweet red cabbage and potato pancakes. . . ."

"They've been callin' all damn day, coach," Deutsch interrupted as he swung heavily into the cab. A huge man

53

with a brush haircut, he took off a western hat and handed it to his wife, his irritation evident as he threw the truck into gear and started down the road, seeking a place to turn around.

"Who do you mean, Albert?"

"The three from New Jersey, Jack Welsh, Carlotta McFadden, Matty Vauchon and even that drunk, Carruthers, from Notre Dame. Plus a few more not on the route goin' East. Some long-lost teammates of ours from New Orleans and upstate New York, to mention just a few out-of-the-way places. The word is out now."

"Albert was very angry, coach," Marta said quietly as he jockied the truck about in the deep snow, then headed back in the direction from which they had come. "And you know it takes quite a bit to make Albert angry."

They came abreast of the Buick again, its taillights barely seen in the whirling snow, then shot past it, Deutsch's jaw set in anger. Magruder watched him in the reflective dash lights. The speedometer showed they hurled along the rutted road through a blizzard at sixty mph, faster than Magruder, who traveled interstate highways, had yet to go.

"Albert, please slow down," Marta admonished, patting his arm. Abruptly the truck slowed, the speedometer needle sank below thirty mph.

"If that damn Carlotta McFadden was my wife, I'd take her out to the barn and whip some of the awful obscenity out of her. I never heard such filth from the mouth of a woman, except when I was in Korea."

"Martin McFadden hasn't got a barn, Albert, but he

seems to manage quite well without it. Carlotta was black and blue when I left Las Vegas."

"Good!" Marta Deutsch said. "I tell you, Coach Magruder, I don't know how Albert could go on listening. I was on the extension and had to put it down and leave the room."

"Carlotta was probably on margaritas again," Magruder said. "What did she want you to do? Kill me?"

"She wanted me to punch you out, turn you around and head you back for California. She kept saying we had no idea what a family was all about and how it needed to be defended against the like of you. God Almighty, what does she mean we don't know what it's all about? We got enough of our own. She's only got two and we got seven."

They pulled off the road and up a long drive between naked elms and a windbreak of evergreens that led to the floodlit expanse of Deutsch's house and farm buildings.

"Jack Welsh was next to call," Deutsch said. "I always did enjoy talkin' with Jack."

"He didn't try to convince you to stop me?"

"No, old Jack just wanted to know if you were safe because of the storm. I promised to call him back tonight."

"I talked with his wife," Marta said as the truck came to a halt in front of the wide front porch. "She sounded very nice. I hope she liked the wedding present we sent. What's she like, Coach Magruder?"

"She's quite pretty. She's also very young. About twenty-one or so, I think."

"And Jack in his forties . . . ?" Something in the notion seemed to delight Deutsch: a satyr doubtless given to his own variety of fantasy. He turned off the truck engine and sat still for a moment, smiling witlessly in the glow of dash lights.

"Jack seems quite rejuvenated," Magruder suggested. "We all smoked pot together and talked quite a bit."

"Do you mean marijuana, coach?"

"Yes, exactly."

They were fascinated, looking at him askance, not in condemnation exactly, but more like wonderment, until Marta Deutsch asked the next question:

"What was it like? Did it make you want to do crazy things, coach?"

"Quite fascinating actually. I've never slept so well in ages as I did that night."

"Coach, don't say anything about marijuana in front of the children, OK? It's not that I question your right to try it, it's just that it's not for everybody. I'd be afraid to try it, especially after what happened to our Ingrid."

Magruder peered out the truck window at the snow that fell softly into the pools of light from the windows in the front of the large rambling house, the rear of the house cutting off the thrust of the wind. Nearby, flanked by tall evergreens, was the Deutsch family shrine, a statue of the Virgin, hauled over from Germany more than a century ago, that stood three feet tall in a kind of Black Forest wood-carver's hut.

"What happened to Ingrid, Albert?" he asked finally, hoping she was not dead, the silence having become pregnant, with no one making a move to open the doors of the truck.

"Ingrid graduated from high school in June last, first in her class. We sent her east to Radcliffe College."

"We were so proud, coach," Marta broke in, sniffling a little. "We're just simple people from Nebraska. Albert never had a chance to finish but two years of college before the Korean War came and then he had to take over the farm when his father died. And I never got a chance to go at all. So you can imagine how excited we were when she was accepted, Radcliffe being such a fine school and all. . . ."

"Well she got to Boston in September. They sent her home for Thanksgiving and told her not to come back."

"What happened?" Magruder asked.

"Everything! It seems there wasn't one rule she didn't break. She just seemed to go crazy when she got to Boston."

Magruder turned sideways to observe their misery.

"Pot and drugs, failin' grades in every course . . ." Deutsch continued. "She ran naked through Harvard Square and when a policeman caught her she scratched his face so bad he had to go to the doctor. She's lucky he didn't use a pistol butt on her. . . ."

"And a baby!" his wife sobbed, burying her face in her husband's hat that she held on her lap. "And we don't know who the father was."

"We don't know if it will be white or black, coach. She can't remember half the ones she lay with."

Magruder gave off a great sigh, revealing tiredness instead. So far, except for Welsh, who was out of it, the lives of his former players had run heavily toward disillusionment and unwanted accident, and they seemed like boys still seeking the locker-room advice of a benevolent coach. He found himself hoping that Vauchon in

57

Chicago, the most controlled and dignified of the bunch, would be in full command of himself.

"I'm sorry, Albert. I'm really quite sorry about your problem with Ingrid. You certainly don't deserve it. Do you think I might have something to eat now, Marta?"

"I'm sorry, coach. We were so wrapped up in our own problems. Let's go inside, now."

They descended the truck and stomped onto the front porch of the house, Magruder able to see through the windows the excited faces of Deutsch's horde of children, the clean-scrubbed and pinkishly healthy variety who probably knew little enough about life to become the captives of actual enthusiasms. Inside, where a fire burned in a blackened brick fireplace with Dutch ovens that might have been part of the original kitchen of the house, Magruder worked his way down a receiving line that ended with a young boy of about four who wore bunny suit pajamas. Ingrid, lately of Radcliffe, was not there.

"Ingrid's gonna have a baby!" the youngest told Magruder excitedly. "She bought it in Boston!" The two next to him concurred just as excitedly; the three eldest hushed them with grave, accusing faces.

"We thought they should know everything, coach," Deutsch said. "This isn't the nineteenth century, after all. The baby's goin' to live with us just like a brother or sister whenever it comes."

"That seems very wise, Albert," Magruder began, only to be interrupted by the young one, who clarified the issue:

"But when it comes, it's gonna be Ingrid's baby, not mommy's."

"All right, that's enough now," Deutsch said, lifting the child and kissing him on the forehead. "It's past your bedtime, buster. And the rest of you mind your homework."

They walked to a hallway closet where Deutsch and his wife together helped Magruder out of his bulky sheepskin before they opened a set of double sliding doors to the next room in their progress toward his dinner —a perfect Gothic museum piece of a place, where the needles of four middle-aged women flew at the work of a quilting bee. Magruder had seen them long ago in upstate New York. When Florence could stand no more of hearing of St. Anselm's football, or the problems of the boys, she dragged him off for one of her recuperative drives through the Grandma Moses villages where women worked the cottage industries subsidized by the state. Now the women looked up, nodding with polite shy smiles to Magruder. He knew they had not missed a single word of what was said in the house that night.

"It's a lovely quilt, ladies," Magruder told them, smiling at each in turn.

"Thank you, Coach Magruder," came the unified chorus of appreciation.

"These ladies are my sisters and sisters-in-law," Marta Deutsch offered. "They've been working on this quilt for three days now. It's to be our wedding present to Aurelia Adnizzio. I wonder, coach, since you're . . . ?"

"Of course, Marta, I don't mind. I've got Jack and Astrid Welsh's gift with me now."

"What did they give her?" As many as six voices seemed to demand simultaneously.

59

"There was a beaded Indian buckskin dress, some silver Hopi jewelry and a rattlesnake skin for courage."

"I told you we did the right thing!" Marta Deutsch exclaimed. "All those Easterners can give crystal glass and silver bowls, but money couldn't by a finer present than this. I know she'll like it. . . . I wonder what the McFaddens gave them? Matty Vauchon is sending a crystal vase."

"Carlotta sent a wormwood statue of St. Francis of Assisi that had been carved in Spain," Magruder told them. "She told me it was over two hundred years old."

"Imagine that!" Marta Deutsch exclaimed. "Sending the statue of a holy saint, and the filth that comes out of her mouth. If I were Aurelia, I'd send it right back to her."

"I'd like to hit her over the head with it!" Deutsch said. "Provided it was heavy enough."

"I'd like some of that sauerbraten, Marta," Magruder told her. "I didn't have a chance to stop for lunch what with the storm and all."

"I'm sorry, coach," Marta said. "Albert hasn't eaten either. Come to the kitchen."

The sauerbraten was fantastic, Magruder thought. He ate with relish, but Deutsch hardly picked at his food. "The three from New Jersey called about five-thirty, coach. They get Walter Cronkite an hour earlier back East, 'n he was tellin' about the blizzard, so they called." Deutsch sighed heavily, less in anger, Magruder guessed, than in plain disgust. "I never heard three grown men so excited. They were praying you were frozen to death by now. They were really disappointed when I told them the storm center was east of here, in Iowa, and that you'd probably lay over for the night in a motel someplace. I really ought to call them 'n tell them you're safe."

"Why bother, Albert? Give them another night of hopefulness. Let's don't be unkind."

"I wouldn't like to be in your shoes, coach, when you get to New Jersey. But I'm glad you're goin' there. It was a crime what they did to Kasprzak and they should be made to pay for it. Only I think you shouldn't have waited twenty-three years."

"Well, the viewpoint seems to be changing as I move eastward. McFadden was adamantly against it, Welsh was more or less indifferent, and you're for it. . . ."

"Matty Vauchon isn't for it either, coach," Marta broke in. "He thinks you've got very little to stand on legally."

"And those three guys are goin' to have a bunch of eastern sharpie lawyers all set to spar with you, coach. See if I'm not right about that."

The word "eastern" seemed to trigger a sort of renewed annoyance in Deutsch, a remembrance of Ingrid at Radcliffe, perhaps, and Magruder watched him stabbing the sauerbraten with a fork and knew that Deutsch was organizing his disparate small rages for a proclamation, just the way he had always done when he was a student at St. Anselm's.

"All the guys on the St. Anselm's team were Easterners except Matty Vauchon and me, coach. Jack Welsh was a good fellow, but the others didn't like us so much. Me especially because they thought I was stupid. I think if there hadn't been Kasprzak then I'd have been last in line in the pecking order. I hope you get to them, though I don't think you will." He turned in a sudden pique to his wife: "I don't know why you're bothering to send that quilt out to Adnizzio's daughter, Marta. It doesn't seem like any of that bunch is worth it."

"It's not any of her fault, Albert. We can't punish her for her father's sin. Besides, that time we went East to visit Atlantic City and New York, they couldn't have been nicer to us. . . ."

"Yes, Marta, I remember. When we wanted to go to the top of the Statue of Liberty, Adnizzio couldn't get off the damn floor for laughin' so hard."

"It's only because they're so used to it. They'd never think of going there."

"No, Marta, it's because we were hicks from Nebraska and only a hick from Nebraska would be fool enough to go to one of their fancy cocktail parties and ask about goin' to the top of the Statue of Liberty."

"Well, we didn't know, Albert. If they were out here they might've said something funny and then we'd have a reason to laugh."

"But they wouldn't want to live out here, so they wouldn't feel a bit insecure about any mistake they made."

"Don't get so riled up, Albert," Magruder spoke through a mouthful of sauerbraten and beer. "You have a much better life than those three guys living in a tight-assed Jersey suburb. . . ."

"What do you mean, coach? We're the prisoners of this farm. After a while, living in Nebraska doesn't make you fit to live any place else. You don't understand deceit enough to live in the East. You trust your neighbors here.

When they say something, they mean only one thing, not two or three other things besides.

"I tell you, Marta!" Deutsch said, suddenly slamming the flat of his hand on the slab of table so their plates leapt, "when it's their time the others are going down to the University of Lincoln to study among their own kind! Ingrid, too, after the baby comes."

Magruder put down his knife and fork with resignation, waiting for the timeless rhetorical question, knowing with certainty what it had to be.

"Where did we go wrong with Ingrid, Marta?" Deutsch asked. "What did we do that we shouldn't have done?"

"Why don't you show Coach Magruder the new milking barn, Albert?" his wife said quietly, a distant, vacuous look in her eyes.

"I'd like that, Albert. I've been cooped up all day in the car."

"Are you sure, coach?" he asked, looking at Magruder's half-eaten meal. There was expectant pleasure rising in his voice. Evidently a wise woman, Marta Deutsch had hit him in a soft spot.

"I'll eat later, Albert. My stomach is upset from worrying about the storm. Some air might do me good."

They stood up from the table, returning to the hall closet through the rooms where the women, heads bent over their work, sewed with frantic industry at the quilt, not missing anything. The children studied with an identically unnatural preoccupation. Passing behind one of them seated on a sofa, Deutsch stopped an instant to reverse a textbook being absorbedly read upside down. They put on their coats and made their way outside.

It still snowed, though, to Magruder, the storm seemed much abated. One of the hands wheeled a snow blower between the house and the fully lit milking barn, widening a lane for the early morning arrival of a milk tanker. Deutsch trudged on with Magruder beside him, blowing out snorts of his anger that smoked in the lighted expanse, pausing only once to ask the hand how the blower worked, then reminding him to hook up a plow to the high-wheeled truck.

They went inside the barn, and the sight of the Jersey herd feeding at grain troughs, lifting heads to regard their arrival with a momentary curiosity, seemed instantly to calm Deutsch. The place had a tiled antiseptic look about it, except for the hay scattered on the floors. The feed was delivered to the animals via shining stainless-steel tubing. Deutsch breezed along a row of swishing tails, slapping at the animals' rumps, then took Magruder to the rear of the barn, behind a concrete wall, to see the farm's stud bull feeding in a pen, an enormous black animal calm again as the cows when Magruder expected him to be in a classic eternal rage. The barn was warm from the accumulation of body heat and Magruder loosened his coat while Deutsch and his stud bull stared steadfastly at each other. The love theme swelling, the bull came forward to be petted, scratching its neck at the same time on the top rail of the steel pen. The fringes of pleasure stealing across Deutsch's face soon became a blatant smile.

"I still think you've got a wonderful farm here, Albert,"

Magruder urged, consolingly he hoped. "A man should be proud to own an animal like that."

"We have twelve hundred acres, coach. There was seven hundred I inherited and five hundred from Marta's place next door when we bought out her brother. We don't accept any government subsidy either. I don't believe in that horse shit. Every acre is under tillage or used as pasture."

"That seems very commendable, Albert," Magruder told him, recalling once that he had been passed in California at high speed by a new Cadillac with a sign affixed to its rear deck proclaiming it was purchased with farm subsidy money.

"Coach, remember how we used to talk in your office whenever I had a problem when I was in school?"

"Yes, Albert," Magruder lied, not really remembering, speculating on how many thousands of Albert Deutsches he may have spoken to over the years at St. Anselm's.

"I mean I was never able to talk with my father, coach. You know how the old German families were. The kids just listened. They weren't supposed to think. I mean one night when I was thirteen I came home from the eighth grade 'n found out I was going to spend the next four years at boarding school in the East."

"Ah yes, Albert, but those days seem gone forever, don't they?"

"I mean I could never go to my father with some of the things I told you. Remember the time I caught the crabs from the lady in Albany, and how scared I was? I've never forgotten how kind you were, tellin' me how to get rid of them. Actually gettin' that medicine for me when I was afraid to go to the drugstore."

"Yes, Albert, but when you look back on it now, it must seem very funny to you. I mean it's all part of the rites of initiation for a young man, wouldn't you say?" But still Magruder found it in himself to laugh. This he did remember: Two had been serviced by the same lady. Deutsch, guilt-ridden and trembling to the marrow, had been infested with them; Vauchon, the strong and elegant black, bemused by sex even in his teens, had not a single one on him. Seeing them out the door of his office, Magruder had howled with mirth when they were gone, deciding only the guilty and vulnerable caught crabs.

"The rites of initiation? Yes, I was a young man then," Deutsch said. The phrase seemed to please him inordinately. For an instant he grinned like a satyr at his brother the bull. "But, coach, what I was getting to was, would you sit down tonight and have a little talk with Ingrid?"

"Really, Albert, I don't think I have much facility in dealing with young people any more. Besides, I don't imagine I'm what you're looking for. I seem to agree with almost everything they think these days."

"Please try, coach . . . ? She was Four-H, always went to Mass, was vice president of her class, had the best grades, and now it's like we don't know her. . . ."

Magruder, wincing at the unexpected whine in the voice, turned to regard him askance: Beneath the brush cut, Albert Deutsch's face seemed gray with pain. Little tears, reminding Magruder of dead Kasprzak's own,

66

coursed down his cheeks, and Magruder feared Deutsch might break down sobbing.

"All right, Albert, I'll talk with her. Why don't we return to the house?"

"Thanks, coach," Deutsch murmured gratefully. He stopped patting at the bull's head and the animal, wanting more, shifted heavily against the enclosure, then angrily stomped the plank floor of the stall as they walked away down the line of contented cows to the outside.

The hired hand had finished his plowing. They walked to the house and entered the kitchen directly this time. Reflexively, it seemed to Magruder, Marta Deutsch removed their warming plates from a wall oven and brought them to the table.

"Everybody feeling a bit better now?"

"Yes, thank you, Marta. It's quite a fine barn, I think."

"The three from New Jersey called again," she said abruptly as she carried more beer from the refrigerator.

"How'd they sound when they heard the coach was here safe, Marta?" Deutsch asked.

"A sound you never have enjoyed, Albert. Three grown men like a steer with a broken leg."

"In their case I would've enjoyed it fine. Anything else?"

"Carlotta McFadden."

"What'd she sound like?"

"Same as usual. I held the phone far away from my ear. Her husband finally cracked her one, then apologized and hung up the phone."

"Good!" Deutsch intoned, his appetite for the sauerbraten evidently returned. "Coach has agreed to talk with Ingrid, Marta."

"Oh, thank you, coach," Marta said. By way of gratitude she remembered bread also warming in the oven, rushed to retrieve it and held the rich prize, wrapped in linen, inches from his nose. Magruder declined, and at the same time heard an actual sigh of relief from the quilting ladies in the next room, if not from the entire state of Nebraska. He chewed at his sauerbraten that now tasted like rubber, and wondered what one said to a doubtless bitter eighteen-year-old girl being smothered alive by an overly solicitous family. He pictured her—who had locked herself away in an upstairs room—gaunt and hollow-eyed yet swelling in the belly, chain smoking, staring in her misery through the night of the waning blizzard toward the East. . . .

"I know it will do her good to talk with you, coach," Deutsch's wife went on. "We asked our priest and her high school guidance counselor but she wouldn't talk to them at all. Wouldn't even leave her room to come down."

"What makes you think she'll speak with me, Marta?"

"She told us she would before you arrived. She knows how much comfort Albert always took from talking with you, coach."

Albert Deutsch sopped up the last of his gravy with a piece of black bread, then pushed away his plate and patted at his lips with his napkin.

"We'd better go up to bed, Marta. Morning comes early," he said.

"Coach hasn't finished his meal, Albert."

"I've had enough, Marta, thank you. I don't seem to have the appetite I did when I was a young man."

"Would the living room be all right, coach?" Deutsch asked, standing suddenly from his place. His wife snatched up the plates and began carrying them off. "I could put more logs on the fire."

"It sounds quite fine, Albert," Magruder said. He heard the bustle of activity in the next room and knew the quilting bee was ended, the women doubtless disappearing, overweight phantoms rushing up the stairs to their rooms where they would lie breathlessly awake until the defiled, yet certainly enigmatic, Ingrid returned upstairs from her consultation. When Magruder followed the Deutsches into the empty living room, the place was soundless except for the crackle of fire in the fireplace. The children also retreated; it was as if no one had been there at all.

"Would you like a nightcap, coach?"

"Perhaps that's a good idea, Albert. Yes, I would."

Magruder watched as Deutsch walked to the sideboard and took out a glass and a bottle of Bourbon, and filled the glass straight to the rim, neglecting to add ice. He handed it to Magruder, then stood with his wife at the bottom of the steps: "Well, we'll say good night, coach. The hands'll have the car here first thing in the morning. The roads ought to be cleared for sure by nine o'clock or so. Are you sure you can't stay another day, maybe?"

"I'll miss Aurelia's wedding if I do, Albert. It's best that I move on."

"OK, coach, sorry you can't stay. Well, as I was saying, we'll go to bed now."

"Yes." Magruder contained a pitying smile. Deutsch's

voice had raised whole octaves, quivering slightly, to announce to the house pretending sleep that the moment was at hand. Why me? Magruder thought, watching them ascend the stairs. Exorcising a demon from Ingrid Deutsch was an awesome task for which he felt so inadequate in his sixty-eighth year. Would that her father, like Welsh, whom he had always admired, had learned disillusionment over old relics of football coaches who gave universally known remedies for killing crab lice, instead of retaining his awe of authority and comfort at its presence, seemingly intact from his days at St. Anselm's.

CHAPTER 5

An Astonishing Paternity

In another moment, as if she had passed her parents on
the way down through some revolving door, Ingrid descended the steps. Involuntarily Magruder winced at the
sight of her. He knew in an instant that she had gone ba-
nanas at Radcliffe.

She was not pretty. An overweight girl with pasty skin
and dark circles beneath her eyes, the ancient Deutsch
wariness was there too. Ingrid was her father's daughter.
She wore a long denim dress, a string of orange beads
about her neck. Her toenails were painted a glaring red.
She puffed like a novice on a cigarette, occasionally
brushing back her long tawny hair, which was unkempt
and dirty. Before she spoke she listened twice to check
upstairs for listeners, perhaps unseen over the railing of
the banister. What a terrible place for her to bear the
stigma of an unwed mother, Magruder thought.

"Hello, Coach Magruder. I met you once at a St. Anselm's reunion when I was about ten."

"I don't remember you, Ingrid, but I'm flattered that
you will talk with me."

"Can I put on a record?" she asked.

"Sure, but something other than country and Western,

all right? I got a bellyful of it crossing the country. There often seems to be nothing else available."

She shrugged: "Country music isn't exactly my bag either. I'll put on daddy's 'Victory at Sea.' That ought to cover up the frankness of the discussion we're about to have unless they've got the place bugged."

She dropped the record onto the turntable, and the multi-speaker stereo hissed and crackled a long moment before the first crash of waves burst upon them, too loud. She lowered it voluntarily and Magruder, faintly amused, watched her shuffle to the sideboard and fill herself a glass of Bourbon, identically straight as Magruder's own. Then she sat on the couch with him, facing him, one leg tucked under her, holding the Bourbon and cigarette in one hand at the same time.

"Are we going to be frank, Ingrid?" Magruder asked. "If you want to talk about an abortion, I'm not the person you want to ask. I'm against it. In fact, I strongly disapprove."

"You sound even more Catholic than daddy, coach. I didn't think that was possible."

"The Church has been a great comfort to me, Ingrid, especially when my Florence passed away recently. You might find it helpful to speak with your pastor. . . ."

"Fuck the Church!" she hissed, sloshing some of the Bourbon on her denim dress. "A big fat mamma with an eternal no! on her lips is all the Church is!"

Magruder was not offended. There were new religions for the young apparently. He preferred his own formal brand of Catholicism.

"What was it you wanted to say, Ingrid?"

She came very close with a sudden intensity in her eyes: "I want you to take me with you when you leave tomorrow. I want you to take me out of this place or I'll die before the baby ever comes."

"It's impossible, Ingrid."

"*Please!* Please don't say no! You're the only one he'd ever let me leave with."

"I am sorry. It's out of the question, Ingrid. I know it's very confining for you here, but it's your home. They all love you very much, and your mother and those women, your aunts, will take good care of you when it's time for the baby to come. Besides, where would I take you?"

"To the baby's father. I want to be with him when the baby comes."

"But it would be far out of my way, Ingrid, to travel to Boston to help you find some boy at one of the universities there."

She wiped her eyes. Tears had started down the furrows of her cheeks: "It isn't a boy in Boston, coach. It's Emmett Carruthers."

"My God . . . not Emmett Carruthers . . ." Magruder whispered hoarsely.

"Yes."

In the same moment he spilled most of his Bourbon onto the carpeting, he thought of the massiveness of Deutsch and the debilitated scrawniness of Carruthers the last time Magruder had seen him. Then he remembered Deutsch listening upstairs, and asked softly behind a crescendo of "Victory at Sea," "But how did it happen? Where?"

"Here. Emmett was here in August to dry out before

73

he had to start teaching again in September. Once he got back on his feet we spent a lot of time together and it just happened one day in that most proverbial of all places, the hayloft. After that we made love every day, just about everywhere."

"And no one suspected?"

"Twelve hundred acres is a lot of ground, coach. Besides, who'd suspect Emmett? Daddy thinks he's a slob and only lets him stay here because he can feel superior to a college professor. And mother thinks he's pathetic, too, but a good moral lesson for us kids."

"And you, Ingrid?"

"I think he's the kindest, most gentle man I've ever met."

"He's weak, Ingrid. He's a very weak man."

"I'm not. I could take good care of him."

"Then ask your father, Ingrid. If he says yes, I'll gladly let you come with me."

She smiled at him, a child grown wise. "If daddy ever found out it was Emmett before he got a chance to hold his grandchild in his arms, he'd rip Emmett's head right off his shoulders. He's that strong."

Magruder sighed for the truth of what she was saying. She took a long sip of Bourbon from the glass which she had not touched since pouring it, then broke into a spasm of coughing. Magruder rose to pummel her back, feigning solicitude when actually something perverse inside him was touched giddy at the profusion of disclosures that the passage of Azrael was evoking: That class of 1950 was full of closet skeletons that rattled and danced and jived about the American landscape to warm up the winter of

'73. What lay ahead with the Vauchons, Carruthers and the three gentlemen of Red Bank, New Jersey?

But then he became serious again, seeing the reality of the sad, pleading eyes before him once more. It was no good: Without the father's permission to go to Carruthers, any intervention on Magruder's part was useless. And even if he were to try spiriting her off the place in a *fait accompli,* Vauchon, the Deutsches' friend in Chicago, would stonewall her progress, perhaps even forcibly return her home when he learned she was to be delivered up to the lover Carruthers. And further, Carruthers might not even want her. . . .

"Unless you confess to your father that Carruthers is the father of your unborn child, I can't help you, Ingrid. I can't pretend we're heading for Boston to find him. It would be unfair to you, don't you think?"

"Please . . ." She put down her untouched Bourbon and collapsed against his chest, her heavy body shuddering with sobs.

"Don't cry, Ingrid," he said, patting her head. "It will work out. It may seem to you like the end of the world, but I've lived long enough to know it never is. I remember when your father was at St. Anselm's, creeping ashenfaced into my office with a problem that he thought would end in the destruction of the universe by five o'clock in the afternoon."

"The crabs?" Ingrid asked wearily, taking a puff on her cigarette and wiping tears from her eyes.

"Among other things," Magruder answered. Then the mirth caught up with him again and he began to laugh:

"How did you find out about those secret awful things in your old man's past?"

"I think everybody in Nebraska knows the story by now. The Vauchons come out here for about three days every fall. The only things daddy and Mr. Vauchon have in common now are the crabs."

"You've got to admit it's funny."

"I'd say it's also boring. Thank God daddy and mother inherited their farms at the right time. I can't imagine how he'd survive if he had to make it in the big world on the outside if life's high point was getting rid of the crabs at St. Anselm's twenty-three years ago."

"Your father, Ingrid, despite the shortcomings you think he has, is probably the most honest person I have ever met."

"That's only because he hasn't got the brains to be wily, coach. Here, take my drink. I'll turn off the music and go up to bed. Sorry to bother you with all this."

"It's no bother, Ingrid. Will I see you before I leave?"

"No. Thanks. I hardly ever leave my room. I have a hot plate and a little fridge and my books, so it's a lot better than going out to face the solicitous mob for meals three times a day."

"They're your family, Ingrid, not a mob."

"The hands eat with us, coach. All six of them. That's a mob. I know what I'm talking about. Good night."

"Good night."

Ingrid turned off the stereo and slowly climbed the stairs to her room. Magruder sat sipping at his Bourbon. It seared his throat on the way down. He composed a lecture to deliver to Emmett Carruthers. It would be old-fashioned and righteous—"You had the fun, now pay the price." . . . Or something like that. In any case, Emmett Carruthers, prime candidate for the world's foremost depressive, was going to assume responsibility for Ingrid's child. Magruder was determined about that.

He awoke just before dawn to the rumble of a plow going past on the road before the house. The storm had blown itself out, and there seemed to be no wind. He looked across the expanse of yard toward the milking barn and saw that his Buick was already recovered, standing in the bright circle of a spotlight, battery cables hooked up beneath the hood. One of Deutsch's hands used a broom to brush off the snow that clung, almost a foot deep, to the roof. The side of the car that had struck the rim of the ditch did not have a single visible dent in it.

He felt hungry from having eaten too little the day before and welcomed the sound of Marta Deutsch knocking on his door to let him know that his breakfast was ready. But he might take plenty of time since the quilting ladies had about an hour's work left on Aurelia Adnizzio's wedding present.

Magruder got stiffly out of bed, wondering if he would arrive in Chicago early enough for a walk to take the kinks out of his legs. He showered and dressed, then started toward the stairs, debating whether he should stop a moment to knock on Ingrid's door (identifiable by a tacked-up poster ruefully urging zero population growth) but decided against it since he knew he could offer her no hope, nor could he stand to see her despair.

Downstairs in the living room, where they worked now before the fireplace, the quilters chanted him a uniform good morning. He returned the greeting, conscious that each of them seemed to be studying his face, trying to decipher what had happened with Ingrid the night before.

He passed through the Gothic room that had formerly held the ladies, then into the kitchen, where he received another greeting from the sixteen people seated at breakfast—Marta, the children, hired hands and hitherto unseen housekeeper of Albert Deutsch, who sat, patriarch of his clan, at the head of the table, gorging himself on a mound of flapjacks and sausage.

"Sit here, coach," Deutsch invited Magruder to an empty place beside him, his eyes trying also for some inkling of the conversation with Ingrid.

"Sleep well, coach?"

"Quite well, Albert," Magruder said. "I see the storm is over. Thank you for getting my car back on the road."

"Yep. We went down 'n got her about an hour ago before the plow came by. She had enough juice left in the battery to turn her over, 'n you don't even have a kick in the side where she slid into the ditch. Nothing hurt underneath either. Hope you don't mind waiting until the ladies finish up the quilt for Vincent's daughter?"

"Not at all. If your road is clear, then the interstate will be for sure. I should make Chicago sometime this evening."

"Matty Vauchon phoned about half an hour ago," Deutsch said. "He wanted to make sure you were coming today. He said not to worry about the directions he gave you. Just drive to the end of the Eisenhower Expressway where it meets the Lake Shore Drive and find a parking spot. You'll find two colored guys in a Lincoln who will lead you to Matty's apartment."

"Where is his apartment, Albert?"

"Right where you'd expect Matty's place to be. Right smack in the middle of the Gold Coast. You can see everywhere up and down the lake from there."

"Oh, coach, wait until you see their apartment," Marta enthused, setting a plate equal to her husband's own before him. "It's like a dream. They have such beautiful things. Every room is different. One is an exact copy of a room from a castle in France. And another one is full of paintings—primitives, they're called—that Matty's family brought from Haiti. . . ."

"I don't care for them so much, coach, that primitive art I mean, but they're worth a fortune," Deutsch interrupted.

"Mr. Vauchon is a colored man, but he's really rich. He's a millionaire," one of the younger sons piped up, banging the spoon with which he ate his oatmeal on the table top for emphasis.

"Damn right he is, buster! A couple of times over!" Deutsch was proud and delighted, Magruder thought, at the notion of being the friend of a bona-fide multimillionaire. "Did you know Matty and Myra own two Rolls-Royces, coach?"

"No, I didn't, Albert," Magruder answered, wary of the very ebullient Marta pouring coffee at his elbow.

"You should see them, coach," one of the hands at the other end of the table chimed in. "They come out to visit in September last in a silver Rolls-Royce convertible that cost more than thirty-five thousand dollars. He paid cash money for it, too. There's a lot of folks couldn't afford even half that for a house, let alone a car."

The admiration at the table was general. Magruder began eating the enormous breakfast he might never finish despite his hunger and stared out through the kitchen windows that looked away from the barns upon the fields of sparkling snow that stretched away to seeming infinity. Perhaps here in the Nebraska dullness where the Deutsches rose with dawn and ate hefty meals in preparation for the long, tedious days of work, they lived vicariously through the wealthy, flamboyant Vauchons with their Haitian primitives and Rolls-Royces, the Vauchons who, it seemed to Magruder, glided effortlessly through life when others faltered often because they were human, whose children would go unerringly off to a Harvard or Radcliffe when their hour came, and return home to present their parents with honors rather than dismissal notices. . . .

Let the monstrous disparity between the Vauchons and Deutsches never turn to hatred, O Lord, Magruder thought.

"I'd be surprised, coach, if Matty didn't try to get you to take a repossessed car one of his finance companies is always taking back. I mean, after all, coach, that car of yours must be twenty years old."

"Eighteen to be exact, Albert. But it's in very good repair," Magruder singsonged wearily, thinking he had uttered the Buick's defense by now in as many places as Carruthers had gone to dry out. "Besides," he added, "Martin McFadden tried to give me a two-year-old

Cadillac that he won in a poker game, and I turned him down."

"You did? Why? That sounds crazy to me," one of the hands judged in disbelief.

"An act of pity is close to an act of contempt, wouldn't you say so?" Magruder asked gruffly.

"Yes . . . well, yes . . ." Deutsch answered uncertainly, signaling the man with his eyes. There was a long silence, broken only by the sounds of eating until Marta Deutsch spoke one of her blank-eyed afterthoughts:

"Myra Vauchon and Carlotta McFadden are very good friends, coach. They call each other up and talk for ages on the phone all the time. Matty is always complaining about the bills."

"I expect this has been a particularly expensive week then," Magruder said, pushing back his plate, half uneaten, and gulping down the last of his coffee. "I'd better be going soon, Albert. How's my gas?"

"Full up, coach. Marta and me will walk you out to see you off. You all packed?"

"I carried my bag downstairs, Albert. It's in front of the coat closet."

Magruder bade everyone in the kitchen good-by, shaking hands with the older children, the housekeeper and the six hands, then walked to the living room, where the four women held up the quilt finished only moments before for them to admire.

"It's quite lovely, ladies," Magruder told them. "I'm sure Aurelia and her husband will like it fine."

"Drive carefully, coach, and say hello to the Vauchons for us."

"I will," Magruder promised, struggling into his coat as the Deutsches struggled into their own. While they watched, the women folded the quilt, wrapped it in tissue paper, then covered that with a heavy wrapping paper that had the notation—Mr. & Mrs. Charles Modesti—already printed in Magic Marker capitals. Marta carried the quilt; her husband carried Magruder's suitcase; the three exited into the bright sunlight where the temperature was now above freezing and water dripped steadily from the eaves of the house.

"This was a freak storm, coach, 'n it's supposed to warm up real good the next couple of days," Deutsch said. "I don't think you'll see too much more snow once you're past Chicago."

They placed the suitcase and the quilt in the back seat since the trunk was loaded, and Deutsch switched off the charger and yanked the jumper cables from the battery. Then they stomped the beaten snow for a few long seconds, and when Deutsch next opened his mouth to speak, Magruder knew the moment of truth was at hand: "Well, how did it go with Ingrid last night, coach?"

"She wanted me to take her East to help her find the baby's father."

"But she said she didn't have any idea who the father was," Deutsch sputtered in disbelief. His wife grabbed at his arm as if for support.

"Well not exactly. But there was one young man she considered rather pliable," Magruder lied. "She thought he would marry her and make a good father for the baby."

"Was he white?"

"Yes."

"But what if the baby's father turns out to be black? What will that white boy say? There'll be a divorce or annulment on top of an unwanted pregnancy."

"I told her I thought the best thing was for her to stay here and have the baby instead of going East on the hope of corralling that boy. She agreed, I guess, but she wasn't very happy about it."

"I'd never let her go East with you, coach," Deutsch spoke sadly, shaking his head. "The chance is too flimsy that the boy would go along with her, 'n God knows what'd happen out there if she got into all that drug business again. You hear all this terrible stuff about deformed babies. . . ."

With a single impulse they looked toward the house: In the window of her upstairs room, behind a lace curtain, Ingrid's shadow could be seen looking eastward, as if—it occurred distantly to Magruder—she waited for the lover Carruthers to come shambling along the road to save her.

He shook hands with the Deutsches who seemed inordinately depressed and forlorn, pecking a kiss on Marta's cheek for good measure, then started up the car, letting it warm a little before driving off. The air was still and there was only the lowing of cows to be heard as they moved out of the barn into the knee high snow. Impulsively Magruder turned to address Marta Deutsch before he slipped the car into gear: "You should have let her get the prescription for the pill, Marta, when she asked you that time."

"I couldn't, coach. It's against all the training of the Church."

"Well, perhaps the Church will be more understanding about the baby, then. But I doubt it somehow."

He drove off sounding the horn and waving to sad Ingrid in the upstairs room. But Ingrid, who surely saw him, did not wave in return.

CHAPTER 6

Chez Vauchon

By the time Magruder reached the interstate again, then headed toward the Iowa line, rivulets of water from the melting snow banks were coursing across the highway, running over the car in great sheets of spray every time a truck whipped past.

He tried the radio, but after the news it was the same country and Western as the day before, so he gave up and found himself thinking without any particular anticipation of the night he would spend with the Vauchons, spiritual kinsmen to the McFaddens in Las Vegas. Vauchon the entrepreneur—lawyer who would care not a moral twitch about the incomplete justice of Kasprzak's dying, be concerned only with the expediency that his circumstances of age and wealth and family required. Expediency was Vauchon's true métier and it served him well. At St. Anselm's in 1950, when he had been a lithe and powerful right halfback, he and Welsh working together might have turned the tide of that season of disgrace, producing one or two wins to offset the column of losses. But Matty Vauchon, who was not a coward, was, better said, a calculator. He set his own levels of exertion. No more. And he was a true genius in judging his limit.

Failing to see the point of scrambling for yardage in the face of a sure loss, he hardly moved at all.

Magruder had hated him for that, raged about it so often to Florence that, in exasperation, she had finally cautioned him that Vauchon the reluctant athlete might not be the root of the problem at all. In response Magruder took special pains in dealing with Vauchon, conceding by degrees that that particular student's superior bearing and cultivated accent had managed to touch an easily annoyed place in him that he never liked to admit. Haitian-born, Vauchon's first language was French. He had learned precise English from tutors so that he spoke it far better than any other student at St. Anselm's, and was the favorite of the rhetoric faculty. To Magruder, it made him seem arch and arrogant. Uppity: the admission then. Surprisingly, Vauchon, the school's only black, and Deutsch had become inseparable friends, a friendship that continued evidently to the present.

Crossing the Missouri from Nebraska to Iowa, momentarily intrigued by the fact that the river seemed not to have a sliver of ice in it, he recalled Vauchon's wife, Myra, a fabled beauty of New Orleans Creole extraction who had come to her marriage with a dowry that Magruder seemed to recall was the only thing anyone talked about at the first reunion after their wedding. Though infinitely more cultured than her friend, the Brunhilde-like Carlotta, she ruled the roost in the same way. He grew suddenly weary, thinking of how it would be: the formal dinner, the children's dismissal, the quiet, purposeful talk of irretrievable time changing everything. There would be no rages, and no beatings either. *Reduc-*

tio ad absurdum was the Vauchon method: In the course of an evening that working twosome would contrive to make Magruder see himself as a witless and ineffectual old fool. . . .

In Iowa, just west of Des Moines, he heard the noise in the car behind him, a long baleful groan of escaping gas that could only have been a fart. Then the sound of coughing came to him, hacking and dry, yet muffled, as if the cougher had stuffed a glove between teeth to deaden the sound. Magruder checked the rearview mirror, tilting it downward, and saw with resignation that the trunk lid was slightly ajar, bobbing with vibration as the car passed over surface cracks in the highway. In a Des Moines suburb, with the capitol building visible in the near distance, he pulled into the parking lot of a small diner and went inside for coffee, not looking out, giving Ingrid time to climb out of the trunk and compose herself in the front seat where he knew he would find her.

When he left the diner she was there, wearing the denim dress, a heavy shawl pulled about her shoulders, looking green, he thought, probably from fumes blowing upward from the exhaust. Still, she munched on a candy bar.

"Hello, Ingrid."

"Hello, coach. I'm sorry, but the fumes were making me sick. I hid the two suitcases I took out of the trunk in the hay barn. Daddy can ship them on to you."

"When I drove off, I thought I saw you sitting at the window of your room, Ingrid."

"It was my sister, coach. She took my place as soon as

you and daddy and mother left the house. I sneaked into the car while everybody was having breakfast."

They watched as a police car drove into the parking lot, eyed them curiously, then turned about to return to the highway.

"You'll have to go back, Ingrid. I can't take you to Carruthers. They'll phone the police as soon as they find out you're gone, and we won't be hard to find in this old car. I'll be in a real pickle trying to explain to the cops that I didn't aid and abet your escape."

"They won't find out for days, coach. We could be in South Bend by tomorrow. They never come to my room. They know better. I'll make sure you aren't blamed."

"You know I'm stopping tonight at the Vauchons, Ingrid. Matty Vauchon will be on the phone to your father in a minute when he sees you there. He'll have you back in Nebraska in no time flat."

"Let me take my chances with Mr. Vauchon, coach. I'm sure I can convince him to let me go on to Indiana with you."

"When Matty finds out you're on your way to hook up with Emmett Carruthers, you'll really have two strikes against you, Ingrid. The Vauchons despise Emmett for his drinking. They think he's a moral degenerate."

She shrugged, munching the last of her candy bar. "So what? All the more reason to try to get to Emmett. Who that knew any better would want to be like the Vauchons? They're whiter than we are."

"I ought to take you to a state police barracks right now, Ingrid, and have them call your home."

"But you won't, coach," she said almost matter-offactly. "Now that I'm here you don't really want me to go back to that farmhouse full of confused, whispering people to have the baby. I think I'd really go out of my gourd if I had to spend the whole winter upstairs in my room hiding from them."

He sighed for the truth of what she said, his mind nevertheless rushing to alternatives as he watched a huge cattle transport full of steers on their way to market edge into the diner's parking lot and stop in a hiss of air brakes. Also he wondered how his neatly planned scenario had managed to get so complicated this far west of his real purpose in making the trip.

"All right, Ingrid, I'll take you on with me. But if we make it past Vauchon, and I have my doubts about that, I'm phoning your father from South Bend."

"Agreed, coach. By that time, though, it will be a *fait accompli*."

"Your father will come after you, Ingrid."

"No he won't, coach. Not when I read him the announcement I've prepared for the St. Anselm's *Alumni Review* stating that the father of Albert Deutsch's first grandchild is Emmett Carruthers. That little blurb will cause a hell of a lot more people to snicker than catty Myra Vauchon can get to."

Magruder snorted. There was humor in this after all. Deutsch, who needed the drunk Carruthers as whipping boy for his bruised ego, was now caught in a hopeless trap of his whipping boy's own making. He smiled at the notion, and turning, he saw Ingrid smiling also, rather impishly he thought.

"And Vauchon . . . ?" he asked her after a moment.

"I know where the chink in his armor is, coach."

"Be responsible for what you do then, Ingrid," Magruder told her sternly. "Whatever you think of the Vauchons, they've been friends of your parents since before you were born."

He started the car, then pulled out onto the street, finding his way toward the interstate access road one more time.

Beyond Iowa City and across the Mississippi into Illinois, Ingrid spelled him at the driving. It grew colder in early darkness and beneath the moon the snow-covered Illinois fields shone with a glaze of ice.

They approached the vast sprawl of the lights of Chicago about seven-thirty and moved effortlessly inbound along the Eisenhower Expressway, turning northward on Lake Shore Drive. Magruder parked in the first available space, according to Vauchon's directions. Instantly, it seemed, two black men materialized in a deep blue Lincoln, incomprehensibly clean, as though it had been carried somehow through the city streets to avoid the splash of slush from melting snow. The passenger got out, effusively smiling a range of gold-capped teeth. He was a well-groomed man in his forties, wearing only a business suit.

"Are you Coach Magruder, by chance?"

"Yes."

"I'm an employee of Mr. Vauchon. My name is Brighton. I do hope your trip wasn't too tiring." He had an islander's accent, Bahamian perhaps. The lilt of it seemed anomalous in the wintry streets of Chicago, where a chill wind had begun rising off the lake.

"The Vauchons are waiting at their apartment for you, Coach Magruder. Just follow us into the underground parking garage and we'll help you with your bags."

"Thank you," Magruder told the man. Suddenly the other had stopped smiling and stared quizzically past Magruder at Ingrid: "May I ask who the young lady is, coach?"

"This is Ingrid Deutsch from Nebraska."

"I don't believe Mr. Vauchon was expecting Miss Deutsch."

"Neither was I. You'll have to trust us. We'll explain it to Matthew later."

"All right, please follow us."

Brighton climbed back into the Lincoln and somehow, not unexpectedly, Magruder saw him lift a phone to call Vauchon as the car moved off. They followed behind and a note of apprehension crept into Ingrid's voice: "Oh God! I hope Mr. Vauchon doesn't call daddy before we get there."

"If he hasn't, then you've got to make sure he doesn't spill the beans if your father calls to see if I made it in one piece."

"I think I'd better tell the Vauchons where I'm going and why just as soon as I get inside the door."

"Yes," Magruder agreed. The Lincoln moved steadily along the lake where the lights of boats bobbed at anchor in the distance, then turned left, crossing the oncoming lane and descended a ramp to a parking garage beneath an elegant new building. Inside—in a school of Cadillacs and Mercedes—the Lincoln drew into a reserved space beside the two fabled Vauchon Rolls-Royces. The driver indicated a place for Magruder to park. In seconds the two black men were at the Buick's door: "We'll take your bags, Coach Magruder," Brighton told him.

"I've got just a single bag on the back seat."

"And Miss Deutsch?"

"Just a small satchel in the trunk. Did Mr. Vauchon say anything when you telephoned to say I was along too?"

Brighton smiled, accomplished servant. His tone was conciliatory: "The Vauchons are quite surprised that you're along, but they're delighted to see you anyhow."

They took the bags, then locked the car that contained the wedding gifts to the Modestis and boarded an elevator to the fourteenth floor. When the doors opened, Matthew Vauchon—leaning to corpulence, Magruder decided, like McFadden in Las Vegas—was already waiting for them in the hallway. Behind him the entry to the apartment was open, one of only two on the entire floor.

"Ingrid!" he said enthusiastically, kissing her forehead, seemingly oblivious to Magruder, "how wonderful to see you! I spoke with your father not forty-five minutes ago, but he didn't say anything about your being on your way here."

"He doesn't know I'm along, Mr. Vauchon. He thinks I'm sulking upstairs in my room back in Nebraska."

"He doesn't know you've left, Ingrid? Are you on your way back to Radcliffe?" The voice came from out of the apartment foyer. It was Myra Vauchon, clad stunningly in a dinner dress that announced to a tired Magruder that a multicourse formal dinner was in the offing.

"I was kicked out of Radcliffe over Thanksgiving, Mrs. Vauchon. I'm pregnant. I sneaked out of the house and hid in the trunk of Coach Magruder's car, so he's not responsible for my being here. He didn't know I was in the car until we got to Des Moines. I'm on my way to Notre Dame to see my baby's father."

"Who?" Vauchon asked. A grim look, like dread, came over his face at the possibility of who it might be.

"Emmett Carruthers."

"Oh, my God . . ." Myra Vauchon gasped out, holding to a wall for support. "Oh, my good God . . ."

"Your father will kill him," Vauchon said. "He will absolutely break him in half."

"That man is a disgusting drunk!" Brighton sputtered involuntarily, his hands fluttering palsy-like before them. "When he came here to dry out that time we literally had to tie him down to the bed to keep him away from the liquor closet!"

"Perhaps we all ought to go into the apartment before we disturb anyone else," Magruder suggested, seeing that the door to the other apartment had been opened a crack. The sound of his voice seemed to startle Vauchon to the reality of his presence for the first time: "Oh, hello, coach. Welcome to Chicago," he said cursorily, shaking hands with Magruder while he continued staring at Ingrid. But Myra Vauchon seemed totally oblivious to him. She shepherded Ingrid into the apartment. "Ingrid, how did it happen? He couldn't have raped you. There's not enough of him there at any one time to do it. . . ."

"It just happened one day last August. I was going East to school and I figured it was time. I got sort of tired of being a virgin."

"Of course, dear. I can understand that. But why didn't you take the pill?"

"Mother wouldn't let me. Birth control is against the Church and all that crap."

"That's ridiculous, Ingrid. Our Lydia's been on the pill since she was fourteen. I wouldn't have it otherwise. Look at the mess you're in now."

"It's not so bad, Mrs. Vauchon. I'm looking forward to having the baby."

"But Emmett Carruthers' baby?" The words came from Vauchon. They were inside the lavish apartment now and while Magruder stared awed through a genuine tropical forest of palms and ferns and riotous flowers in front of the huge plate-glass windows that gave out onto a spectacular view of the arc of lights along the lake shore, and the ships' lights in the water beyond, Matty Vauchon stood narcissistic prisoner before a full-length antique mirror and surveyed the pained grimaces that the name Carruthers evoked on his face.

"Ingrid . . ." Vauchon spoke, staring wide-eyed at his image but probably not seeing it. "Ingrid, I seem to have read somewhere that a growing number of doctors consider it possible that alcoholism may be transferred genetically from generation to generation. This is said to be the case of W. C. Fields. If it's true, that isn't much of a life for your baby to look forward to. . . . Perhaps you might like to stay with us a few days and have a little talk with Mrs. Vauchon?"

"I'm not having an abortion, Mr. Vauchon. That's out of the question."

"We could call it a miscarriage, Ingrid," Myra Vauchon said stonily. "A bad spill on a patch of ice. That way your parents, who don't believe in birth control and obviously wouldn't condone abortion, wouldn't need to be compromised. And they would never need to know about Carruthers either."

"What are you two up to?" Magruder demanded in disbelief. "You haven't got the right. She's carrying a human life inside her."

"You hypocritical old son of a bitch!" Myra Vauchon said sharply. "Don't play holier than thou with us! How dare you belabor us for trying to help Ingrid with her problem when you're on your way to New Jersey to wreck three existing lives, not to say anything of their wives and children, for the sake of that fat zero Kasprzak, who's better off dead!"

"Kasprzak had a life and soul also, Myra!" Magruder thundered at her. "No one had the right to take them away!"

"Some lives are more valuable than others, coach. Some are more beautiful, more intelligent, and have lots more money. And you know damn well what I'm talking about. . . ."

"Myra—silence!" Vauchon ordered. "We talked about how we would handle this, remember?"

"Yes, I'm sorry, Matthew," she demurred. "I lost my temper. I've been so edgy all day and Carlotta has called three times already, which isn't helping things. We're all so incredibly embroiled in this."

95

"Yes," Vauchon agreed. "Yes. . . . Coach, why don't you let me take your coat? You must think we're poor hosts. Brighton, you and Ramsey wait around a few minutes until I call Nebraska and find out what next to do about Ingrid. You may have to drive out to Omaha with her in the morning."

"Please don't call daddy, Mr. Vauchon," Ingrid begged.

"Are you willing to accept our little offer of help, Ingrid?"

"No, not that."

"Then I've got to call your father. I can't let you go on to that degenerate Carruthers. It's my responsibility as your father's friend."

Ingrid sat down on the edge of a gilt chair and drew her shawl more closely about her shoulders. She stared at the Vauchons, pityingly, Magruder thought, even though it seemed to him every deck in the world was stacked against her now.

"You're making a mistake, Mr. Vauchon. If you tell him about Emmett Carruthers being the father of the child, then your fabulous friendship, such as it is, will really be kaput. Daddy never liked you anyhow, and now that he knows you know all the shoddy details about his tramp of a daughter and are sure to impart them to everybody on the old St. Anselm's circuit via Carlotta McFadden, he'll really hate your guts. . . . You'll hear the word 'nigger' all the way here from Nebraska."

"Ingrid, that is absolutely preposterous!" Vauchon insisted, stomping ineffectually into the thickness of an oriental rug. "Your father and I have been friends for

96

over twenty-five years. I know exactly what kind of man he is. He would never say such a thing about me. . . ."

"Bullshit, Vauchon! Are you kidding? He hates your money and your Rolls-Royces and your Haitian primitives and your dusky rich wife and the annoyingly superior way you two speak French that nobody else understands right in the middle of somebody else's conversation."

"But, Ingrid, we do that only because Matthew is translating some of the patois your parents speak for me," Myra Vauchon said, pleadingly, Magruder thought. "We're not being superior. There are simply many words and idioms your parents use that I don't understand."

"Bullshit again, Mrs. Vauchon. We know why you do it."

"Ingrid!" Magruder raged at her. "If you don't stop this, I'll smash you myself!"

"They're not lies, coach. What do you know? The Vauchons stay with us for three days and daddy gets drunk for the next three. He's always bitching about the fact that he was so low down in the social order at St. Anselm's that his only friend was a nigger. And you should hear him going on about the crabs. . . ."

"What crabs?" Myra Vauchon demanded, narrowing her eyes at her husband.

"The crabs daddy caught but Mr. Vauchon didn't when they both balled the same prostitute in Albany, New York, one time."

"Ha!" Vauchon snorted his pleasure for the benefit of the two black men who looked on. "You should have seen that honkie corn husker Deutsch! He was infested with them! And I had not a single one anywhere on me!"

The three howled with mirth, the one called Brighton stomping his foot repeatedly on the exposed pattern of a parquet floor, the other, Ramsey, bent double with his arms folded into his stomach.

"Was the prostitute white or black, Matthew?" Myra demanded angrily, grabbing her husband's arm and spinning him around.

"She was black," Vauchon said automatically.

"Bullshit! She was white and you know it, Mr. Vauchon," Ingrid threw at him.

"Matthew!" Myra screeched. "You swore to me you have never lain with a white woman!"

"Myra, it was nothing. She was a prostitute. It was a lark back in prep school. Every young man does that sort of thing. I didn't look at her color. It was dark in the room. . . ."

But to no avail: Myra Vauchon, looking for a moment as if she might assault her husband, instead turned about and ran from the room through an open door, slamming it hard behind her. In the wake of her leave-taking, Vauchon stared at Ingrid Deutsch, disdain written all over his face: "Did you know, Ingrid dear, that your father used to polish one pair of my shoes each evening after dinner in our room?"

"No," Ingrid answered, a trifle uncertain now, as if she began to fear the monster she had set loose.

"Yes, dear. You see, I had many pairs of shoes, and your father derived a certain pleasure, given only to imbeciles no doubt, in keeping them clean and in good repair and in orderly files in my closet. You can readily see why I consented to be his roommate for four long years."

"Matthew, I think we should be leaving. I'm truly sorry about all this," Magruder told him.

"Yes, I guess you should be leaving, coach. There's a Howard Johnson Motor Lodge not too far from here where you can stay the night. Brighton will show you the way. Ramsey, you stay here to answer the phone when those three honkies from Jersey call, then slam down the receiver as hard as you can. We will only speak with Mrs. McFadden from Las Vegas. She has Mexican Indian blood in her veins."

"Matthew, please . . ." Magruder said. "She's desperate. . . ."

"I won't call her father, coach. I have no intention at all of interfering. The hell with them. And as for the three in New Jersey, I hope you have an unrivaled success in the business of their punishment. I absolutely hope all three end up quite dead for their horrendous crime against our dear departed brother Kasprzak. I was supposed to read you the riot act tonight on the statute of limitations and the caseloads of county prosecutors, etc., but I won't waste my breath. . . ."

"We'll go now, Matthew. I'll call you in the morning before we leave Chicago. This whole thing will probably seem much overblown to you by then."

"No need to call, coach. I won't be here. But sleep late because it won't take you more than a few hours to get to South Bend. And when you find that bum Carruthers, please offer him our congratulations on the occasion of his paternity. Tell him we didn't think he had it in him."

99

"Yes, Matthew. Good night now."

"One last thing, coach. There was a present for Aurelia Adnizzio. We hear you're going to her wedding."

"Yes. I'll deliver it for you, Matthew. I've picked up a few others along the way."

"Fine." He nodded to Brighton, who retrieved the present from a nearby table, a styrofoam container that evidently contained the promised vase.

"It's a really lovely crystal vase," Vauchon said to no one in particular; then in the next instant he flung the container furiously against the wall so that they heard the tinkle of shattered crystal despite the protection of styrofoam.

"Damaged in shipment, coach," Vauchon said, handing it over.

"I'll try to glue the pieces together, Matthew, and call it an accident. It's the thought that counts, after all."

"Yes, coach, you're right," Vauchon replied, a momentary grimace of pain sliding over his face, "and we have always fancied ourselves to be very thoughtful people."

Then the phone rang, and Vauchon, prescient with pleasure at who it might be, lifted the receiver.

"Carlotta dearest, how are you? Yes, he's here and he's just leaving. And have we got a little smidgen of news for you. I'll switch you over to Myra and she can provide the gory details. I hope you're sitting down. You'll need to be. Speak to you later, dear."

He pressed a button, evidently to transfer the call, then shook hands gravely with Magruder: "Good-by, coach. Good-by, Miss Deutsch."

"Good-by, Matthew, it will heal," Magruder said, patting his shoulder with one free hand, holding the contemptuous offering in the other. Vauchon saw them into the hallway, then softly closed the door behind them as Brighton wordlessly pressed the elevator call button. When it arrived the three descended silently. Ingrid stared at the floor, with the edge of her shawl wedged into her mouth. In the garage Magruder opened the Buick's trunk and deposited the wedding gift. Brighton threw in their two bags, then went to start up the Lincoln while Magruder opened the passenger door for Ingrid.

Inside he hunched wearily over the wheel for a long moment prior to inserting the ignition key, then flew awake and smashed Ingrid Deutsch fiercely across the face with the back of his hand. Blood spurted instantly from her nose and she collapsed shuddering against the window pane.

"You hurt that man so cruelly, Ingrid. That was a wicked, wicked thing to do."

"What else could I do?" she sobbed. "It was the only way I could think of not to be sent back to Nebraska. I'll kill myself if I have to go back there and have my baby."

He handed her a handkerchief: "Is your nose broken, Ingrid?"

"I don't think so. I just bleed easily, that's all."

"I have never struck a woman before this in my entire life. I'm sixty-eight years old," Magruder said morosely. He turned his head sideways to see Brighton in the blue Lincoln regarding them thoughtfully.

"Don't worry about it, coach," she sniffled. "Oh, God"— she burst into real tears now—"Mr. Vauchon was so hurt.

I know he's a tough trial lawyer and all that, but he was practically crying when we left."

"It will heal. They've been friends too long. Your father will crawl to Chicago if he has to, to reconcile things."

Brighton sounded the horn and Magruder switched on the engine.

They followed Brighton out of the garage, back into the slush of Lake Shore Drive and perhaps half a mile farther on to the familiar orange and blue decor of the Howard Johnson Motor Lodge. Brighton pulled into a parking lot beyond the entrance and came back to stand at Magruder's window.

"Coach Magruder . . . ?"

"Yes, Brighton?"

"None of it was true, was it?"

"No."

"Somehow I thought not. I have gas for you in the trunk of my car. I'll fill your tank while you check in. Your rooms are reserved. They are charged to Mr. Vauchon. Don't try to pay for them. By the way, Miss Deutsch's room is reserved under the name of Artwald. . . ."

"Why?"

"A small precaution. The police may be looking for an Ingrid Deutsch by morning for all we know. Mr. Vauchon phoned me as we were driving here. He says it's imperative that she make South Bend in your company."

"I see . . ." Magruder said, though in truth he did not. With Ingrid, who had stopped her bleeding and reversed her shawl to hide the spotting, he went inside to confirm their reservations. He sent her upstairs to her room, then came outside again to stand beside Brighton, who emptied the last of two jerry cans into the Buick's tank.

"A dippy world, ain't it, Magruder?" Brighton asked, his eyes reddened from the gas fumes, his breath smoking in the below freezing temperature. Behind them came the muted roar of traffic on Lake Shore Drive. Someone played a TV set too loud in a nearby downstairs room of the motel.

"Yes. It's too bad. The Deutsches have a tremendous admiration for the Vauchons. They need them," Magruder added as an afterthought.

"The Vauchons need the Deutsches also."

Magruder was bemused: "What could the Vauchons possibly need from the Deutsches?"

"Those three days of rest every Fall on that farm in Nebraska. Sometimes it seems to me Mr. Vauchon talks of nothing else the entire year from the day he returns until the day it's time to go out again. It's the only place he's completely able to relax. Well, good night, Magruder."

"Good night, Brighton," he said as he went to retrieve their bags and carry them upstairs to their rooms. Gas cans in the trunk, the Lincoln sped quickly out of the parking area as Magruder mounted the stairs.

In the morning they rose about nine, breakfasted and were on the road by ten, heading south briefly on Interstate 90 until they regained Interstate 80 again, heading eastward. The day was chill and overcast, and passing by the belching stacks of industrial Gary, Indiana, just over the line from Illinois, where the smoke rose upward to flatten out against the overlay of clouds, Magruder chanced to look behind them in the rearview mirror and felt a nameless surge of fear ripple through him.

The blue Lincoln and the silver Rolls-Royce convertible, both seen for the first time, followed behind them, each carrying a full complement of blacks. On closer scrutiny Magruder perceived that all the passengers were husky-looking younger men.

CHAPTER 7

The Drunkard
of Notre Dame

"Matthew Vauchon is following us, Ingrid," Magruder told her quietly. "Along with two carloads of black men, that is."

She winced at the news, then swung around and involuntarily crammed the end of the shawl worn about her shoulders into her mouth.

"Oh God, look at them all. Coach, do you think he'll try to take me back to Nebraska?"

"No. If that's what Matthew intended doing, he could have caught up with us long before this. I guess, though, that it's about time to find out what he wants."

Ahead, in another mile, was a roadside rest. Magruder turned off the interstate and parked before the entrance to the rest rooms. He ordered Ingrid into the ladies' room without really knowing why. Then he went to the men's room and stood up to a urinal to relieve himself. In a minute more he was joined on either side by seven black men, the fury of their collective relief sounding to Magruder like the boiling of an angry rapids. In another moment, Vauchon, his expensive cashmere overcoat first removed by Brighton, stood in place beside Magruder on the right.

"Good morning, Matthew. Sloppy day, isn't it?"

"Good morning, coach. Yes, it's grisly, all right."

"Well, Matthew. Evidently you're not trying to take her back."

"No, I'm not. In fact we're going right on into South Bend with you."

"Why?"

"To make sure that Carruthers assumes his responsibility for her."

"From the looks of it, I'd say he doesn't have much choice. Why are you doing this? Why all these men?"

"They're not for Carruthers. They're for South Bend. As a black man I'm always filled with a vague dread of the presence of so many of our blue-collared co-religionists in that town. But otherwise, as far as Ingrid is concerned, after we'd had a few drinks to calm down last night, Myra convinced me she was faking it. When Brighton came back and told me what had happened down in the garage, I was certain of it. I owe this to her father for the sake of our friendship."

Magruder flushed the urinal and zippered up his fly: "Did you call Albert and Marta last night?"

"No. He didn't call us either. Which probably means they don't know Ingrid is gone yet."

"I've got to call him as soon as we find Carruthers, then. With Carlotta McFadden in possession of that knowledge, it'll just be a matter of time before somebody lets them know second hand."

"Yes." The room convulsed in a massed exclamation of flushing urinals. Vauchon stepped regally back from the apparatus that was flushed by the man beside him to the right, and accepted first a wet, then dry linen towel from

Brighton, washing, then wiping with meticulous care his long elegant hands with their manicured nails before he slipped back into the overcoat. Magruder grew irreverent at that spectacle of ablution that seemed to awe Vauchon's followers. "Do you know where Carruthers lives, Matthew?"

"Brighton knows the place. He went there once to pick our friend up to bring him to Chicago for one of his dryouts."

They all filed outside and Vauchon knocked on the door to the ladies' room: "It's all right for you to come out now, Ingrid."

"Is it, coach?" she asked, the trembling evident in her voice. "There are some women in here. I could ask them to stay with me."

"No need. Come out, Ingrid."

She pushed through the door, eyes downcast as she stood before Vauchon: "Hello, Mr. Vauchon. Why are you following us?"

"To make sure your paramour is ready to accept the responsibility for what he's done."

She looked warily about the half circle of unsmiling black men: "Don't hurt him, Mr. Vauchon."

"I'll absolutely have him broken in half if he chooses not to see the light. Let me know it now, Ingrid. Do you really want to set up housekeeping with him?"

"Yes, I love him, Mr. Vauchon."

"God Almighty! It seems there ought to be more promise for a young life than the misery of waking up every morning to the sight of Emmett Carruthers with the shakes trying to invent a reason for not going to teach his classes that day."

"I'll straighten him out, Mr. Vauchon. He only drinks because he's so alone. When we're married and the baby comes he won't be alone any longer, so he won't have so much reason to drink. . . ."

"And the other principal reason he drinks is because he's so terrified of women. How old are you now, Ingrid?"

"Eighteen, Mr. Vauchon . . ."

"Less than half his age . . . hmm. Well, at least he'll have only half as much reason as before to booze it up on that score."

There was a universal sniggering from the blacks behind them until Vauchon whirled about in anger: "Shut up, all of you! This is no goddamn joke!" Then he turned about again to Ingrid: "Really, Ingrid, I should call your father from here and have Brighton take you right back to Nebraska! You've caused me a lot of trouble."

"Boss, it's too damn far to go to Nebraska, and South Bend's just up the road apiece," Brighton pleaded, out of character, reminding Magruder of radio-time Jack Benny's Rochester that he and Florence had enjoyed ritualistically when returning home in the car from summer Sunday outings beside the Hudson. Vauchon eyed the other with startled disbelief, his mouth forming a reprimand perhaps, when Magruder cut him off, wearying now of Ingrid, Carruthers and Vauchon when he meant to be in New Jersey the very next night: "Brighton's right, Matthew. We've got to act quickly. In Nebraska they may already have found out she's gone."

Vauchon ordered his protection to the cars with a jerk of his head, then told Magruder to follow them, nodding compliance to Magruder's request that they not go faster than fifty-five miles per hour. They followed after the Rolls, falling a convenient long distance behind where the spray from the road slush was minimal since the Buick had no windshield solvent. In forty minutes perhaps, just before they turned off the interstate at South Bend, Ingrid broke the heavy silence for the first time: "Do you think they'll hurt Emmett, coach?"

"As Matthew implies, it depends on how co-operative he is," Magruder said stonily. "Hurting Carruthers a bit might be just what the doctor ordered at this stage of things."

"Would you let them?" she demanded.

"Do you really want him?"

"Yes."

"Then I'd let them."

They entered South Bend, Magruder looking for the Notre Dame campus and its trademark of the Virgin's statue atop her cupola that he had only ever seen in pictures. Ingrid was fascinated and childlike at the apparitions of toy soldiers, Santa Clauses and animal faces painted on the town fire hydrants. Seeing the forlorn face of a clown on one of the hydrants when they halted for a traffic light, Magruder uttered a silent prayer to himself that they would not find Carruthers already wrecked for the day, drunk unto unconsciousness.

When had the real boozing begun? Magruder suddenly wondered. When had the certainty arrived in Magruder's mind that Carruthers had ceased to become a joke among

his classmates, was no longer the overindulging sopho-
more moralist, unbelievably shy of women, and chary of
argument, to whom they all introduced their new or future wives with the easy certainty of coming off the better
man? Perhaps at the tenth reunion of that class of 1950
that Magruder remembered with absolute clarity: when
Carruthers had passed out standing up and cleaved a bartender's table in halves, knocking out two of his front
teeth, spraying the table's linen cover with a geyser of
blood, prompting an early, embarrassed end to the day's
events.

At subsequent reunions, his behavior, if anything, was
predictable and worse. Still, his former teammates had
not given up on him completely, mixed solicitousness
with their criticism, left open the door to their homes for
Carruthers' periodic dry-outs, when (Magruder suspected) the wives secretly enjoyed the prospect of rein-
troducing the child Carruthers to solid food.

All told, though, Carruthers' saving grace was the fact
he was not a mean drunk. He was a sad, ironic drunk instead and Magruder knew with certainty whence the
drinking had sprung. He had been a menaced child: A
timid boy who was pushed to the limits for any kind of
excellence in scatter-shot directions by a father who
raged and screeched, apoplectic-faced, from the side lines
during every football game, Magruder had taken to
benching Carruthers where his vomiting had easier recourse to the locker-room toilets. Not impressed by that
message, Carruthers the elder had so cajoled and
harangued Magruder via the alumni association and the
administration that Magruder, apoplectic in turn, had or-

dered him not to set foot on campus during a game, and put his own job on the line to emphasize to the headmaster that he meant business. Ironically, excellence occurred during the first game after his father was barred from observing: Carruthers intercepted two passes for St. Anselm touchdowns thrown by the same witless quarterback into a hole where Carruthers alone was trying to evade the action.

They arrived at a poor neighborhood of identical houses where Carruthers' small one-story clapboard place sat squeezed between two enormous naked trees whose protruding roots looked ready to pick up the structure and heave it into the street. Before the house the Rolls-Royce seemed ridiculously incongruous. Magruder, Vauchon and Brighton stood out of the cars and stomped onto the tiny front porch where three floorboards together were broken through to the crawl space below as if they had collapsed all at once beneath the weight of someone peering through the front window. Inside, past lace curtains gray with age, Magruder beheld the squalor of Carruthers' existence. Ancient, stuffed, dirty-looking furniture, a litter of whiskey bottles on two end tables, the blue books of some doubtless uncorrected test spread about the floor. The screen of the TV set had been kicked or punched in and shards of glass still lay on the floor beneath. Vauchon pounded on the door for a long minute, but there was no stirring from within. Magruder scanned the ugly sky and shivered in the cold despite himself: Perhaps it was always colder than a bank thermometer's reading in a mean, poor street like this.

"Now where?" Brighton asked. "To his department at the university?"

"Yes, I suppose so," Vauchon answered. But then the door to the next house opened, and an old woman wearing a faded housedress and man's hunting jacket, high socks, bedroom slippers with smiling foxes sewn to their fronts and a kerchief on her head, studied them closely for a minute.

"Are you lookin' for Emmett?"

"Yes, we are, madame," Vauchon told her.

"Is one of you Coach Magruder?"

"I'm Magruder."

"Good. I've got your gas right here in the parlor beside me."

"Who's she?" Vauchon asked Brighton as she ducked inside the house. "Have you seen her before?"

"She's his mother-in-residence. Carruthers told me she also corrects the tests he gives."

She returned in a moment with two glass one-gallon wine jugs filled with gas, their labels still attached, that she put down side by side on her porch. She re-entered and came out again with two one-quart plastic juice containers, also filled, and lastly a plastic salad bowl with snap-top lid that she also put down on the porch.

"There was two more gallon jugs for you, Magruder, but they broke when Emmett was tryin' to carry them home from the gas station in my shoppin' cart. The poor lamb wasn't thinkin' when he came to a high curb, 'n he dragged the cart right after him 'n the bottles broke. But there's still two and three quarters gallons left."

They stood for a silent moment staring at the meager

collection of gas, Magruder thinking that the offering of Carruthers was perfectly appropriate. Brighton began to laugh, uncontrollably now, grasping the porch rail for support, and turning, Magruder saw that the two carloads of Vauchon's men had begun laughing also, perhaps understanding immediately from the offering the ilk of their adversary they had come to persuade. But Vauchon shook his head in dismay, staring at the gas: "Some people are quite beyond conquest, coach. It suddenly occurs to me that we may not be able to convince a man who proffers gas in wine jugs and salad bowls to do anything. . . ."

"Where is he now, madame? Teaching?" Magruder asked.

"No, it's his day off. He got nervous waiting for you, Magruder, so he went down to Dutchie Dougherty's to calm himself down."

"Is it far from here?"

"I'll go with you and show you. What are all those black men in the car for?"

"Persuasion, perhaps," Vauchon said.

"Well, you better leave 'em here, mister. Dutchie doesn't like the colored in his bar. They've got their own bars in their part of town."

"He'll make an exception this time," Vauchon said flatly.

"Well, yes, you're right about that, I guess. It's about six hours before quittin' time for honest workingmen, so there won't be anyone much in Dutchie's to mind."

"Can we go now?" Magruder asked.

"Just let me leave a little note for Emmett in case he happens back. I'll tell him to wait here for us."

She left the neighboring porch and hobbled through the lumpy snow onto Carruthers' porch, walking past them to remove a broken piece of window sill and the key that was hidden beneath it. She opened the door and they followed her inside, Magruder and the others recoiling involuntarily at the musty booze smell of the place. The blue books were everywhere, hundreds of them, the one neat pile of ten or so of them stained red where a wine jug had tipped on its side and glugged out until the level of the neck was reached.

"Emmett must have been correcting tests last night," Magruder suggested.

"No. Emmett does the teaching. I correct the tests. It depresses him so to have to do it, poor boy."

She looked, squinting for a moment at one of the booklets on the edge of the table, then seized it, dramatically, as if she had plucked a live rabbit from its warren by hand. She removed a red marking pencil from her coat pocket, licked the end of it and rewarded an emphatic D to the blue book's owner.

"That seems unfair," Vauchon said. "You haven't even read that test."

She flung the booklet into his hand: "You wouldn't think it was unfair if you knew the witch who wrote it. One of those 'freedom of choice' abortion people. Every word out of her mouth is a goddamn blasphemy against the Church's teaching. She's goin' to flunk that course if I have anything to say about it."

"Then doubtless she will," Magruder heard himself say.

"Yes," the woman agreed. While they looked on she scribbled a note to Carruthers, merely tearing out the last page of someone else's booklet, which was half covered with handwriting, then pinning it to a frayed curtain with a paper clip.

"Let's go," she ordered. "Emmett ought to be half out of it by now 'n Dougherty will be gettin' set to ship him home."

Cowed in the face of her authority, they followed her out of the house, then stood beside her on the porch while she surveyed the three cars parked at the curb, her brows knit in some unfathomable consternation: "I don't want to have to ride in that old car," she said, pointing to the Rolls. "Those old-fashioned brakes aren't worth a damn these days."

"That happens to be a one-year-old Rolls-Royce," Magruder told her dryly. "But you'll be riding in my car," he pointed to the Buick.

"Who's that girl sittin' in the car there?"

"We anticipate that very shortly she'll be Mrs. Emmett Carruthers," Vauchon said.

The kerchiefed woman turned to stare dumfounded at Vauchon: "Are you out of your goddamned mind there, blackie? Emmett doesn't need to get married to any teen-ager. I can take care of him well enough."

"He's getting married to this teen-ager because he happens to have impregnated her. Quite in opposition to the Church's teachings, I might add," Vauchon said, "and as chief grader for an eminent moral theologian, I'm sure you'd be the first to agree that somebody's got a debt to pay."

"That house isn't big enough for the three of us!" she

snarled, actually pointing one finger of each hand at the two identical houses behind them.

But Vauchon was in full gear now, barely able to conceal his pleasure; Magruder had no thought to stop him: "It might not be a problem, madame. After the wedding Emmett and Ingrid probably will move to Nebraska. He'll teach there at the university and she'll take courses."

"Well, I'm not movin' out to goddamned Nebraska 'n neither is Emmett. Let's get that straight right now."

She headed for the Buick, opened the back door before Magruder made it to the driver's side and bounded inside. Vauchon and Brighton returned to the Rolls. Magruder took his seat behind the wheel and turned to introduce the woman, whose name he had not thought to ask, to Ingrid. But there was no need.

"Hussy! Seducing poor Emmett! She isn't even pretty!" she hurled, reaching forward to slap Ingrid's face. In response, Ingrid the gentle lunged halfway across the seat back, grabbing the other's hair through her kerchief, and began beating her furiously about the head. Magruder, trying to separate them, saw through the rear window that Vauchon and his henchmen were gleeful and clapping with laughter.

"Stop it!" Magruder yelled. "Stop it or she'll miscarry."

"Good riddance! That child was conceived in sin!" the corrector screeched, removing Ingrid's grip from her hair and shoving the other across the seat back. "Let's go," she ordered again. "I want to hear Emmett say this is all a lie. It's got to be! He's a goddamn professor of theology."

"Brace yourself, lady," Ingrid told her.

But that was all. Magruder drove to Dutchie

Dougherty's Bar in another section of town slated for urban renewal, getting his first look at the Notre Dame campus on the way.

They entered Dougherty's en masse, the kerchiefed corrector leading the way, the baldheaded bartender reflexively flattening back against the racks of bottles that ascended against the blue-tinted mirrors (etched with drink prices of a forever gone past) of an old-fashioned oak bar. Seedy-looking Christmas decorations were spread across the top of the mirror, nearly a full month in advance of Christmas, and it occurred distantly to Magruder that they may simply not have been taken down from the year before, or years before.

Two long-haired students playing pool were the only patrons besides Emmett Carruthers, a ghostly specter, who sat alone in a wall booth, staring down at what was certainly a beer with a raw egg in it.

Magruder winced at the sight of him. For sure there was nothing left to joke about in Emmett's drinking any longer: He was looking like a man headed for the terminal place. The two young pool players racked their cue sticks and began edging toward a back door with an exit sign over it, frightened perhaps at the initial inrush of so many determined-looking black men. But now there was hardly a need; they were no longer determined-looking at all: Their collected faces covered a spectrum from revulsion to outright pity. One of them even said inadvertently, "Holy shit! Is this here the guy we come to put the screws on?"

"Keep quiet," Vauchon ordered with an annoyed wave of his hat. Ingrid slid into the seat beside Carruthers and he smiled benignly upon her, though Magruder thought perhaps he might not even recognize her. His corrector plopped into the opposite seat and slammed a hard fist on the table: "Emmett! What's this all about?"

"Ingrid goin' have a baby," Carruthers slurred. "My baby. A little boy baby."

"How do you know it will be a boy?" Vauchon asked distantly.

"I jus' know. The man in the liquor store figure it out for me on last week's sales slip. Look," he offered proudly, pulling a rolled-up register tape from his pocket and handing it to Vauchon, who unraveled it. With Magruder he studied the reverse of the itemized side where a gibberish of numbers, algebraic signs and arrows raced down its length to end in the single word "Boy!" with exclamation point. Vauchon shrugged and Magruder concurred. The flip side was more convincing, a long list of articles that added up to (Magruder considered) a whopping $219.79. Vauchon, a rich man, may have thought so also: "Did you have a faculty party last week at your place, Emmett?"

"No, Matty, it's all for me to drink. Two weeks worth."

Vauchon whistled, eyes cast heavenward at the bar's tin ceiling.

"I'm too shy to give a faculty party," Carruthers said. "What if nobody came?"

There was a silence, Magruder's mind racing for a balm to kill the rush of pain in the voice. Instead, Vauchon handed the bill to Ingrid, pointing to the total with one manicured finger, and said quietly, "You're about to have your first faculty party, Emmett. To announce your wedding. Ingrid will make all the arrangements and I can assure you the party will be quite successful. From curiosity, absolutely no one will stay away."

Carruthers stared a long moment at the egg yolk floating atop his beer, then his face broke into a large wreath of a smile and he stared up at Vauchon.

"Ingrid 'n I are gettin' married?"

"Yes, Emmett, you sure are," Vauchon spoke evenly, narrowing his eyes and shaking his head in concurrence. Two carloads of his henchmen also nodded in concurrence. Magruder thought it appropriate to nod also.

"We exchanged love letters," Carruthers told them.

"How many?" Vauchon asked.

"Three times," Carruthers said, putting up four fingers.

"That many in this day and age is a quite sufficient courtship."

"What about me?" Carruthers' neighbor begged.

"You can be the mother-in-law," Vauchon said, "and help Ingrid prepare the buffet for the party."

She thought a moment and the words seemed to placate her somewhat.

"And can I keep on correctin' the tests?"

"Only if you agree to compromise on the abortion issue, birth control and the business of priestly celibacy. Those tests are subjective, you know."

"All right," she grunted after a long wheeze of a sigh. "I'll go for a B minus on that witch's exam, but no more."

Little tears started down Carruthers' cheeks and he asked finally, "Is everything all right now?"

"Yes," Vauchon and Magruder answered at the same time.

"Good." Then he picked up the beer and quaffed it, the egg yolk disappearing inside him with the ease of an oyster. Carruthers evinced no nausea, only smacked his lips with apparent satisfaction at the taste. Curious the parceling of gifts and talents in this universe, Magruder thought, guessing he might have vomited the evil-looking thing right back upon the table top.

Vauchon ordered the Lincoln and its complement back to Chicago. Then, from Dougherty's Bar they drove first to an Avis Rent A Car and picked up a compact to return the remaining henchmen who had come to South Bend with Vauchon and Brighton in the Rolls. The next stop, at Carruthers' emphatic request, was the Notre Dame campus.

The day was quickly darkening and chilling still more, and flurries of snow were falling, powdery and clean, settling onto the frozen slush of the snowfall of two days before as they crunched across the lawn before the administration building where the Virgin's statue atop its dome was already spotlit. Before anyone thought to stop him, Carruthers plopped to his knees in the snow. Magruder, Vauchon, the corrector, Ingrid and Brighton all stood in a half circle behind him. By now, students had begun halting to stare at the curious gaggle of people. From the snickering, Magruder decided Carruthers was a widely known bad joke around campus. Then the snickering turned to outright guffaws as Carruthers stretched out, Muslim fashion, toward the Virgin's statue, his arms before him, his face buried in the snow.

"Emmett! What the hell are you doing?" Vauchon demanded testily.

"I'm prayin' to her. I'm prayin' that our son, l'il Emmett, don't take to the drink like his old dad. . . ."

"Well, why don't you pray in a church like anyone else would? You're making a spectacle of yourself. Think of your job, Emmett. Let's go to a church."

"No. I don't pray too often, but when I do, this is the way I have to do it. Besides, I'm praying for special things. Big things. Not all mine either. You just don't go to a church and light a ten cent candle to pray for Coach Magruder's problem. Those three guys in New Jersey are goin' to try to kill you, coach. . . ."

Magruder thought to speak, but Ingrid's new mother-in-law usurped the privilege: "He knows what he's sayin', Magruder, 'n you better listen to him. Them three're desperate men."

"How do you know so much, lady?" Magruder asked, testy now himself.

"Because I made a deal with them on the phone one night when Emmett was passed out on the couch to make sure he convinced you to turn around. They wired the five thousand bucks the next morning. That's desperate, I'd say."

"You took five thousand dollars from them?" Vauchon demanded incredulously. "You promised them that Carruthers would talk to the coach and dissuade him?"

"Well, it's not like taking money from honest people, is it? And Emmett was nine hundred dollars into the hole with the liquor man and behind on his payments to that lady whose car he ran into that time last year when the bastards wouldn't renew his insurance. After all, their money isn't goin' to do them any good if Magruder gets his way and puts them in the pokey, so it might just as well do somebody some good. . . ."

"Whew . . ." Magruder sighed, a long trail of vaporized breath hissing into the air. Then he looked down at Carruthers, who still prayed Muslim-like toward the Virgin, not knowing where exactly to begin chastising him. But Carruthers began a singsong praying instead:

"Lovely lady dressed in blue, teach me how to pray.
God was just a little boy, tell me what to say. . . ."

Small sobs came out of Carruthers, his body convulsing in rhythm, and Magruder thought of reaching down for an arm to haul the suppliant to his feet. But an angered Vauchon acted first, kicking Carruthers fiercely in the ass, sending him sprawling flat into the snow.

"Get up, you honkie drunk, and stop making a spectacle of yourself!"

"I'm prayin' for you, too, Matthew," Carruthers whined. "I'm prayin' for better treatment of all minority groups."

"Come on, honkie. The longer I live, the more I prefer my minority status. If nothing else, it implies some sort of moral superiority. There weren't any black men mixed up in that Watergate horseshit if you remember."

With Brighton, Vauchon dragged Carruthers to his feet and began wiping the other's face with the sleeve of his coat. About them, the students had drawn closer and now were openly jeering at the event. Vauchon glared at them for a long moment, turning in a slow circle, then pronounced imperiously, "Shut up, all of you! Proceed directly to your classes!"

Incredibly, they drew back, moving off in groups of confused mutterers, trying to figure out who Vauchon was. Not unaccountably, Magruder heard himself asking Vauchon, "What do we do now, Matthew?"

"We take him home and phone Albert Deutsch with the glad tidings about Ingrid's forthcoming marriage. You, coach, had better be the one to handle that call."

"Yes, I suppose I must."

They returned to the cars, then drove back to Carruthers' house, where Ingrid, seemingly unapprehensive, began cleaning up the cluttered, dusty living room. Carruthers lurched to his bedroom and fell fully clothed across the disheveled length of his bed and began snoring almost immediately. Magruder, Vauchon, Brighton and the corrector went to the filthy kitchen and stood about the walls as Magruder dialed the Nebraska number. The phone rang a brief moment, then was lifted to the expected voice of Albert Deutsch: "Sergeant Foster?"

"No, Albert, this is the coach."

"Coach . . . coach, Ingrid is gone. I thought it might have been the state police. They've been looking for her since early this morning when we went into her room and she wasn't there."

"She's with me, Albert. We're in South Bend, Indiana, with the baby's father. They're going to be married very soon."

"Who . . . ?" Deutsch demanded hoarsely, Magruder certain from the whisper in his voice that he already knew.

"Emmett Carruthers, Albert."

"Nooool!" came the terrible whisper. Then a scream, maniacal, the certain threshold of a heart attack flung itself across the late afternoon darkness of the American landscape from Nebraska to Indiana, hurling Magruder away from the phone, pinning the others in awe to the walls. Everyone in the kitchen heard the resounding clunk of Albert Deutsch dropping to the floor nearly a thousand miles away.

Magruder prayed he was not dead. In the next room the farmer's daughter worked away with seeming unconcern at stacking the disorderly blue books.

CHAPTER 8

A Little Town
in New Jersey

Eagerly, Magruder prepared to flee the carnage of Carruthers' life, leaving Ingrid to the great test of her strength, hoping Albert, her father, was not dead.

Outside the tiny house, in the darkened South Bend street, distracted by the gaucheness of a Virgin's statue standing in a grotto of an upended bathtub trimmed with winking Christmas lights, he shook hands good-by with Vauchon and Brighton, wordlessly accepting a replacement of the Modestis' shattered wedding gift from the latter.

"I hope Albert isn't dead, coach," Vauchon said distantly, uncharacteristically tapping a puffed-up cheek with an extended finger.

"You guys were better suited to being preppies, Matthew. Right now I'm feeling a little sorry for you that you all grew up."

"Save your pity, coach. Albert is probably alive and well, and Ingrid may even manage to pull our brother Carruthers off the bottle. Yes, in fact, save your righteousness as well."

"You seem rather testy, Matthew."

"Who wouldn't, coach? If you're annoyed with us,

don't doubt for a moment that a good many of us are annoyed with you. I don't know what the hell we owe to each other after all these years. This trip of yours isn't merely fruitless, it's beginning to seem like a good old-fashioned case of senility. . . ."

"Good-by, Matthew . . ."

Vauchon did not answer.

Magruder drove from South Bend to the environs of Cleveland, turning into a motel for the night about 11 P.M., certain from the increasing dimness of his headlights that the Buick's generator was on the blink though the dashboard indicator showed nothing.

In the morning, his suspicion confirmed, the engine refused to turn over. The car was towed to a local garage and spent most of the day there until the mechanic found a rebuilt generator from a junk yard. At four-thirty, Magruder headed eastward again, the vastness of Pennsylvania still before him. He would not be arriving in New Jersey that night as he had intended.

He spent the night in an eastern Pennsylvania motel near Allentown. Magruder rose early to complete the last lap across New Jersey to Red Bank near the Atlantic, arriving to the three identical houses of Adnizzio, McFarland and Matland in cul de sac, about fifteen minutes after the nuptial Mass was to have begun.

There were assorted cars in the driveways and along the curbs, and before the middle two-story pillared colonial—evidently Adnizzio's—the contents of two caterers' trucks were being unloaded and carried to the side entrance of an enormous and eerily billowing tent attached to a part of what was evidently a rear veranda on the house. From tanks of helium, Magruder supposed, a workman was inflating a final section of the tent, the fan-shaped end of which was a plastic window looking out on a pond and a small wood lot beyond.

Magruder parked and followed two workers carrying a plywood arch covered with doves and plastic flowers inside the tent and watched them place it in a near completed row of arches that gave the illusion of holding up the serpentine innards of the thing. Beneath the arches a double row of tables stretched the considerable distance away from the veranda toward the head table, raised on a dais, that spread before the window of the fanned-out end. Occasional heating units, standing between the arches, blew off and on to warm the inside of the tent. Privately, Magruder was amazed at the bucolic helium palace whose walls above the arches ambled and flowed like jelly.

"How do you find all this, Magruder? I'll bet it'll be a real bacchanal when they get back from the church."

Magruder turned to see an old man, older than himself, imp-faced and watery-eyed, dressed all in a black suit, fedora and a black overcoat drawn loosely about his shoulders, seated on a white wrought-iron chair on the raised portion of Adnizzio's veranda. He seemed benignly demonic-looking, if such a thing were possible, and Magruder responded to him pleasurably. Moreover, he was perfectly balanced. His left hand was gripped firmly about the head of a gnarled cane. His right held an iced-tea glass of red wine from an unlabeled bottle on the flag-stone beside him.

"Wonderful, isn't it? It's supposed to resemble a cave in Calabria where a famous wedding feast was held during the Renaissance for the son of an important bandit. At least that's what the caterer told Vincent. It looks nice anyhow. The ceiling is supposed to look like it leaks water, but that's just a comfortable illusion. You could create a whole city by blowing up these things full of helium and adding them one to another. Look there." He pointed to a large tent room off to his right with a wooden floor and platform for the band. "They don't even have to bother heating that one. When the young people start dancing in there, they'll be rolling up the sides, even though it is December."

"How did you know my name?" Magruder asked him.

"Everybody knows who Magruder is. You're the most important guest at this wedding. More important than the bride and groom. Don't doubt that for a moment."

"Who are you?"

"I'm Nicholas the Tedesco. My real name is Nicholas Morelli. I'm the uncle of Vincent Adnizzio, the great-uncle of his daughter Aurelia."

"What does Tedesco mean, Mr. Morelli?"

"The German. Apparently as a young man I had an obstinate nature and no decent sentiment and I refused to go to Mass. All this was very un-Italian, so given the level of their reasoning, my relatives nicknamed me 'the German.' Would you like some wine, Magruder? I make it myself."

"It's 10:30 A.M. It seems early in the day for a drink, doesn't it?"

"Do you wake early, Magruder? Like me? Before dawn, unable to sleep any more?"

"Yes," Magruder admitted.

"Then the day is already long for old men like us. Have some wine. Pretend it's later."

Magruder shrugged. Nicholas the Tedesco poured another iced-tea glass of red wine and handed it to Magruder. Magruder sipped it, his eyes tearing instantly at the onslaught of the alcohol.

"Why aren't you at the wedding Mass?" Magruder asked him.

"It's too embarrassing. These days I'm too sentimental, if anything. Evidently people's natures change. I cry at weddings. They have to carry me away from funerals. Even when I didn't know the dead."

"Oh, then you're here for the happy part. For the reception and dancing."

"No, I'm here to read a love poem. Apparently, notable poets of the day read love poems when the bandit's son was married in the Calabrian cave, so they needed one today. Otherwise I'd never be invited. For my part, I say thank God there is a poet about, someone with an aesthetic and ameliorating nature. I can help to temper the storm of emotion raging all about this place over your coming. Particularly the storm emanating from the wind chambers of Vincent's father, old Gennaro, because of what you've come to do to his son. Watch out for that one, Magruder. A dangerous man. In his youth he was a sentimentalist, an aesthete. He even studied for the priesthood. But his nature changed from sentimentality to obstinacy. It's as if our two ships had passed in midocean.

Now he packs a gun where he formerly kept his rosary, so to speak. Here, have a bit more wine. . . ."

"I don't think so, Mr. Morelli. I should go to the church for the service, or what's left of it."

"I wouldn't, Magruder, if I were you. I checked over the guest list. There might be as many as ten guys carrying an iron in that church."

"They're not going to use a gun on me in a church."

"Maybe not. But there's not much to stop them from taking you outside and beating the hell out of you on the frost-hard lawn."

"It's not possible, Mr. Morelli. Vincent would never permit that to happen to me."

"It's not his prerogative, Magruder. Vincent and his wife Angelina, they're decent enough people, humanists even, though their taste in art and music begs questioning. And Vincent would like to pay for his crime if you'd come up with a reasonable way other than having to go to jail. But old man Adnizzio isn't going to let you put his son in jail. He'd kill you first and a lot of people in that church would think he's right for doing it."

"How would they know about it?"

"Everybody knows, Magruder," Morelli said, sighing deeply and pouring more wine. "When old Gennaro heard you might be coming to collect a debt years ago, he told everybody about the childish prank that Vincent and his buddies played on Kasprzak of St. Anselm's. And he's managed to convince everyone that Kasprzak is better off dead, too, so that if you make trouble he can write you off as a madman and put a bullet between your eyes."

"He's a clever man, old Adnizzio. Strange, I used to remember him as being very obsequious when he'd come up to St. Anselm's. He was always trying to slip somebody some money."

"He hasn't stopped," Nicholas the Tedesco said, suddenly spitting in fury on the flagstone. "A real *pet-zanovanti*. Fingers in every pie. I'm a subsidy of his, too. He pays me five thousand a year to write new poems then read them at funerals, weddings, etc. He's crazy. He had me work all one winter on a twenty-verse memoriam for an associate in Jersey City. When it was finished he had the guy bumped off and Gennaro himself read the poem at the graveside, tears streaming down his face all the while. . . ."

"What do you think of my mission, Morelli?"

"I'd like to help you, Magruder, if I could. But I'm an old man. We're both old men. All I can do is go to Mass every morning and pray for your soul. It saddened me so much, poor Sterling Lloyd's death. I even went up to St. Anselm's to his funeral. Look, I carry his Mass card in my wallet," he said, flipping open the wallet to reveal sad Kasprzak's face. I even wrote a poem in his honor. Do you want me to read it to you?"

"I don't think I have the time."

"It's a short poem. It won't take a moment. . . ."

"All right," Magruder sighed.

Nicholas the Tedesco removed a single sheet from a sheaf of papers in a brief case at his side and read, "For Sterling Lloyd Kasprzak, dead from exposure at St. Anselm's School for Boys, in 1950 A.D. year of Our Lord."

Magruder heard the words, frowning at their familiarity, until the recognition came to him: "That's Dante, Mr. Morelli. . . ."

Nicholas the Tedesco shrugged: "Ah, so you know the literature, Magruder. . . ."

"A little."

"Thank God the Adnizzios are aestheticless goons. If they knew they were getting Dante when they were paying for Morelli, I'd probably be copying the masters on the bottom of Newark Bay right now. I like you, Magruder. Do you still want to go to the church?"

"Yes. I was invited to the wedding after all."

"You're a brave man. But we old ones have little left to fear. If the Adnizzios kill us now or later, it only means that they've saved us from the indignity of the inner crumblings that relatives and friends would be forced with embarrassment to watch. The sphincter goes, you know."

"I have things to do yet in life, Nicholas the Tedesco. I have no intention of letting myself be killed. And the sphincter remains firm. After I've finished the Kasprzak business, I'm going to Florida to retire a second time."

"To which part, Magruder?"

"I'm not certain about that."

"Naples is nice. On the Gulf coast. A lot of old people there, like us. The climate is good and it's less expensive than the Atlantic coast."

"I'll have to think about it," Magruder said as Morelli stood, leaving his brief case and instead taking the jug of wine and two glasses with him. They walked together through Adnizzio's house that was—somehow expectedly —gleaming white, with wall-to-wall carpeting, Naugehyde furniture, bad seascapes, Vincent Adnizzio's framed medical degree, and too few books. Then out the front door onto the crunching gravel of the circular driveway to the curb where they climbed into the Buick.

"Tell me, Magruder . . . you were the football coach of that place, St. Anselm's, yet you know the literature. How is it?"

"I turned to it for survival when we moved to Barstow, California, right after my retirement. My wife, Florence, was quite ill with asthma and I was out of sorts with no more team to coach, so I worked it off in the library."

"What did you read?"

"Everything." Magruder smiled. "I had a previous forty years to make up for. Forty years of reading almost nothing but the sports page."

"Your wife passed away just recently, did she not?"

"Yes, it was a merciful death, I think. Trying to get a breath was an agony for her."

"My wife died also," Morelli said, pouring one glass half full of the dago, then holding it between his knees while he poured the other, handing it to Magruder, who did not refuse.

"I'm sorry," Magruder said, taking a swig of the wine as he drove the car from the cul de sac.

Morelli shrugged: "It was two years ago now. She even asked me to kill her. . . ."

"Did you do it?"

"Yes. After a fashion, that is. She had the kidney disease and was on the dialysis machine nearly all the time and her pain was terrible. So one day when she asked me for perhaps the hundredth time, I simply kissed her good-by, went to the cellar of our house and put in a bad fuse so it would look like the thing had blown from an overload, then went off and read poetry with some colleagues at an espresso bar. When I returned it was over. I was happy for her."

"Yes. Yes, it was good," Magruder agreed, taking another sip of his wine. "Was there any blame?"

"The electrical contractor who did the wiring, if anybody," the Tedesco laughed. "I never liked him anyhow. The insurance adjuster told me afterwards the wiring had been a shoddy job. All the better. At Mass I glared at him openly and everybody understood when he wept from shame."

Magruder found it in him to laugh also. He drained the wine and asked for a little more, bemused, rather than astounded, at his realization that he had never drunk alcohol, not even a beer, while driving a car before. He finished the refill as they pulled up before the church where long lines of bunting-draped limousines stretched out on either side of the street, their drivers shuffling about and clapping hands against the cold in little conversational knots.

Nicholas the Tedesco instructed one of the Adnizzio drivers to park Magruder's car, and the two hurried up the front steps of the church. Inside, at an altar set in the middle of the edifice with octagonal rows of pews ringed all about it, the nuptial Mass had already progressed to the offertory. Beside Magruder, Nicholas the Tedesco whipped out a handkerchief and began immediately to sniffle. He placed one hand on Magruder's arm for support.

"Steady yourself, Morelli," Magruder urged him. "Where shall we sit?"

"The ones facing us are the Modestis. The Adnizzios have their back to us. We should go round to the right and come in from the side."

They crept along the outer aisle, then started to edge their way into a pew as the priest, a slight young man with inflamed-looking ranges of acne on his face, intoned the offertory prayers in the most timorous voice Magruder had ever heard in the service of the liturgy.

Nicholas the Tedesco was first to take his seat. Magruder closely scanned the Adnizzio side of the church, found his three victims and watched, at first not unpleasurably, the dawn of recognition of his nearness on the faces of Adnizzio, McFarland, Matland and their wives. The reaction—it seemed to him—was a kind of collective dread, unexpectedly intense, as if they were responding not to Magruder the coach but to some metaphorical presence like the unknown reveler with the trump card in Poe's *The Masque of the Red Death*. The hushed buzzing of voices and turning of heads spread like brush fire through the Adnizzio side of the church (even the youngest child riveted him with the most knowing, fearful look) then leapt the wide firebreak of the main aisle to the Modesti side until Magruder began to think he should not have come to the church at all despite his invitation, especially when the young priest lowered the host in the midst of the offertory and peered all about to decipher the cause of the disturbance.

"I shouldn't have come here," Magruder whispered to the Tedesco. The other only shrugged, but Angelina Adnizzio, Vincent's wife, made that judgment absolutely certain. Magruder, thinking to flee what must needs be coming, watched hypnotically, unable to move, as Angelina removed a hand from her mouth, then began rising from her kneeler as the scream prepared to hurtle out of her: "He's here! A hangman in the house of God! Can anyone actually believe he dared come here on this day of all days!" The plea ended in a long shrill scream and Angelina Adnizzio collapsed in a dead faint into her husband's arms.

"*Dio mio*, evidently a miscalculation!" Nicholas the Tedesco winced at Magruder. "Look who's just lumbered into action now . . . the *dottore* himself. Notice how he resembles a rhinoceros."

The description was apt: An enormous figure, the patriarch of the Adnizzios, heavier easily by one hundred pounds than the last time Magruder had laid eyes upon him, lurched to life from the blur of confused, whispering faces, rumbled onto the satin of the center aisle covering and staggered, apoplectic-looking and wrenching open the collar of his tuxedo, toward the altar, where he admonished the young priest to halt the reading of his Mass, then hauled the two young Modestis to their frightened feet, standing between them and gripping each by an arm.

"Magruder!" he raged. "You have the sensitivity of a pig! How dare you ruin the happiness of these two godlike young people by coming here on their wedding day! I command you to apologize at once to them and all here present for this intrusion!"

"I apologize for nothing, Adnizzio," Magruder snarled back at him, at the same time irritably pushing away the hand of Nicholas the Tedesco, who tugged insistently at his coat, hissing at Magruder to hold his ground. "I was invited to this wedding, and if I wasn't meant to be here, I shouldn't have been invited. The business I've come on doesn't concern these young people at all. Now let's don't ruin their happiness as you suggest, and get on with the ceremony."

"I give the orders, Magruder! Not you! Right now I'll give you the chance to leave this sacred place with dignity for the sake of old times when my son Vincente and his friends had great respect for you! Otherwise you'll be carried from here and pounded ignominiously to a pulp beyond the boundaries of church property! Take your choice. . . ."

"Papa! Stop it! Stop it or you'll have a heart attack with all your ranting!"

It was Vincent Adnizzio who had shoved off his fainted wife to another family member and come to his feet in the first pew: "He's the coach! I invited him to the wedding. Papa, he's a guest. . . . We can't insult a guest!"

Angelina Adnizzio revived suddenly in a wrath and pulled herself upright by grabbing a handful of her husband's tails: "Yeah, you invited him all right, you idiot! But he isn't prostrate with blubbering sentimentality like you figured he would be, so the invitation is obviously worthless!"

"Angelina is right," the elder Adnizzio bellowed. "I side with my daughter-in-law completely in this matter. I'm thinking of you, too, Vincente, even though you seem to be always too stupid to do so. You think I'm gonna let that old fool send you to the electric chair for a schoolboy prank that happened twenty years ago when the *bestia* that's dead is better off dead? Look at this Modesti who is marrying your daughter, Vincente! See his handsomeness! Think of your grandchildren! Think how handsome and well formed they will be! More godlike still! What if it were the first son of Sterling Lloyd Kasprzak standing here instead, Vincente? Preparing to deflower your beautiful Aurelia on the altar of their marriage bed this very night?" Gennaro Adnizzio's face turned grotesque with loathing: "Think of the revulsion you would feel toward your own grandchildren. . . ."

"That's the most preposterous argument I've ever heard!" Magruder hurled, raising a demonstrative arm toward the church rafters. "And as to whether Kasprzak is better off dead than alive isn't for you to decide. That's the province of God alone!"

"God . . . ?" old Adnizzio questioned. He may have meant to scorn the notion, only a blank look instead came momentarily into his eyes: Then as if the word had triggered a remembrance, he turned obsequiously to the hapless priest, who steadied himself on the altar by an elbow, and sought out the cleric's free hand, kissing it reverently, eyes closed, then announcing, "Father, forgive me for interrupting Holy Mass. I'll have this bum out of here in just a few seconds and you can go back to your job. . . ."

"Come on, Magruder," the patriarch commanded, "you're leaving!"

He began a great shambling stumble from the altar steps and across the front row of pews, meaning evidently to charge down the side aisle to the pew where Magruder stood now, to evict the intruder bodily from the church. But he never made it. Before Magruder could even let free the final "never!" that was forming on his lips, the seizure was upon Adnizzio. Still center stage, he looked suddenly as if he had been struck by a bolt of lightning. Dancing a tiny jig step all the while, he reached both hands to his throat as if to aid the process of his dying, made, though an obese man, a definitive single leap into the air, then flipped backwards with a resounding crash onto the satin of the floor. Stupefied by his own shock, Magruder was vaguely aware of the chorus of shrieks and screams that had erupted in the church; also he felt the talon hand of Nicholas the Tedesco dig into his left arm and heard the man's intense hissing beside him: "Die, you dirty son of a bitch! Die!"

Magruder turned to see the bulging of the Tedesco's eyes and decided on the instant it was the most venomous look he had ever seen on another human face: The Adnizzios' poet truly hated his patron, then. Magruder jabbed him sharply in the ribs to shake him out of his fury. "Morelli, get that look off your face or they'll kill you before they kill me."

On the floor before them, Gennaro Adnizzio thrashed a final time, then presumedly died, just as his son Vincent and the young priest reached him. The younger Adnizzio broke into sobs and wails on his father's chest, pounding a fist repeatedly, then as Magruder strained to see him over its railing, Vincent's ashen, anguished face appeared to the neck over the pew's front: "Coach . . . coach . . . papa's dead. . . ."

"I'm sorry, Vincent. I didn't come here to kill him."

"But still he's dead. . . ."

"I had better intercede right now, Magruder," the Tedesco said in a level, normal voice, "or you're going to be dead, too, *paisan*."

Morelli edged out of the pew past Magruder, who reflexively sat down to be less conspicuous. The poet moved center stage near the body slowly and dramatically, his long coat still thrown about his shoulders, using its folds to the same effect as a cape with his right hand, thumping out every step of his measured progress with the cane he held in his left. He stood a long moment, eyes closed, evidently praying, over the lifeless hulk of Gennaro Adnizzio, then strode to Vincent, who still knelt staring over the pew railing at Magruder, and clasped a tight, comforting hand on his shoulder.

"*Coraggio*," he urged the kneeling wounded.

He went next to the priest, who had stuffed the end of his vestment into his mouth from fear, took the cleric's other hand and pressed it to his lips as had the dead one before him, pleading with the other, who looked conclusively ready to faint, "*Eminenza* . . . forgive me. . . ."

Then he swung about, stern-faced now, raising his cane to halt the advance of a flying wedge of five burly men from the Adnizzio guest list who were making their way toward Magruder: "Halt, all of you! Do not dishonor the dead by violence in this sacred place! Let me speak first. My muse is shrieking within me, screaming to be loose. The moment is so noble and profound!"

Gesturing, palms downward, he urged the wedding guests to sit again; then flailing his cape at them, he banished the flying wedge to the wings, though they still stood. Finally, he fixed a long gaze on Magruder, repeatedly shaking his cane at the intruder: "God himself has sent this man to us!" he proclaimed loudly.

"What? Are you mad, you gooney bastard?" screamed out the leader of the wedge, slapping a hand to his head. "Why in hell would God send this guy to kill Gennaro Adnizzio?"

"Not to kill him directly! Certainly not that. But to be the catalyst of his dispatchment, for his time was surely at hand. Look at him, the *patrono*, sleeping and at peace now before us, joining his beloved Jenny in heaven. Death, I tell you, at the zenith of his power, the consummate hour of his life, his moment of most perfect happiness. . . ."

Magruder, astounded, watched the awed hush come over the church, watched the flying wedge shrink still farther back, watched Vincent Adnizzio rise slowly to his feet to stand in noble sorrowing beside his fallen father. Nicholas the Tedesco swept pastorally by the priest, breaking open the knot of the two young betrothed who clung to each other for safety, taking each of them by the hand beside him.

"Did I say his moment of his most perfect happiness? Yes, I believe it to be this! Look at the symbolism of the day. He dies in the splendid company of family and worshiping friends before the very altar of God, bursting with tearful joy at seeing the first of his granddaughters, the beautiful Aurelia, daughter of his son Vincent, youngest of his sons in whom his pride had always been most boundless—though indeed he loved his other sons no less —led to the altar by that same son to be married to a

worthy and handsome young man of impeccable family
background. These Modesti, the *dottore* told me this very
morning before he left for the Mass, are a noble people!
There are none finer!"

At that moment, a pause in the oration, an old woman
on the Modesti side of the church raised her arms skyward, shrieked, "*Che buon 'homo!*" then sat back, sobbing, in her seat, joined instantly by an Italianate chorus
of other women who wailed the primitives of a funeral
dirge in the midst of the nuptials. Nicholas the Tedesco
took out a handkerchief, dabbed it to his eyes, then blew
his nose loudly, a trumpet of his apparent sorrowing:
Huge tears rolled down the planes of his wizened face.
Everywhere in the church now, handkerchiefs flashed to
tearing eyes, there was a general chorus of sniffles and
sobbings. Morelli turned again to address the corpse.

"How I envy you, Gennaro Adnizzio. To have died on
this day. For after today, *dottore*, even for you, it would
be all downhill. Downhill to an end of crumblings, senility and pain. Physical pain?—yes, certainly. But worse the
pain of unremedied exasperation, the recognition of
ineffectualness that must needs come to a virile and powerful man like yourself, *dottore*, when the specter of
death hovers a long and tormenting time about you, when
the life force wanes. The worst pain of all, I tell you. That
pain, if I may, of having the privilege of picking up the
dinner check at a table of friends usurped by another, a
younger man. . . .

"The *patrono* is dead," the Tedesco intoned, pointing to
the hulk on the floor. "Long live the *patrono*," he intoned
again, walking over to a stupefied Vincent Adnizzio, lift-

ing his unwilling hand and kissing it in a kind of homage. Then he turned to face a frowning Magruder: "We thank you for your coming, Coach Magruder. I believe still that you are God-sent. Gennaro the elder leaves for his eternity at your arrival in a blaze of glory. In his wake a new, young and strong *dottore* Adnizzio is given to us. Let no man bear malice in his heart for Magruder. He is but the deity's hit man. I say that Gennaro did not die of a stroke or apoplectic rage, but rather he choked on a bottomless pride, a pride that is not sinful, a pride so intense that it had no expression in life, a pride whose only true expression is given to us this day in the profundity of death. Bless you, Magruder. Thank you again for what you have done for us."

"Thank you, coach," Vincent Adnizzio said earnestly, tears coursing down his face.

"You're welcome, Vincent," Magruder told him softly. "You're welcome, I'm sure."

Nicholas the Tedesco, his oration done, stood wiping his brow, leaning heavily on the railing of the first pew. The church was rent again with the sounds of coughings and blubberings into more handkerchiefs; a paroxysm of grief had overcome the newlyweds, who cried into each other's faces, and also the priest, who wept, racked with sobbing, wiping his eyes with the end of his vestment.

There was a dramatic pause until the Tedesco, looking down, grimaced irritably for a moment, seeming to remember that old Adnizzio still lay there. He raised his hand, calling for silence, and spoke again: "Wedding guests! Hear me one moment longer, I the interrupter of this august nuptial beg you. Let six strong men come forward, three from the Modesti, three from the Adnizzio. Let them bear the *patrono* in accordance with the dignity of his station from this church; let them remove him to the mortician's establishment; let the mortician prepare him, cosmetize him, place him to rest in a sumptuous coffin; let that coffin, the ship as it were of his voyage into Eternity, be returned to the house of his son Vincent for the wedding reception; let it be placed upon a dais in the great inflated chamber reserved for the dancing so that he may be with us who are sorrowful, yet joyously celebrating the happiness of the newlyweds. Then let his smiling spirit bear witness to the dancing of the young and old, let him be one with us in our feasting, drinking and merrymaking. Thus, though he is gone from us, he shall be one with us at the same time. I avow to you we can pay him no higher honor."

Nicholas the Tedesco was done. He placed a kiss on his fingers, imparted it to the dead one, then sang out, "Now let the bearers come forth. . . ."

All hell broke loose. Magruder, bemused now beyond belief, laughed inwardly, barely concealed, at the spectacle of grown men from both wedding parties fighting openly beside the altar for the privilege of carrying the corpse from the church. A smirking Nicholas Morelli winked at Magruder. But a moment later, fearing perhaps the monster he had let loose might turn into a gunfight in a holy place, or produce a mob attack on Magruder, who had started the whole thing from the outset, Morelli interceded again, taking up the altar bells and ringing them loudly to gain attention.

"Let the three brothers of Vincent Adnizzio carry out

their father. Let the three eldest sons of the Modesti aid them. Stop this fighting that gives sacrilege to God and Gennaro Adnizzio at the same moment!"

Chastened-looking, the six designated men emerged from the squabble and walked in two files before the altar to retrieve the dead one. Straining, they lifted his bulk between them to their shoulders. Weeping anew, the Tedesco planted a kiss with his fingertips on Adnizzio's forehead, then launched the procession on its way out of the church, everyone standing and lowering their heads as the body was carried past them. The young priest, remembering his function perhaps, blessed Gennaro Adnizzio as he floated by atop the bearers' shoulders. When Adnizzio was gone, after descending the church steps, his head hung far back, open-eyed, surveying the wedding guests behind him, Nicholas the Tedesco made his final pronouncement: "On Tuesday morning, let all of us here today and hundreds more besides come to honor the dead one at a solemn requiem Mass. But now let us be about the task at hand. Good Father, these young people crave the legitimacy of holy wedlock."

Morelli urged the betrothed to their kneelers and escorted Vincent Adnizzio to his pew once more. The priest took up the reading of his Mass. The Tedesco returned to Magruder, patting at rheumy eyes with his handkerchief.

"Jesus, Morelli, you are really crazy," Magruder whispered to him as the other knelt down beside him.

"I'm not through yet, Magruder. I hated that pig Adnizzio. His wife was my sister. He drove her to her grave. Poor Jenny," Morelli sniffled, then began crying in earnest so that others, seeing him, cried openly also, though for the wrong reason.

During the exchange of vows, when Nicholas the Tedesco had stopped crying, he spoke to Magruder in a muted voice above a whisper so that others turned their heads to eye them: "If you died, Magruder, how many would come to your funeral?"

"Not many, I think."

"I think no one would come to mine. My friends, with whom I read poetry, probably couldn't raise the price of a taxicab to come here from Newark. . . . Will you be around here Tuesday for the funeral?"

"I suppose so. I really can't expect to begin implementing Sterling Lloyd Kasprzak's justice until after Vincent's father is at least buried."

"That will be some funeral, Magruder, let me tell you," Morelli said, weeping again, as they stood for the tumultuous exit of the married ones. "You'll see on that day what it profits a man to lose the price of his immortal soul. Thousands of mourners, mountains of flowers, every politician in the state and half the goddamned clergy. Gennaro Adnizzio was one of the biggest crooks in all New Jersey."

Magruder, standing, found it in him to weep also: hopeless, hopeless tears of irony as Charles and Aurelia Modesti marched down the aisle toward Life. His new friend Nicholas the Tedesco was truly a soul brother, as the young people said.

CHAPTER 9

More of the Enemy

"What do I do now?" Magruder heard himself ask his new friend.

"Try to look like an emissary from God, Magruder. You aren't out of the woods on this thing yet."

They were the last to leave the church. Outside, at their approach, the low drone of generally grim-looking wedding guests fell to a complete silence and a line parted automatically between the twosome and the newlyweds standing in the cold, having their pictures taken against the slab side of a limousine.

"I might die today," Magruder spoke reflectively, "somebody might shoot me dead."

"*Che sera, sera, paisan.* It must be admitted that you walked into the lion's den on your own two legs. Still, my oratory has a certain magical prowess. . . ."

"Yes," Magruder agreed, deciding on the instant that since his careful progress toward Sterling Lloyd Kasprzak's justice was gone dangerously atilt, he would simply accede to the rest of the day's events, whatever they were, and hope the special madness of Nicholas the Tedesco would protect him. Also, he was bemused by the notion of his new tolerance, thinking that he might have

147

feared the energies of the man Morelli, his apparent indis-
cipline, not so long before in the past.

They walked through the parted sea, Magruder wearing, he hoped, a wan, ironic smile that he considered best
befitted a proper emissary of God. It seemed to work:
Many of the guests nodded shyly at him, a few men shook
his hand and he was addressed as "coach" as often as
Nicholas the Tedesco was called *"dottore."*

At the limousine, Magruder kissed the bride, as did the
Tedesco before him. She collapsed against his chest, a
frail, lovely girl, dark-haired and olive-skinned, whose
body shuddered with sobs as she chanted the name of her
grandfather over and over again. Magruder patted at her
back consolingly, trying at the same time not to step on
the lace folds of her wedding gown and to conjure up the
required cooling platitude. Absurdly, hardly believing the
voice that issued from himself, he told her that this was
supposed to be the happiest day of her life as it had
doubtless been for her grandfather. Complying with the
lie, she rearranged herself and Magruder patted dry the
tears that fell from her eyes with his handkerchief, taking
special care to remove the blots of eye liner the tears had
dragged along with them. Then he shook hands with her
visibly quivering new husband, declining to kiss him on
the cheeks as the Tedesco had done.

They posed for separate pictures with the bride and
groom, then with the entire wedding party before the
cars bore the lot of them off to the reception. In the wake
of their parting, as the guests who had stood absorbedly
watching the photographing session began moving off in
straggling groups, Adnizzio's cohorts in crime, McFarland

and Matland, together with their wives, appeared from among the tombstones and monuments of the neighboring churchyard. McFarland, a bank vice president in one of the surrounding towns, and Matland, an insurance executive in Manhattan, seemed somehow identical to Magruder, an uncanny likeness that touched everywhere on the extremities: the amount of hair that each of them had lost, the girth of paunch, the type of suit they each wore, even to their wives—two short-haired, small-breasted, athletic girl types who had the special look of playing lots of tennis on any given day.

"Hello, coach," McFarland spoke first.

"Hello, Justin. How are you? And you, Eric?" he shook hands with Matland.

"Rather amazed that you're still alive, coach, considering that you just pulled the circuit breaker on old Gennaro Adnizzio in church back there. Our friend Vincent is a soulful moderate. But the rest of that gang . . . well, one hears whisperings about Mafia and other such things. . . . It could all be illusion, theatrics of course. Old Gennaro had a neat flair for the robust big time. Still, I'm pretty sure I know what those bulges are under the jackets of some of the Adnizzio minion. Not fat, I mean, even if some of those guys are pretty hefty."

"I think I understand what you're trying to say, Eric. But as you say, it might be theatrics," Magruder told him stonily as McFarland and the two wives began a kind of nervous giggling. The hands of Matland's wife began fluttering before them, involuntarily certainly, and she took a cigarette from her purse, fascinating everyone with her tremble as she tried to get a lighter's flame within range.

Magruder took the lighter from her and lit the cigarette. She drew in the smoke in a long, grateful gasp. It came to him then, seeing their fear, a real monster compared to the degrees of concern he had witnessed in the others during his trek across the continent, that they supposed perhaps that any punishment by law would be the ultimate, a sanctioned pummeling of their lives and families and careers into leavings of dust. Instantly guilty, Magruder considered that there was a certain irresponsibleness on his part: He had not actually considered what the punishment might be, had only wanted them brought to court for a start. He thought somehow to assuage their fearing, but Matland, growing visibly more angry, was off on a new tack.

"Nice job you did back there in church, Morelli, you stupid bastard. I still don't believe you got away with it."

"You're a goddamned fake, Morelli!" McFarland's wife hurled. "You were reading Keats at that christening for Vincent's brother's kid last month. I should have blown the whistle on you then. Old Gennaro wouldn't have taken too kindly to the knowledge that he subsidized a bum who copied the greats when he's supposed to be composing."

"It's only because my talent doesn't hold a candle to Keats and the occasion was so solemn and momentous that I consented to read Keats instead of Morelli. That, I would say, is true humility, Mrs. McFarland."

"No, it's just some more of that damned involuted reasoning of yours that squeaked you through this morning. But if anything happens to Vincent, it won't wash. One Adnizzio is something, but two . . ."

"Do you actually think Vincent or any of you will have to die because of what you did to Kasprzak?"

"If it's left to you, you old fool, we might," McFarland raged. "You shouldn't know a person like this, coach. Even Italian people think he's crazy. I knew he'd find a way to hook up with you. He wasn't even involved, but he's had nothing but Sterling Lloyd Kasprzak on his god-damned mind since it happened. He even went to the funeral twenty-three years ago. He was the only outsider there!"

"That's not completely right, McFarland. I brought Vincent back to school from New Jersey for the funeral. He came to talk with me when he was so upset. He could never go to Gennaro with a problem. Gennaro didn't listen. He . . ."

"Do you understand what you're doing, Morelli?" Matland demanded. "You're conspiring with Coach Magruder to wreck your own nephew's life."

"I'm not conspiring with anyone. All I want is simple justice. It's Vincent I'm thinking of. I have nothing against him. He's a good boy. But he suffers too much. His conscience needs unburdening. The thing has to be done with now, one way or the other. If he's convicted and serves his time, his debt is paid. If he's acquitted, then justice has at least been attempted and he can live with that consolation."

"If he's convicted . . . ?" The words came out of Matland's wife in a tremulous snort, edged with ready tears that warned she might advance to the full-blown theatrics of hysteria. "If Vince is convicted, then this balding bedwarmer of a husband of mine who looks like a used-car salesman is convicted too. I mean this husband and father whose three kids actually like him and used to fight for the privilege of the olive in his martini when he came home from work at night. I mean you're not breaking up my home, Morelli, or you either, Magruder, with your stupid fucking old men's games . . . !"

"Judy . . ." Magruder vaguely heard the low growl of Matland's warning to his wife: His eyes were riveted instead on the flaring tip of her cigarette that zoomed through the chill air, describing arcs and ellipses of her fearing and rage. He thought perhaps that she meant to use it as a weapon. She did: The lit end raced toward him, and as his eyes blinked involuntarily shut, a prayer for safety accompanying, the cigarette thudded painfully into the center of his forehead in the same moment she got off a fierce kick in the shins. He yelped with the pain but evidently did not suffer alone: McFarland's wife assaulted Nicholas the Tedesco. Before her husband dragged her off, she cleaved four lines of instantly bleeding scratches across his right cheek with a talonlike swipe of her hand.

"Coach . . . Mr. Morelli . . . forgive us!" McFarland pleaded. "Rita's just so upset. She doesn't really mean this."

"Yes I do! I damn well do mean it!" Rita McFarland screamed, spitting at Morelli and hitting one lapel of his coat. "We've got two kids in college now and another on the way in a year. What am I supposed to do if their father ends up in some damn jail in New York state?"

Then she calmed down on the instant, it seemed to Magruder, and began looking at him reflectively instead:

"Do you know something, Magruder? Justin told me about this crap years ago before we were married. He wanted me to know what might happen so I'd be sure. But I was never really unsure. The whole thing was such a preposterous-sounding business for grown men to be worried about, and when I got a look at old Sterling Lloyd in the class yearbook, I was more certain than ever. I mean, Jesus Christ, Magruder, what if he'd actually found a woman to marry and fathered children? There'd be a race of cretins wandering about upstate New York. God-damned necrophiliacs or something. These three guys did the world a favor. It was humanitarian. They should've been welcomed back to those class reunions at St. Anselm's with trumpets instead of having to go up there with a bad case of the shakes every time."

Magruder, declining to answer the absurd argument yet another time, probed the dime spot of pain on his forehead instead. Nicholas the Tedesco bent down to study his scrapes in the side mirror of a nearby car, clucking to himself at first in annoyance, stamping one irritated foot on the sidewalk, then warming up, perhaps to some vaster poetic possibility: He twisted his face every which way—bizarre narcissism—alternately grimacing, wanely smiling or pouting back at his apparition. The remaining five watched him fascinatedly. McFarland and Matland had each released their wives. Simultaneously the two women lit up a cigarette, neither one's hands shaking now, both sharing the same lighter flame. Judy Matland began giggling a little, then shuddering with barely concealed laughter as the cigarette smoke escaped her mouth in staccato puffs. Rita McFarland began laughing also, then their husbands—gales of mirth shucking off the tension. Magruder, too, found it in himself to howl at the spectacle and the impulse toward humor spread to the last knots of wedding guests who had observed the violence of the assaults on Magruder and the Tedesco with open-mouthed stupefication.

In another moment, replacing his fedora, Morelli returned to confront them: "These wounds are annoyingly rendered, yet not unattractive. Notable poets of the past have always enjoyed tempestuous liaisons with women. Lord Byron, for example. These scars, I suppose, will serve to give the artist a certain meritorious badge of authenticity."

It was too hilarious. Magruder guffawed with laughter, patting at his eyes with a handkerchief, and he watched as McFarland's wife, weak with laughter, moved to support herself on the front fender of a nearby car, kicking small dents in the aluminum hide of its wheelcover. McFarland and Matland together did a giddy little jig, a real hopefulness growing in them perhaps that the whole Kasprzak affair was about to dissolve into formless absurdity. Magruder thought to restate his purpose, but Judy Matland, obviously the most determined person there, stepped before him, poking a hard finger into his chest, obviously past being amused by Nicholas the Tedesco: "You watch out, Magruder! You're in enemy territory now, and except for this nut, Morelli, you're all alone."

"I believe there is an established code of laws in New Jersey to protect people like me from people like you, Mrs. Matland."

"Yeah, well sometimes that code is at work and sometimes it's on vacation, and right now it's gone skiing and I'm feeling very extra-legal. If you and I and an aluminum tennis racket ever got locked into a small room together, you'd be dead in about two minutes, Magruder."

"That's enough now, Judy," her husband said placatingly. "This business will all be resolved one way or the other in a few weeks I think and we'll all be embarrassed that we went around threatening old friends with tennis rackets and such."

"Old friends, bullshit!" McFarland's wife, Rita, chimed in. "When some intelligent judge up there in New York acquits you guys, I'd still like to go after this crazy old bastard with a hockey stick for all those years of nail biting he put us through."

"The women are always the worst," Nicholas the Tedesco began extemporizing before Magruder could shut him up. "The home is their kingdom where they reign as virtual queen. They'd kill us if they knew how. And come to think of it, Vincent's wife, Angelina, she'd know how. She was the only daughter of that family. Her father and uncles, they worship the ground she walks on. . . . Sicilians, that bunch. Enough said. A single phone call would do the trick."

"I'd still like two minutes alone with either of you in a small room," Judy Matland hissed. "To make up for lost time."

"I'm not impressed," Morelli stormed on. "A hockey stick or a tennis racket. Bah! You Anglos are ineffectual. I have a low regard for passionless people. Now the Adnizzios, they would use a *garrotta,* for example. In the instant of death they say your entire life passes before you with brilliant clarity. That's because your eyes usually pop right out of your head."

"Delightful!" McFarland's wife enthused. "I think I'll try to get together with Angelina for a few moments today after the reception and see what we can arrange."

"We should be going now, coach," Matland spoke. "There's feasting and dancing in the offing, after all. Perhaps we can get together at our own place tonight for a sandwich and some coffee. You'll want to go up to New York state soon, I take it?"

"If the funeral for old Adnizzio is Tuesday, I'd like to go up on Wednesday morning. I'll call for an appointment with the headmaster and county prosecutor."

Matland shrugged: "No use wasting any time, I guess. See you at the festivities."

"Yes."

The four walked away to a white convertible with vanity plates that spelled MATLND. They were about to get inside the car when Judy Matland opened the trunk lid and fished out—not unexpectedly—a tennis racket that she flashed furiously through the air, unimpaired by the weight of a wooden frame that contained it. Beside her, Rita McFarland had twisted a long scarf about her neck and tugged the ends of it in opposite directions, simulating the agony of choking. With Nicholas the Tedesco, Magruder began walking thoughtfully off toward the Buick as McFarland and Matland tried pushing their wives into the convertible.

CHAPTER 10

Some Allies

Nicholas the Tedesco made a phone call for help.

Then, instead of returning directly to the rippling helium-filled caves of the bacchanal at Adnizzio's house, they went up the Garden State Parkway toward Newark, where they were to pick up the members of a string quartet who would play soothing Vivaldi during the lavish five courses of the wedding feast.

"It's touch and go, Magruder, right now. The pendulum could swing either way. Those two women who just attacked us are dangerous enough, more so if they commence some sort of lobbying effort at that banquet. If the Adnizzio brotherhood and some of Angelina's relatives, to say nothing of that cretinous newly arrived tribe, the Modestis, all come to their senses on the same glass of wine, the least you can expect is a beating on that frost-hard lawn I keep speaking of. *Moi aussi, je crois . . .* he who hoodwinks is no less guilty. . . .

"Anyway, music doth calm the savage beast, and this transition from blessed death to painless life still needs a little help. My friends of the Celestiale String Quartet of Greater Newark will play 'The Four Seasons,' beginning with 'Fall.' During the 'Winter' movement, if timing be propitious, and the mortician is done stuffing him, they can carry in Gennaro's casket and place it before the head table, where I, acting in my capacity as master of ceremonies, will read a poem by way of reverant eulogy over that pig's body."

"A poem of your own creating?" Magruder asked impishly. They flew up the extreme left lane of the parkway, declining to stop for the toll baskets, faster than the Buick had ever traveled in eighteen years of its existence. Nicholas the Tedesco drove. Magruder was warden of the wine glass on the passenger side. He alternately sipped at it, then passed it to the driver. Soon they were at Perth Amboy near the ranges of fuel tanks. Magruder breathed in gulps of air, holding his nose, against the awful odor that overwhelmed them.

"I say, Morelli, a poem of your own creation?"

"No alas, another borrowing. A hijacked stanza from Tennyson's *Lotus Eaters*."

"Have you ever read a poem of your own anywhere?"

"Not one that could be called exceptional. But I will soon. I've been working for more than fifteen years now on a memoriam for Sterling Lloyd and it's almost finished. The meter is dactylic hexameter, a work longer than two hundred pages. It's exhausted me though, needless to say. Stolen my energies from the lesser commissions that old Gennaro was always throwing my way."

"I wouldn't have thought there were two hundred pages worth of the pitiable memory of Sterling Lloyd Kasprzak to eulogize."

"The geneology was considerable. His American nationality was only the tip of the iceberg. Below were Poles and Bulgars, Ukranians and Khazars, a vast gutteral-tongued cacophony of middle and eastern European types, to say nothing of periodic Mongol and Tartar rapings and pillagings. A female antecedent who boiled oil on the battlements when the Turks were repulsed from Vienna's gates nevertheless reportedly lay with a Turk all during that siege. Sterling Lloyd was an incredible composite. He was an amalgam of most all the races and people of the earth. I've made him into the very symbol of mankind itself. . . ."

"I take it the quartet will continue on into 'Spring' of 'The Four Seasons'?" Magruder asked gruffly, abruptly slamming the cork back into the bottle, trying to shake the wine dimness from his head: He needed to catch up with himself again. The Buick zoomed along now at just over ninety miles per hour.

"Yes, that's when I'll have the coffin borne out of the place. By then, if we're still in one piece after the depths of Vivaldi's February, we should survive. Who would attack us during 'Spring,' after all? That season of the young betrothed first coming together, the hushed expectancy of their shy coupling in breeze-kissed fields of lavender. The wedding guests will understand, be breathless with anticipation. No time at all to permit a dead man or his vengeance to steal the day's thunder. Old Gennaro will be exiled to the larger room of the dancing, his coffin placed squarely atop draped saw horses to await the revelers when the feasting is done. Gone but not forgotten, Magruder, believe you me. I've got further plans for that *strutz*. . . ."

"He's dead. Isn't that vengeance enough?" Magruder

demanded sourly, his head aching now, thinking that crazy Morelli's hundred-headed vision of almost anything might surely wreck the simple plan he had brought with him from California.

"No. That's good enough for simple people perhaps. But this is an artist's revenge. In fact, a poet's vengeance. It needs a crowning of metaphors, icing on the cake, so to speak. But I digress. After 'Spring' comes the final move-ment, 'Summer,' the full-blown symbolic time of mar-riage's joys and sorrows, the pain and exultation of chil-dren and home life. The heady time of life's fruits fullest ripening. While the newlyweds hold hands before me, I'll read a poem of consummate optimism."

"Your own?"

"No. Sadly, another purloining. Dante again. *Il Paradiso* this time. Another instance of this poor poet's profound humility. . . ."

"Morelli, do you have a driver's license?" Magruder asked suddenly. Approaching Newark they still careened along at more than ninety between the tunneled walls of a succession of overpasses. Nicholas the Tedesco swept clean the highway before them with the flashing of his lights and blaring of the horn. Miraculously, not a cop anywhere, he had still not paid a single toll.

"No I don't. Not for about ten years now. Why?"

"I just wondered," Magruder said weakly.

They paid up a meager fifteen cents at the final exit-ramp toll booth off the parkway and navigated the grim Newark streets of a badly run-down section where few pedestrians walked in the sunless December chill and a whole cyclone of discarded newspapers blew everywhere through the air. At a corner bar where a curved and badly peeling wooden turret graced the building from sidewalk to roof, the Tedesco pulled up and began sounding the horn. Tarnished-looking, tinsely Christmas decorations with winking lights framed four old men in dark old-fashioned overcoats and fedoras like Morelli's who came to the bar's single window to peer out at them with undisguised suspicion. Nicholas the Tedesco got out of the car to prove evidently that he was not an apparition: The four quaffed their drinks and headed for the door. To Magruder, each of the members of the Celestiale String Quartet of Greater Newark seemed, inexplicably, to be a kind of mirror image of their friend Nicholas Morelli; he hoped fervently they were not equally crazy.

Magruder stuffed the two wedding presents that remained in the rear seat into the trunk as the foursome emerged from the bar with their instruments. For the moment Morelli declined introductions. The bass fiddler carried a heavy quilt and lengths of rope in addition to his ponderous instrument, and everyone helped spread the quilt on the Buick's roof, raise up the fiddle and lash it forward and aft to the bumpers. Then they piled into the car. The bass fiddler, a huge jowly man with the atrabilious circles beneath his eyes of a bad liver perhaps, sat up front, sandwiching Magruder against the Tedesco. The two violinists sat on either side in the rear, small wizened old men with wispy white hair whom Magruder considered looked enough alike to be brothers. The viola player was center rear, directly behind Magruder, and held his instrument across his knees. All were Italians with Old World accents; none removed their fedoras in the car; the two violinists were brothers, named Scanella; the viola player was called Pernelli, the bass fiddler, Volpone. Volpone belched loudly by way of a greeting to Magruder. Then he picked up the wine jug, pulled a cork and took a long swig of the evil grape. He passed the jug to the rear and wiped his mouth on the sleeve of his coat. They all seemed quite giddy with excitement as the driver-poet shot back onto the parkway south. The bass fiddler squirmed about to regard Magruder closely.

"So you've finally come, Magruder. We gave up on you three years back, you know."

"Why all the intense interest in one old man's last mission?" Magruder asked. The angry bells of the Parkway Authority began screaming again as Morelli shot untaxed through the first toll booth.

"Why? Not for an abstract like justice's sake, let me assure you. It's because we've been listening to Dottore Morelli's epic—*Reflections on Life's Pitiful Short-changing of Sterling Lloyd Kasprzak*—almost every Friday night for about fifteen years now, and even he agrees all it needs is an ending. Which is why I and my companions would do almost anything to help you, since one way or the other an ending would be provided and we wouldn't have to listen to Morelli's piss-pot readings any longer."

"*Zu fungu!*" the poet hurled, flashing an arm past Magruder's nose and catching the bass fiddler with a sharp crack on his cheek. But the fiddler only laughed, tears racing from his eyes as the car slalomed at ninety plus across three lanes from Nicholas the Tedesco's inattention. The three in the back seat howled mirthfully as Magruder grabbed the steering wheel and saved them from sideswiping a bridge abutment. Incredibly, they traveled in a vehicleless vacuum. Waves of cars, three abreast, fled ahead of them, off to the break-down lanes in hopes of safety, or cowered in fear behind them. Magruder took another gulp of wine from the glass between his knees as the Tedesco returned the car to the left-side passing lane.

"Hey, Nicholas," the viola player in the back called after another turn at the jug, "I hope to Christ you're not going to write in a complete new section about Gennaro's heart attack. God, if you start composing your way down that old crook's family tree, we'd be at it for another fifteen years."

"I intend to dismiss his death in one single line: 'Ironically, Gennaro Adnizzio died in a church.' Not one word more. Then all the world will know my sister's vindication is absolute."

"Then why play the master, Vivaldi, over his miserable remains?"

"Not to honor that pig, believe me. It's to help Magruder stay alive so he can effect Sterling Lloyd's justice. The master would approve of the use he's being put to, as long as it's for the sake of Magruder, who's our champion of righteousness. Nothing is defiled."

"You must hurry, Magruder," a violinist spoke up, the Scanella brother who sat behind the driver, staring raptly out the window and fastidiously drinking the awful wine from his own collapsible plastic cup. "We joke and kid about the Tedesco's epic, but even so, after listening to it for so many years, Sterling Lloyd's cause has become my own. When you didn't show up in the twentieth year, in

1970, I took to my bed in severe depression. If you fail me yet another time, I can't say what will happen, Magruder. I'm older than you yourself. It will probably be the end for me."

"Your nature is too sensitive, Scanella," the bass fiddler told him, squirming his huge shoulders about to address the other in the rear, crushing Magruder against the Tedesco. "Not mine, though. A man who has to waltz around the massiveness of a bass fiddle through life cannot afford the luxury of recognizing he's an ineffectual artist, then languishing so he's crushed to death by his own instrument. That's your problem. You see yourself as ineffectual."

"Perhaps. But at my age corrective therapy is ridiculous. I know too much about myself. That's why I need Magruder. He's not ineffectual. He was a football coach. As dispenser of justice, he's my surrogate."

"Mine also," the viola player said. "I've waited for your coming like the others, Magruder. I'm seventy-two years old. Justice must be served before I die. Please hurry as Scanella says. Remember those lines from Nicholas' poem that described the coming of the avenging angel?

He came from out the desert vastness of the New World
    West,
Bronzed skin, eyes blue and calm, fair ringlets of
    medium-length hair. Blond.
His chariot drawn by the fleet-footed steeds of the
    Apocalypse.
On his shield the flaming apparition of the Savior's Tree.
His loins covered over with wrappings of the Fiercest
    Mail . . ."

164

"Inspired. Truly inspired verse," came out of the rear seat in a chorus of muttered approval.

"Yes, credit must be given where credit is due," the bass fiddler intoned, "and this is truly inspired poetry, though it should be admitted, the rest of the work is often not." Still, he planted a kiss on the fingertips and reached across Magruder to touch the cheek of the broadly smiling poet. In another moment, his muse evidently appeased, Nicholas the Tedesco slowed to the speed limit and actually placed a quarter in a toll-booth basket. But Magruder found it in himself to laugh in the midst of the general rapture until Morelli and the bass fiddler asked at the same moment, "What's wrong, Magruder? Why are you laughing?"

"Because everything is so damn unreal and ironic. Your Magruder come out of the New World West is sixty-eight years old. My eyes are brown and watery, not blue and calm. My hair, when it wasn't white, was black, not blond, and my poor loins are girded in long johns, not wrappings of the fiercest mail. . . ."

"Poetic license, Egil," the Tedesco assured him, shrugging. "Merely a metaphorical language."

"It's still an awesome responsibility. I'm an old man like yourselves."

"Old age is a blessing, I think," the poet extolled, taking a long sip of the dago. Ahead the Perth Amboy bridge loomed up, the promise of awful stink again assured by belching clouds of smoke that climbed through the girders. "Only the old can feel the way we can about justice and morality. We've started back along the down side of the arc again toward zero and there's no need to compromise any longer. We're free to concentrate on avenging Sterling Lloyd. There's nothing more to fear losing."

"It's true what Nicholas the Tedesco says," the other Scanella brother spoke now. "When I was most vulnerable, when I would have compromised my conscience and broken any laws was when my wife was still alive and my children were growing up and had to be educated no matter what. But now my wife is dead and my children are moved away and married to Anglos and I never see them or my grandchildren because they don't want to admit their father is just an old wop violin player from Jersey. Believe me, Magruder, I've got all the time in the world until the hour of my death to help out with Sterling Lloyd's justice if there's anything I can do. It would be doubly satisfying. I'd be getting in a few licks of my own. How can children be so ungrateful? I kissed my father's hand until the day he died, and I was fifty-five years old when it happened. . . ."

"That's the wrong attitude, Scanella," the Tedesco told him. "Please remember that one of the guilty is my own nephew Vincent, who's always been a good boy, an obedient boy, properly respectful in the old tradition. The principal justice I want is the one that will unburden his mind one way or the other and let him out of his private prison of fear. That same justice will also prove that we, sensitive artistic men of good will, humanists truly, did not forsake the tragic memory of a fellow mortal, poor Sterling Lloyd."

"Bravo! Well said, Tedesco!" the viola player enthused, clapping the driver's shoulder. "It's a noble thing to be kind to Sterling Lloyd's memory, but Sterling Lloyd, even dead, can serve me well in return. No man is motiveless, after all. I'll make him my surrogate, too. For everything. Before I die, Sterling Lloyd's justice will serve to obliterate the terrible toll of all the infamies and injustices of this world during my lifetime that pricked my conscience yet left me, a simple violinist of Newark, New Jersey, powerless to do anything about them. That's why I'd do anything I had to to help you, Magruder."

"What the hell do you think you could do for me, sir?" Magruder demanded annoyedly. His head throbbed now like hammer blows from the dago and the fierce whine of radial tires traveling again at ninety miles per hour and he was tiring of them: They were all a bunch of loons, Nicholas the Tedesco the worst of the lot, even though he had doubtless saved Magruder from reprisal at the church that morning. It was imperative to disengage himself from the Celestiale Quartet and the talentless poet as soon as possible before they ended up totally confounding the vindication of Kasprzak.

"What could I do for you, Magruder? Well, I and my friends for a start are going to try to keep you alive for the rest of the day despite your annoyance because you think we're crazy old men. Nicholas may have moved the mob this morning and got you off, but that was a church, a holy place, and those Adnizzios hadn't had their first drink of the day. I'll bet sometime today, with all that booze, somebody's sentimentality is going to run shallow and you'll be in trouble. Something like that happens at nearly every wedding I've ever been to."

"I apologize, gentlemen," Magruder said conciliatorially, "but if a flying wedge makes for me across the dance floor today, I'd say Sterling Lloyd's justice is already blunted, if not over with altogether."

"I could kill a man with my bass fiddle!" the huge one beside Magruder avowed furiously. Magruder stared: He slammed two heavy hams of fists together and his knuckles went bone white with the effort of crushing the enemy between them.

"Look, Magruder." One Scanella tapped him on the shoulder. Magruder edged about, heard the rapid chanting of "*Uno, due, tre*" . . . then gaped open-mouthed as the two violins and the center viola were upended toward the roof: Stiletto blades, about six inches worth, shot out of the base of each instrument at a turn of a peg, the viola's blade ripping right through the ceiling upholstery.

"You see, Magruder," Scanella said, trembling with an infectious excitement, "we have been preparing for your coming. If we used the knives, it would be the least expected event in the universe. Just imagine the element of surprise!"

For their last mile on the parkway the car swerved all over the road in accompaniment to their evident delirium. Their notion of prowess was gone mad. Flying off the parkway at the Red Bank exit, Morelli sounded the horn deafeningly; the wine jug made its final round, a terrified toll collector leapt inside his cubicle for safety.

Magruder, basically reserved, a conservative by nature, recalled his ancient fear about New Jersey that uncoiled each time he had had occasion in the past to visit there: a sense perhaps of a dangerous capacity for anarchy that seemed to run always through the populace of that small state.

CHAPTER 11

Feast of Lupercal
Feast of Mars

That evening, about 10 P.M., and alone at last, numbed by exhaustion and drinking and preparing to sleep in a motel room in the nearby town of Rumson, Magruder capsuled the day's events, storing them away in his memory bank. Hilarious recall, he would infuse them defiantly into maudlin, depressive days of the future:

Barring no other, it was the most irreverent day of Magruder's life.

It was set to music.

The young Modestis would never forget their wedding.

Nor doubtless would any of the wedding guests.

Magruder was threatened by a dark, surly man playing cat's cradle with a *garrotta;* the same man later got drunk and almost strangled himself with his own *garrotta.*

A corpse arrived at the wedding; he stayed for the feasting and dancing, and later left with the bride's garter and a jug of Nicholas the Tedesco's wine.

In life, apparently, the corpse had been something of a rouè; he had lain, it was said, with half the women

169

of Red Bank, New Jersey; three of these included his daughter-in-law and the wives of McFarland and Matland.

Hearing that, the three women's husbands grew compliant and anxious to aid Magruder in the quest for S. L. Kasprzak's justice.

All three wanted to go to jail; their punishment, in point of fact, would be their wives' punishment.

The poet Morelli read two of his own compositions; one was Tennyson's, the other Dante's.

Homage to the dead one and homage to the newly-weds was given jointly; the ritual was elaborate and smacked of Old World solemnities; everyone participated, and everyone was duly impressed; Nicholas the Tedesco invented it as he went along.

The lover Morelli began the formal courtship of fat Theresa Bugalli, a widow in her sixties with lovely eyes and a mustache; the Celestiale Quartet played Viennese waltzes and schottisches for the two during the intermission of The Beached Boards, a rock band for the young people, and Harry Simon and the Ship's Lights, who gave familiar comfort to the middle-aged.

Theresa Bugalli was chaperoned by two older sisters, also widows, and an aunt, Olympia, who was reputedly ninety-eight years old; they watched the stiff, unsmiling dancers with an unrelenting gaze.

A great windstorm, a sudden squall off the winter Atlantic, announced the end of the festivities to the few who remained about 8:00 P.M. by ripping up the ambling jelly helium-filled tents and depositing them

in the trees about Adnizzio's house; the para-
phernalia of decoration was spread for blocks
around.

Stoned on pot they had graciously offered to
Magruder, The Beached Boards played out their
souls in competition with the storm's frenzy as the
tent blew away from around them; Harry Simon and
the Ship's Lights lost all their music and music stands
as well when they ran fearing into Adnizzio's house;
a length of siding got loose, by its color from
Matland's house next door, shafted the Ship's Lights
abandoned base drum.

The storm, eerie, sudden and God-sent perhaps, departed as abruptly as it had arrived, its task completed, evidently.

Thereafter, Nicholas the Tedesco and Theresa
Bugalli danced on the spotless wall-to-wall carpeting
of the living room of Adnizzio's house; the Celestiale
Quartet played in the kitchen; the chaperones knit-
ted in the dining room, watching fiercely through an
open door.

The caterer, an intense, emotional man, devastated
by the destruction of his Calabrian cave, lay sobbing
face down on the floor near the dancers; in time,
driblets of blood, doubtless from an ulcer, sputtered
out of his mouth onto the rug.

Angelina Adnizzio, weeping, admittedly, over the
loss of her father-in-law, did not think to ask him to
remove himself to a more impermeable floor; she simply followed his squirmings about her carpeting with
a can of rug cleaner, erasing the trail nearly as soon

as it was created.

Magruder laughed so hard at everything that once he even vomited.

Nicholas the Tedesco drove Magruder to his motel for the night, then borrowed the Buick to take Theresa Bugalli and her three chaperones home to Secaucus in North Jersey. . . .

Magruder doubted he would be allowed to stay the night.

In the morning Magruder came awake to the sound of more laughter. His own again. He had dreamed in perfect recall of the primal event of the day before, the revelation that Gennaro Riccardo Adnizzio was the uncontested satyr of Monmouth County, with primal lusts and a penchant for dazzling exhibitionism that, in the case of his daughter-in-law, Angelina, had violated the sanctity of his own household, to say nothing of a good number of others besides.

It happened during the "Fall" movement of "The Four Seasons" when Magruder sat down with an assemblage of more than three hundred to begin the first of five courses, privately wincing at the sounds that came from the Celestiale group. They played the master, Vivaldi, in much the same way that Nicholas the Tedesco punished the language, corrupting already melancholy notes into a minor-toned kind of Semitic keening or wailing until Magruder grew ashamed for them: Old men with burdens that were now endemic to the marrow, comfortable even from familiarity, woes that they channeled into the strings of their instruments. His allies infuriated him.

But no one else seemed to care or notice.

Magruder sat alone at the end of one long table, facing the dignitaries of the head table when all others were at right angles to them; the McFarlands and Matlands sat immediately on either side of him. Hardly a preferred place, Magruder considered, but one in which Angelina Adnizzio had pointedly placed him for safekeeping (actually removing his place card from the head table, where Nicholas the Tedesco had installed him) and his proximity to her relative who played cat's cradle with his *garrotta*.

"Why here, Angelina?" Magruder asked her as she led him firmly to the new seating. He judged that she had drunk quite a bit during the reception and, remembering her furies, he thought to make a small joke.

"This seems quite a vulnerable place, Angelina," he chuckled as she slammed him fiercely into his chair.

"The better to keep an eye on you from up there, shithead! I didn't buy any of that shit at church this morning that Morelli was selling. And that wop string band up there isn't goin' to help you one bit either. Those gentlemen over there at the other table who are glarin' at you so unabashedly are my father, two uncles and two brothers. The guy with the *garrotta* was a childhood sweetheart. They'd like to kill you, shithead!"

She was weaving in place on her feet now, and the assault by her tears on her makeup had given her the mask of Medusa in return. They watched as she lifted Magruder's steak knife, absorbedly slit about six inches of tablecloth with it, then returned it precisely to its place.

"It's no use getting so overwrought, Angelina, on the day of your daughter's wedding. The business of Kasprzak will be resolved soon enough. Then the whole thing will be over with once and for all, do you see?"

"Kasprzak? What the shit do I care about Kasprzak?" she slurred. "Nothin's goin' to happen to these three bad little boys anyhow 'cause anybody could tell you the case is never goin' to make it to court for a starter. What I'm overwrought about—that was the word you used, wasn't it, shithead?—what I'm overwrought about is that you're responsible for the death of the man I'd rather be married to than the one I was married to for more than twenty years. Twenty goddamn years!"

"Angelina, think what you're saying!" Matland tried. "For God's sake how do you think Vinnie's going to feel if he hears you talking like this?"

"I don't care how that soft-voiced, milksop shithead feels about it. Twenty years of being married to the son when I tossed and turned in bed at night panting for the father. . . . Gennaro was all man. If it had been Gennaro instead of Vincent, Magruder would be a dead duck long since. Gennaro was a man of action, too!"

"He sure cut himself a wide swath through the ladies of this pleasant little suburb. I think that's why he built the goddamned place," Rita McFarland tittered. "If old Justin here can get it up as many times all next year as Gennaro did in the month before he died, I'll nail up a public notice of ecstasy at City Hall."

"He had a dick that long," Judith Matland proclaimed aggressively toward Magruder, describing the member of a pony perhaps rather than that of a man in the space between her hands. "I could get off just looking at the damn thing!"

"What are you saying?" Matland demanded incredulously, seizing his wife's arm. "Are you saying that you had relations with Gennaro Adnizzio? With that old man? That greasy gangster?"

"Greasy gangster, shit! He was a man!" Angelina shouted, so that more faces looked upward in amazement from their plates. Then she slapped Matland hard in the head with a purse she carried on her arm. Matland made as if to hit her from his seat, but his wife hauled down his fist with a fierce grab: "Don't you dare hit her, Matland! If you want to hit someone, hit Magruder, the way Gennaro would have done."

Then Vincent Adnizzio arrived, pinning his wife's arms behind her back: "Angelina, what's going on here? Leave coach alone."

"It's all right, Vincent. We've all become privy to the knowledge that these three ladies have enjoyed the sight of your dead father's sumptuous member, fully extended evidently, in the recent past," Magruder told him dryly.

"Vinnie," McFarland said witlessly, "Vinnie, they say your old man put it to half the women in this town."

Adnizzio smiled broadly, clapping Magruder on the shoulder, puffing delightedly on a thick cigar: "He was a tremendously potent man, daddy was. And you're right, fantastically endowed! Was he hung! Conversation would just sort of stop and all sorts of guys would be sneaking shifty glances whenever he changed clothes in the locker room at the country club. Men's rooms were a gas, too. It made me so proud. And the business of his prowess, that was kind of an open giggle at home while we were growing up . . . Petzanivan, as the old people say."

"He may have balled our wives, Vinnie, you dope," Matland hissed at him.

The idea broke Adnizzio up into gales of laughter.

"Yours, too, Vincent," Magruder told him softly.

"Angelina . . . !" Adnizzio started.

"He did! And I loved him. You aren't half the man your father was, Vincent."

"I should have guessed," Adnizzio said distantly, though not angrily, analyzing a cuckolding now. "They always spoke Italian together when I was around. I was never allowed to learn the old language when I was growing up. . . ."

"Remember that first time he showed us the thing up in your bedroom, Angelina, at that party? My God, I almost died," Matland's wife exclaimed. "I was blushing so badly after I went downstairs, I thought everybody in the place knew why for sure."

"Coach, I'm on your side now," Matland said suddenly. "I'm not going to thwart justice for the likes of this wife of mine."

"The same for me, coach," McFarland assured him. "The defense rests. Rita and those kids of hers can go to hell. I hope they lock me up for good." A pleased smile came over his face, the faraway look perhaps seeing himself somehow happily ensconced in a jail cell. "You know, they say prisons aren't so bad any more with this new reform business. Perhaps they'd let me read, all the books I've wanted to read so much, but never had the time for. Kierkegaard and Sartre, even Thomas Aquinas. I could become the warden's friend since I wouldn't exactly be categorized as a hardened criminal, and we could play chess and discuss philosophy and criminal justice in the evenings. . . ."

"Oh Jesus, listen to him!" McFarland's wife howled. "The man who blends his own coffee and requires half a fifth of Chivas Regal every night before retiring is set on joining the chain gang to become a thinking philosopher and friend of the enlightened warden. What a joke! In the long run, Magruder may be doing us a greater service than we realize by bringing reality home to these gentlemen. . . ."

"Shut up, Rita, or I'll bring some reality home to you and your dentist," McFarland raged, whole octaves higher than even Angelina Adnizzio's slurring, so that by now no one among the wedding guests could fail to know there was an altercation in the works. Magruder for his part grew giddy at the surreal quality of the day and the feast, then was convulsed with silent laughter, tears streaming down his cheeks, at the notion that, like Daniel, he now sat in a perfect, safe isolation in the lions' den, the lionesses having stolen the bait and turned the trick that set the Furies racing to throats other than Magruder's. Overhead the cave's roof rippled and flowed, the Celestiale Quartet scraped and sawed its way to the end of the first movement, the concerned wedding guests nevertheless attacked great platters of antipasti that were being set down on the tables. Vincent Adnizzio threatened to punch his wife.

"I'm going to break your nose for you, Angelina," Adnizzio informed her evenly.

"Hey, Papa, *tio* Nicki," she called loudly to her family

members at the next table, "watch closely. Vincent's going to break my nose for me. Isn't that nice?"

"Maybe I'll wait till later," Adnizzio conceded weakly as her father, two uncles, two brothers and the childhood sweetheart with the *garrotta* stood up simultaneously.

In the midst of the drama Magruder discovered he was laughing harder than he had ever laughed in his life. At the head table, Nicholas the Tedesco was smitten with mirth also, tears rushing down his cheeks and a handkerchief actually stuffed between his teeth to stifle the sounds. He was absolutely anomalous beside the newlyweds, who still clung to each other with the same look of fearing that had never left their faces since old Gennaro dropped dead in the midst of their nuptial Mass. When he caught Magruder's eye, the poet pointed rearward to the string quartet laboring away at their instruments. All of them, understanding the joke, were laughing and tearing identically.

Matland stared levelly at Magruder for a long moment, detaching himself from the verbal fracas that raged all about him, then simply opined, "Coach, I never thought I'd have to say this to you, but I think you're becoming a cruel old man."

Magruder, sputtering now with absolutely uncontrollable laughter, could not think of a single reason to contest this judgment.

In the same instant it occurred to him also that a wedding, as it was often said, was not really intended for the newlyweds at all.

In bed in his Rumson motel, Magruder thought of

gathering himself together for Sunday Mass until his friend Nicholas the Tedesco, wildly exhilarated, burst into the room to tell Magruder that he had spent the night in Secaucus in the very same bed with fat Theresa Bugalli.

CHAPTER 12

Alma Mater

On the brilliant sunlit Tuesday morning after Saturday's death-scarred wedding, Gennaro Riccardo Adnizzio was laid away to final rest in his family's grotesque mausoleum where four black and scowling life-sized angels guarded the portal against the living. He took with him his granddaughter's garter and Nicholas the Tedesco's wine into Eternity, and the idea was generally applauded (for the most part a merry crowd of mourners) that he was going to have a fine old time when he got there.

Beside the crypt, the God-sent one, Magruder, was moved only to a look of hopeless irony with his friend the poet: The latter's prediction of hundreds of mourners seemed trebled, quadrupled if anything. There were certainly almost two thousand people in attendance. The three Kasprzak culprits, become even more committed to their own punishment by now, Magruder decided, obviously saw no irony in the proceedings at all. They were too distracted, standing side by side before the coffin, dry-eyed and collectively infuriated, glaring at the nearby huddle of their wives, who were weeping and faint-looking and held each other up from collapse. Halfway through the requiem prayers the three women had to be helped to waiting cars by the pallbearers. The black-clad monsignor finished officiating over the mobster, Adnizzio was placed in the crypt beside the wife Nicholas Morelli affirmed he had driven there and the bronze doors closed upon the united dead with a heavy clank.

Magruder and the Tedesco were last to leave the cemetery. It was time for their parting. Magruder made a formal retreat, leery of the dam-held lake of sentimentality he felt ready to burst out of the poet, anxious to be off, following what looked like a hot trail to easy compliance that led toward justice for S. L. Kasprzak. This before Morelli began extemporizing again on life, morality, justice, poetry, vengeance or anything else. But the other only handed him an address card, bussed him fleetingly on both cheeks, then headed home to Newark to wait. . . .

Only Magruder's hot trail turned cold and died the very next day at St. Anselm's itself, of all places, the first bridge they came to, mined and blown out from beneath them as they galloped across.

With Adnizzio, McFarland and Matland, Magruder left early the next morning for upstate New York, speeding up the wintry thruway in Adnizzio's Cadillac, the silence within the car virtually unbroken except for the incessant playing of Frank Sinatra albums on the stereo tape deck. All were sad songs, and Magruder, a self-admitted, quite compartmentalized Sunday night romantic in the days of his marriage, did not recognize any of them. They spoke of loneliness, unrequited love, insomnia generally and booze. At the wheel Adnizzio sniffed copiously into a packet of Kleenex on the dash. McFarland and Matland in the rear used handkerchiefs. Magruder in front stared out at the scenery.

The suggestion of snow ahead in the last miles of northern New Jersey became a certainty ten inches deep as they pulled into the grounds of St. Anselm's, which Magruder had not seen in six years. Inside the gates, a pleasant expectancy filled the car despite their purpose and the unhappy tomes of Sinatra, and uncompelled, Adnizzio halted the car a hundred yards or so beyond the fence. They sat a long moment staring up at the school's main complex of buildings on the crest of a hill, the Romanesque chapel front entrance connecting through porticoes in either direction to Neoclassical and Gothic additions strung on as the seasons of revival styles had changed over the years, and the trustees, more or less well connected, responsible for the building fund drives, came and went. A dash of Rococo with gaudy statues in niches made for the corners, then twin wings of classrooms swept back to form a quadrangle where the outdoor plays, commencements and pep rallies had been held. All told, it was a bizarre arrangement, Magruder considered, though sectionally beautiful: A proper place even, its design stolen from the legacy of Europe and kings and courts, for the conspiracy and conniving and backbiting and intrigue that alternately whispered or thundered through the halls and along the porticoes of dear old St. Anselm's among the administration, trustees, faculty, athletic department and physical plant for all the forty years Magruder spent there. The recall wearied him: Only the students (innocent minds given over to ghouls, in some cases) seemed untainted. Extraneous, almost.

"I loved it here at St. Anselm's," Adnizzio whimpered. "I wish I never had to leave it."

"Yes, that would've been very nice," Magruder concurred. In the next instant he noted with annoyance that someone had painted an indelible peace sign on the statue of St. Anselm. When they rounded the first curve on their way up the switchback of road that led to the parking areas near the administration offices, they saw one of the other changes. Adnizzio brought the Cadillac to a halt again and the four stared speechless out the windows for a time, then actually got out of the car: There on the practice ski slope the old rope tow still functioned, though there were few practicing skiers. Instead, upper form boys chased girls through the snow, one boy tackling his quarry, then disappearing with her in a jumble of legs over a bank and into a range of evergreens.

"What in Christ's name is that all about?" McFarland demanded. "It's the middle of a school day. . . ."

"You may not have heard, Justin," Magruder told him mutedly, not expecting it to be quite as bad as it seemed, "but we went coed last year. You know about this women's lib business and all that . . . ? Well, apparently some of the students' mothers are rabid feminists, especially the ones with rich husbands. . . ."

"This isn't right. I'm not sending any more money up here," Adnizzio whined. "St. Anselm's was for us boys."

"I didn't know anything about this, though I never get a chance to look at the alumni magazine any more," Matland said. "Now I'm glad I don't have any sons. If I did I'd never let them come here. It's for the discipline and sports I'd want to send them. Sports build character. Not this stuff."

"Yes," Magruder agreed, recalling that Matland was just plain yellow at football.

"It was the discipline I liked best, too," McFarland spoke. "The square meals when we were bad, the straight-line walks between classes, the silence we had to keep in the halls. You always knew where you were going or where you were supposed to be. And the required readings in the common room after dinner, before study hall. . . . Remember how wonderful it was with the fireplace burning and snow falling on the outside . . . ?"

"You used to sleep all through the goddamned readings, McFarland," Adnizzio told him.

"I was meditating. Not sleeping. How could I sleep? Remember when Brother Proteus used to read *Great Expectations* to us? I used to dream about how my whole life would seem before me . . . that somebody would leave me a lot of money, and I'd go to New York and live like Nicky Hilton. . . ."

From below, the shouts and laughter of young people, doubtless more realist than romantic, hurtled up the hill in mockery of McFarland's recall with its suggestion of pain.

"I used to think about the Friday night socials, too," McFarland surged on. "Remember when we'd go to the dances at St. Evangeline Academy or their girls would come here? Like USO girls. A whole bus load of them . . . that was nice. That's the way young people should go to school. Five nights of study, one night social and the other night in town to see the girl for a Coke. That way there was an expectancy created. Something to look forward to. But look at this business. . . ."

"I hope all these girls are on the pill," Magruder said quietly.

"You do?" Matland demanded.

"Wouldn't you if one of them were your daughter?"

"The issue's never going to come up. My daughter won't be coming here, either. Much too dangerous."

"We'd better go now," Magruder advised. "Father Headmaster will be expecting us."

They returned to the car and drove the remaining distance to the parking area, marched through one of the admitting archways and then were inside the snow-heaped quadrangle where more students threw snowballs on their way to and from classes, something forbidden in the old days because of all the window glass about: wooden signs advising against that infraction of rules were peeling and almost illegible now.

"Everything is so changed. I just can't believe it," Adnizzio sputtered.

"There's one thing that hasn't changed." Magruder pointed across the glaring snow where an old priest bent almost double over his cane, plodded along before the rear of the chapel, invincibly safe, it seemed, beneath the arcs of snowballs that whizzed over his head. It was Brother Proteus. A great sorrow welled up in Magruder at the sight of him: If Magruder was sixty-eight, then Proteus was ninety-five at least. Incredibly, he wore only a thin sweater against the cold.

"It's Brother Proteus," McFarland blubbered, instant

tears flashing to his eyes. On cue perhaps, the three were pummeling their eyes with handkerchiefs.

"Poor Brother Proteus. Remember how kind he was to us?" Matland sniffled. "When he was boss of the kitchen, he used to let us sneak down there and have cookies and milk with him."

"He was so kind," Adnizzio said. "Once when my parents came, he changed the menu right in the middle of the afternoon and everybody ate lasagne that night in their honor. . . ."

They advanced along the walk toward Proteus, who raised his head to squint at them. He had removed his denture piece so that only the remaining upper molars were to be seen, making him look unnaturally fanged and wolf-like.

"Brother Proteus, hello," Magruder greeted him.

"Who is it?"

"Magruder. Egil Magruder. Remember? I was the football coach."

"I remember, Magruder. You were a lousy coach. I wrote the trustees many times, pleading for your removal before St. Anselm's went under. But you were well connected and they wouldn't listen and St. Anselm's did go under just as I said. There's no more football and we've got girls instead. Boys chase girls, not the old pigskin now. . . ."

At that moment of rebuff, a young girl wearing jeans, a ripped parka and a clacking of beaded necklaces sauntered by, and Proteus raised his cane as if to strike her. But she neatly evaded his swipe, laughing delightedly, and as she skipped off, Proteus smiled inanely, chuckling at his act. The others laughed also, and Adnizzio spoke:

"I'm Vincent Adnizzio, Brother Proteus. You once cooked lasagne for the whole school in honor of a visit by my parents one weekend."

"Your father was a wop gangster, Adnizzio. They made a movie about his life. I saw it. He died of a heart attack in his tomato patch. The plants were about six feet tall. It must have been about mid-September, I reckon."

"That was about somebody else. My father died just last Saturday morning. In a church. We buried him yesterday."

"Good. Damn greaser. Always trying to get somebody to put up a plaque around here to commemorate the peanuts he gave when others gave whole buildings or filled the library with books. Once I baked him a plaque and mailed it to him down in New Jersey."

"That was very kind of you, Brother Proteus," Adnizzio said hopefully, "but when it came it was all in pieces."

"That was the idea, Adnizzio. After I wrapped it, I whumped it a few times with a skillet to get the point across. . . . Which one are you?" he pointed the cane at Matland.

"I'm Eric Matland, Brother Proteus."

"You were yellow at football, Matland."

"I wasn't . . ."

"You were," Magruder assured him. Then he took McFarland by the arm: "Brother Proteus, this is . . ."

"It's OK, coach. I can stand the anonymity," McFarland protested with a kind of fearful laugh.

"He's Justin McFarland," Proteus identified him. "Justin was a good boy. He used to come to the kitchen for cookies and milk and tell me about his girl friend from St. Evangeline Academy. Justin graduated last in his class of eighty-one boys. He lost his virginity when he was a senior at Georgetown to the girl from St. Evangeline."

"How do you know that?" Magruder asked.

"He wrote to tell me. It was a nice gesture, I thought. Why are you here, Magruder? Sentimental journey?"

"We're here about Kasprzak. Sterling Lloyd Kasprzak."

"Kasprzak is dead. He ate himself to death in my food locker. It was awful." Proteus trembled, pulling his sweater more closely about him. "He ate a whole side of beef raw, then died halfway through a smoked ham. It was a pig's death."

"He died of exposure, Proteus. He froze to death."

"That's not possible, Magruder. Not possible. The door could be opened from the inside. All he had to do was push the knob."

"Not much point to that when it was padlocked from the outside. He couldn't get out."

"You're wrong, Magruder. Everybody knows how it happened. Father Headmaster Rowley, may he rest in peace, told me himself. Everybody's known for more than twenty years. Father Headmaster Morton, who sits in that office now, told me the same thing. Kasprzak was a slit-eyed little piggie of a boy. He had blood lust. A necrophiliac, he was. I looked it up in the dictionary. All the time he was here they found the disemboweled remains of rabbits and foxes. Sheep and cattle were forever disappearing from the neighboring farms. I think he ate them, bones and hoofs and all. Thank Jesus we're rural, or it might have been children. . . ."

"We have to see Father Morton now," Magruder said stonily. "We'll have to leave you."

"I'll go with you and end this argument for good and all."

"It's too far for you to walk, Proteus."

"There's an elevator now. Come on, Magruder. The rest of you, too."

They followed after the shamble of ancient Proteus across the rest of the quadrangle into the administration building, then took a modern elevator that hauled them speedily to the third floor. On the outside, in a hallway, the new headmaster, Morton, was already waiting for them: A youngish man, forty-five perhaps, he was unexpectedly handsome. His eyes were very blue, bemused-looking after a fashion, his hair blond as a tow-headed kid. Magruder saw that his nails were manicured; his cassock was of expensive cloth, too perfectly cut. He smiled the smile of the consummate optimist, the inveterate fund raiser, reminding Magruder, not unaccountably, of the slack-memoried realtor who had sold them the trailer in Barstow. On the instant it occurred to him that he was sizing up some variety of natural enemy.

"Coach Magruder! Welcome back to St. Anselm's! I'd know you anywhere from all those team photos in the field house. How old are you now? Sixty-nine? Seventy?"

He had a lilting voice that invariably ended every sentence on the upbeat: Magruder did not like the sound of him either.

"I'm sixty-eight, Father. I took my retirement a year early because of my wife's asthma."

"And we hear your poor wife has passed on. I'm sorry,

Magruder. But still at sixty-eight you're a testimony to the value of a life spent on the playing fields. What do you want, Brother Proteus?"

"The truth for Magruder. He says Kasprzak didn't eat himself to death."

"He didn't, Proteus," the headmaster lilted warily. "He was a very obese boy who had a heart attack and died twenty-three years ago. That's all there was to it."

"There were dead sheep and stock found all about these parts. Disemboweled! I know it was Kasprzak. I once caught him eating sausage I'd just stuffed. It was raw. It hadn't even been smoked yet."

"Go to your quarters, Proteus!" the headmaster ordered; his face became menacing-looking, belying the original suggestion of total aplomb. "These gentlemen have come here to talk about our fund-raising campaign and haven't a great deal of time. Gibbons," he called to a man pushing a broom and pretending industry at the far end of the hallway, "take Brother Proteus home and give him a nap, will you?"

They watched a moment as Proteus was led away unprotestingly into the elevator. The doors closed behind them, then Morton gave off a long whistle: "Cripes Almighty, you think the old nut would keel over and die. He's ninety-six years old."

"He was a good horse once before he went round the bend," Magruder said defensively. "He cooked and ran the kitchens for thousands of hard-paying alumni before you ever showed up, priest."

"Ah hah! The boys from the old school. The better days, the wiser days, the more disciplined days.

Recherche du temps perdu. Crap! If those were the better, wiser and more disciplined days, why didn't you rock-rib moralists take care of old Sterling Lloyd Kasprzak's little problem back them? Why does it have to show up on my desk so many years later?"

"Because you're Father Headmaster now," Magruder growled at him.

"I'm not a headmaster. I'm a hotelkeeper. If those liberal jackass trustees go one step further, they'll change the name of this place to Mount St. Anselm's and start selling vacation ski weeks. Let's go into my office and get this over with. I've got a squash date in about an hour."

He ushered them into the high-ceilinged range of three offices where the gray ladies—the women secretaries to the headmaster and bursar—rose from their desks to greet Magruder, each proclaiming a condolence over Florence's death, then addressing the long-departed Adnizzio, McFarland and Matland correctly by name: after so many years. Everybody was in on it, Magruder decided ruefully, and, from the sightless gazing of the gray ladies' eyes, it looked as if the case was indeed closed.

In the headmaster's office the judgment was to be quick and complete. The heavy door swung closed behind them, Morton bade them sit down, then glided across the faded oriental carpeting of the paneled room and sat on the edge of the massive desk. With the others, Magruder sank resignedly into the deep pile of an over-long couch, the only seating available, thinking perhaps the trick was passed from headmaster to headmaster on succession day: Sitting so low down in bottomless cushions, with one's head almost at the level of one's knees, the process of disarming and weakening protestors and complainers was already begun.

"Now, gentlemen, what do you want from me?"

"Access to the files concerning the investigation into Kasprzak's death," Magruder spoke, trying to hunker aggressively forward.

"Alas, they are no more. They were declassified."

"How do you mean declassified, Father?" Magruder demanded.

"Burned. They're dust and ashes now."

"When did this happen?"

"About three years after you folded your tents in these parts, coach, and headed for California. The day that Father Rowley and I exchanged the kiss of peaceful transfer. It happened right in that fireplace over there."

"But why?"

"Because Rowley wanted it over and done with and I just didn't want it. That's why. If you want materials, go to the sheriff's department. I'm sure that they'll be glad to oblige you, coach."

"Father, you've got to know as well as I do that his death was classified as a heart attack by our estimable ancient school doctor and the coroner had no reason to order an autopsy. Kasprzak had a history of illnesses. That's what the records in the sheriff's office will say."

"Then if the blame needs to be put somewhere, stick it on the doctor. He died ages ago."

"It wasn't his fault. He never even got a look at Kasprzak. Rowley was in the midst of one of his fund drives and wasn't going to have any scandal, so he just told the doctor what he wanted him to know and the doctor signed the death certificate between two babies he was delivering at either end of the county in the middle of a blizzard. . . ."

"So other than Rowley and the first string of that season of seasons, who are haphazardly bound to this imprecise 'justice' concept by your oath, there were only you and the old guard who knew. And now the guard's dead, and of course Rowley's dead also. . . ."

"Correct, Father Headmaster."

The priest smiled, looking through a window, squinting at the glare of sun from the snow in the quadrangle.

"I'd say, if I'm not being indelicate, that you compromised yourself somewhat, Magruder, by not speaking out at the time."

"Yes, I guess I did, Father." Magruder shrugged, remembering how hysterically Florence had cried at the prospect of his job being lost.

"What a perfect Catholic you seem to me, coach. A sterling example of Holy Mother the Church's deepest penetration of the mind. Whose expiation have you really been thinking of these twenty-three years, I wonder. These three guys or your own? Coach?"

"Some of both, I'm sure," Magruder admitted gruffly. "But the point remains that Kasprzak's justice is still incomplete. Will you help us with what you know?"

"No, I won't. Humble Headmaster Morton, whom you see before you now, is stuck right in the middle of his own fund-raising drive and so far the stillness of money is absolutely terrifying. We just can't afford to bring old Sterling Lloyd back from the dead. The bad publicity wouldn't help us a bit, and believe me, boys, applications

194

are way down. We don't pick and choose any more, we send out raiding parties after other folks' rejects. Black kids, Chicano kids, warm bodies . . ."

"You're a priest!" Magruder interrupted angrily. "You're supposed to care about justice and morality."

"I do, Magruder, I believe in the necessity for them absolutely. But in this case I just don't believe in the necessity for police, prosecutors, judges and courts. Let's take another tack. Let's say we harness these guys' energies for the duration of the, say, one-year sentence, suspended or otherwise, they'd probably get, to the new fund-raising drive for St. Anselm's. Wouldn't that make more sense to you? Think of the good they'd be doing for old alma mater instead of languishing on the inside of somebody's jail, or hiking it up here a couple of times a month for a chat with their probation officer. . . ."

"Bullshit!" Magruder hurled.

"Why don't we hear from them, Magruder, for a change? You've done all the talking so far. How do you see it, Dr. Adnizzio? Wouldn't you have your punishment a productive period?"

"No. Not if it meant raising money for St. Anselm's. I don't like what's going on here now. St. Anselm's was for us boys. I wouldn't send any of my sons here if I had any more to send. Do you know what's going on right now out under those trees, Father?"

"I don't think about it, Adnizzio. A priest shouldn't. Still, it has its compensations. Homosexual incidents are virtually unknown these days. What about you, Mr. Matland?"

"Hustling a fund drive isn't enough. I want real justice.

I want to be punished, but good. I want to go to jail. It's the only way I can think of to get even with my wife. She had an affair with Vincent's father."

"Phew!" the headmaster whistled, eyes beseeching heaven. "Twenty centuries of Catholic guile, the legacy of the Borgias and popes like Alexander VI, and all this guy can think of is going to jail to get even. . . . Be more conventionally intelligent, stupid. Take a mistress. Flaunt her. Like in the movies. How about you, McFarland?"

"Same for me, Father. I want the justice that punishes my wife."

"It's just as well," Morton said reflectively. "I pulled your file, McFarland. You're dumb. We'd be headed for a sure loss with the likes of you working the phones."

"I don't like you, Morton!" Magruder told him fiercely.

"I don't like you either, Magruder. In fact, I don't like any of the old guard around here who just let St. Anselm's idle toward disintegration with never a thought for the future or the possibility of change in the world. I don't like it one bit that they pulled me out of my brilliant department chairmanship with a fantastic library just around the corner and sent me to this Godforsaken funny farm to put it all back together and save the place. Then to add insult to injury, one of the former petrified minds shows up needing my help to solve a problem from the days of blue blazers and white buck shoes that nobody had the guts to take care of back then. . . . Gentlemen, the interview is concluded. There are no files. There is no one here left to help you. You're on your own."

Magruder stood up as did the others: "I'll have to warn

you, Father Headmaster, that I'm scheduled to see the county prosecutor. This thing isn't dead yet."

"Yes, I know you're to see him. His name is Ed Mc-Kitrick. Recognize the name, Magruder?"

"No, I don't think so."

"He was somewhat short. Apparently you found him dispensable three years in a row when he tried out for football. He's never forgotten it. We carry certain scars indelibly into our adulthood, it would seem."

Magruder smiled, bemusedly now: "Ah, yes. He was a student here not all that long ago. His father was the old county prosecutor for a time, I believe. Have you gotten to him, Father?"

"No need for me to strong-arm him, Magruder, if that's what you mean. He's an enlightened young man, fresh out of law school, with a caseload that would collapse an elephant. But go to him. He's waiting for you now. In fact, you're late. . . ."

Magnificently, pastorally, Morton swept them out of his office and into the anteoffices where the gray ladies fell instantly to their typing. Magruder could still hear the echo of their footsteps in the intercom. Morton spoke to them, perfecting the lie: "Say good-by to Coach Magruder and these three gentlemen, ladies. Our new fund campaign got a fabulous boost because of their generosity today."

"How wonderful!" the oldest of them, a Mrs. Whiting pronounced. "Poor St. Anselm's just isn't as solvent as it used to be when you were with us, coach. Times change and absolutely everything costs so much these days, and . . ."

"Do you remember Kasprzak?" Magruder nearly shouted at them, enraged at the insipid pretense.

"Kasprzak's dead," Whiting said, a mourning in the voice, speaking to the other secretaries now. "He was a student here who died of a heart attack about twenty years back. He was only eighteen at the time."

"So young! Can you imagine?" another gray lady chortled.

"It was bizarre. He died in the big kitchen food locker. Brother Proteus sent him there for a ham and I guess the strain of lifting it was too much for his heart, poor thing."

He was murdered! Magruder wanted to shriek at them. These three did it! Only he saw the sad shaking of heads, the closed-case, handsomely smiling mask of Morton beside him, and simply acknowledged, "It was a terrible thing. A black day for St. Anselm's."

"Yes," Morton agreed. "Best left to faded memory when St. Anselm's has produced such fine alumni as these."

"Yes," the gray ladies chorused.

"Yes," Magruder pretended to agree. Then they turned and walked to the corridor and the elevator. The headmaster did not follow. The clacking of typewriters began collectively an instant later.

In the elevator, when the descent began, McFarland pounded the wall furiously: "Does anybody ever let you forget? I graduated last in my class because I wanted to. I wanted the anchor money. . . ."

"Bullshit, Justin," Matland told him. "You used to study with a flashlight under the covers at night. You couldn't get the work. The only reason you passed calculus was that Brother Martin caught you reading a calculus text in the john when he thought you were jerking off and rewarded you for the relief he felt at not having to punish you for sexual abuse by pushing you through."

The sharp crack of a slap resounded in the cage of the elevator as McFarland struck Matland.

"Take it back, Eric! Take it back or I'll break your fucking nose!"

"Why should I take it back? You did graduate last. Everybody knows it. . . ."

But the doors opened and McFarland was immediately on top of Matland on the outside, pounding his head with ringed fingers. Adnizzio wandered about in small circles, proclaiming, "I want to be punished. . . . I want to go to jail for at least a year. . . . Not for Kasprzak. For Angelina. Angelina's a bitch! She deserves any punishment she gets."

Magruder tried half-heartedly pulling McFarland from Matland, thinking some kind of punishment should begin somewhere, but gave up when he felt the insistent tug of other hands trying to pull him upright. It was Brother Proteus, evidently not put to bed for a nap, the strength of his urgency impressive despite being ninety-six years of age.

"Magruder! You were wrong about that business of Kasprzak being locked in the freezer to die. It couldn't be that way. Who would lock somebody in a deep freeze and forget about them? None of our boys would do that!"

"These guys did," Magruder told him quietly, watching McFarland pound away with unrelenting fury at Matland's face; the other, beneath him, was crying now, and Adnizzio, like a drunken martinet, lurched an ever-widening circle about the entire grouping, tears streaming down his face, doubtless from thinking of the traitorous Angelina.

CHAPTER 13

Unfortunate Rejection

They got McFarland's and Matland's bruises patched up at the school infirmary, compliments of Headmaster Morton, who phoned down from above (a considerable pleasure in his voice, Magruder thought) to inform the nurse the treatment was gratis. Then they fled St. Anselm's to the courthouse for their appointment with McKitrick.

The prosecutor was shorter than Magruder remembered, his diminutiveness accented now, into his young thirties and newly married, by a girth of baby fat and a hastening baldness. Magruder recalled one sad conversation with his parents about how their son seemed finally able to master his stutter: Now the stutter was completely returned, a disturbing malady given the intentness of McKitrick's dark eyes. They shook hands. The prosecutor's was clammy and cold. Magruder understood he would get no justice here either.

"Hello, coach."

"Hello, Edward. Sorry I didn't recognize the name when I made the appointment with your secretary. Otherwise I would've tried speaking with you directly."

"I couldn't . . . couldn't expect you to remember, co . . . coach. . . ." Before them McKitrick's face twisted grotesquely in an attempt to control the stutter. Magruder knew they were making it worse by eying him so frankly. But he drew it under control: "After all, Magruder, you never had much time for the rest of us who weren't on the team. You ate and slept football. I can remember all those history classes that turned into study periods because you were working on some game plans."

"Well, that isn't exactly true, Edward. I mean the part about not having time for the other boys."

"I would've made a hell . . . hell of a center, coach. I was small, but I was fast, too."

"Nevertheless, you seem to have compensated for any inadequacy you imagined rather well, Edward," Magruder tried, embracing the ornate, old-fashioned room with a sweep of his hands. They sat plaintively before small, stuttering Edward McKitrick, who ruled a legal roost of a high-ceilinged, paneled-wall domain that his father had procured for him. The value of a connection, after all, Magruder decided. At that moment he suspected McKitrick of sitting atop a stack of law books for height.

"What happened to this guy?" McKitrick asked, jerking his head toward Matland, who wore two bandages above one eye where McFarland had pummeled him continuously with ringed fingers.

"An altercation of sorts," Magruder said.

"About Kasprzak?"

"No," Magruder answered wearily. "About some ancient history at St. Anselm's that somehow seems more important than anything that's happened since they left the place. . . ."

"What about Kasprzak, Magruder?" The voice was unexpectedly harsh, the embittered schoolboy become prosecutor again.

"His death wasn't an accident, Edward."

"What was it then?"

"Well, a prank that got out of hand. These three guys got drunk the night of the season's last game and padlocked him inside the food locker. The death certificate says it was a heart attack. He died of exposure. He froze to death. We want justice now, Edward. It's been too long already."

McKitrick surveyed them for a long moment, his eyes narrowed to tiny slits that bespoke menace. On the instance it appalled Magruder that government consented to put power in the hands of such people. McKitrick stood and walked from behind the desk, taller than expected. He wore the newfangled lift shoes with multicolored laces that Magruder considered too effeminate for men's wear. Before them the prosecutor hiked himself onto the desk top. His legs rotated slowly, banging the heels of the shoes annoyingly into the leathered front panel of the desk.

"Father Headmaster Morton phoned me last week to say he thought you were headed my way with that story. He thinks it's a case of senility."

"Perhaps I am, but do these gentlemen look senile to you, Edward?" Magruder demanded fiercely. "They can't be more than twelve or thirteen years older than yourself."

"To tell you the truth, Magruder, they don't look like they've got it all together either. These two guys are battered and bruised and this one"—he indicated Adnizzio—"has been on a crying jag about something since he got here. . . ."

"Since before that, Prosecutor, sir," Adnizzio whined. "Since last Saturday at my daughter's marriage when I found out my wife had an affair with my own father, God rest his soul, who dropped dead in church when Coach Magruder walked in the door with my uncle, Nicholas the Tedesco. . . . That's why I want the case reopened. I'll go to jail, but my wife gets punished. See?"

"Me, too!" McFarland and Matland chorused together. The prosecutor drew up his legs beneath him, Indian fashion now on the top of the desk, grinning openly as he stared at McFarland and Matland. Inwardly Magruder groaned at the impossibleness of it all.

"I take it your wives also had liaisons with this gentleman's father, gentlemen?"

"Yes, they did," McFarland assured him.

"I won't let the law be used for a common vengeance!" McKitrick snarled at them furiously. "The law is sacred!"

"Listen, you goddamned runt!" Magruder rose out of his seat. "How about letting the law be used for some common justice as it was intended? I want that case opened. Father Morton is lying to you. He knew the circumstances of Kasprzak's death on the day he succeeded as headmaster."

"I'm sure you're lying, Magruder. Morton is a priest. But even if Morton did know about such a possibility, he's known it for only three years or so, and you've known it for about twenty-three, if my arithmetic is correct. I could have your ass for complicity or obstruction of justice. You wouldn't come out of any proceedings I was running scot-free. Believe me about that. In fact, I wonder if we couldn't make a case for yours being the greater responsibility? You were the parent elder, after all. . . ."

"It's your vengeance we're really talking about now, isn't it, McKitrick?" Magruder demanded dumfoundedly. "You're the one with the responsibility to decide if this case is going to be opened or not. And you obviously don't want to do it. Can it be all because of the fact that you weren't eligible for the team so long ago? There has to be a selection process, you know. Everybody can't be an O. J. Simpson or a Y. A. Tittle."

McKitrick looked as if he were ready to hurl himself off the desk top at Magruder's throat.

"What fucking process of selection turned up three assholes like these?" the prosecutor nearly wept. "Look at them! Do you mean to tell me that fat slob knew anything about forward passing . . . ?" He pointed with a shaking finger at McFarland, who sat beside Magruder. The fat slob looked as if he might rear up and strangle the prosecutor. Magruder held him to his seat with a firm grip on his arm.

"Look, McKitrick, I don't remember after all these years what he knew about forward passes. He was a tackle anyhow. All I can remember is that the year these guys were first string was the worst in St. Anselm's history. I hope that's some consolation to you. Now, are you doing anything about opening the case?"

The news that St. Anselm had held up the league that

year seemed to mollify the prosecutor somewhat. He climbed down from the desk top and walked around to his seat.

"Let me ask you something, Magruder. . . ."

"Ask away, Prosecutor."

"Were you a witness to this prank-cum-crime we're talking about?"

"No. I only found out about it the next day."

"Then which of these winners actually put the padlock on the door? A small technicality, if you see my point. Judges tend to interest themselves in such detail."

"They all did," Magruder said quietly, baffled now that he had never actually considered the possibility that a court would need to differentiate.

"Which of you gentlemen actually padlocked the door? . . . Gentlemen?"

"We all did it together," McFarland said mutedly.

"Then it's a genuine act of criminal collusion. Not just a prank. You premeditated Sterling Lloyd's death. Altogether you put him in the food locker, then six large first-string hands placed one comparatively small lock through the handle and closed it. . . . What a scramble that must have been."

McKitrick smiled his victory at them now: No one of them would ever volunteer.

"We all did it," Matland urged. "We were drunk. Who can remember? Why is it so important?"

"Let's make a little hypothetical case." The prosecutor smirked on. "Suppose you three fellows rob a bank together, but only one of you shoots the bank guard dead. Is everyone equally culpable? Or is somebody going to turn state's evidence to save his ass? The point is, six hands on a four-inch lock makes a lousy case. Any judge would call it insubstantial evidence and throw us out of court. Why waste my time?"

"Aren't you being a bit too technical, McKitrick? These three guys admit their guilt. They'll sign confessions. Couldn't we at least have a hearing in a judge's chambers on the strength of those confessions?"

"Confessions, Magruder? All sorts of nuts admit to almost every crime that happens hereabouts. It's appalling to comprehend the prevailing guilt we live among. My father was prosecutor when Sterling Lloyd took the freeze. He could have dredged up ten confessions back then, I'll bet, and none of them would ever have set foot inside the gates of St. Anselm's. And don't forget that I heard these gentlemen say not ten minutes ago that they wanted a punishment that would punish their wives, not themselves. That's first-class nut reasoning in my book. No, courts want decent evidence, Magruder. Like this."

He removed a padlock from his desk drawer and flipped it to Magruder, so stunned by the neatness of the trick that he dropped it to the floor.

"Recognize it?" the prosecutor asked.

"I gather . . ."

"Right. Yale Lock Company, manufactured in 1946. Compliments of Headmaster Morton. Twenty-seven years old and still going strong. If you can get six fingers on that thing in any reasonable way, let alone six hands, then we're that much closer to the threshold of possibility."

Magruder sighed a dismal sigh, squeezing the lock in his hand. It disappeared easily in the curve of his fist.

"Well, McKitrick, where are we now? A person is still dead. You're the prosecutor. You've got a responsibility under law."

"Save the lecture, Magruder. We're out of school now. And as I implied, I didn't get to be a ninetieth percentile prosecutor by shoving vagaries at juries. But I'd like to help you. It requires two things, though."

"Which two things?"

"One, decide which one of these guys gets thrown to the lions. . . ."

"I think it was you, Vinnie," McFarland said so quickly and emphatically that Magruder whipped his head about in shock.

"Bullshit, McFarland! One Adnizzio gone to heaven for the sake of that strutz Kasprzak is enough for this week. Matland must have done it. He was just that way. Always so sneaky and underhanded. One time on a Sunday during training he got me to jog about ten miles with him, then when we were far enough away from school he tried to get me to roll naked in the snow with him. You were queer, too, Eric."

"I wasn't! I got laid before any of you!"

"You were and you are. Angelina says so, too. She's got good antennae. She always knows about those things."

"Oh yeah! Just great! If we were talking about my Judy instead, you can bet your sweet ass she wouldn't be fucking her own father-in-law. Hell of a moral barometer that fat peach of a wife of yours is."

A certainty, despite being wronged by his woman, Adnizzio hit Matland, swinging about in a swift arc, smashing his neighbor hard in the nose and drawing blood instantly. Behind his desk, McKitrick pounded his elevated heels into the floor in delight. Magruder despaired. McFarland laughed hilariously until Matland lunged out of his chair and knocked his other neighbor over backwards into the carpeting. McKitrick pressed his intercom and ordered the single word, "Officer!" In moments a lawman entered with his gun already drawn. Order was restored as Magruder raged at the prosecutor:

"All right, half pint, you've got your revenge! What was the other condition?"

"That you get Mrs. Kasprzak to press charges opening these here proceedings. I'm leery of your private motive, Magruder."

Mrs. Kasprzak: She still lived, then.

"Of course!" Magruder suddenly enthused. "She never knew anything other than her son had a heart attack! She'd be the absolutely logical one to contact. Let me use your phone. I can call her. She lives in Albany, doesn't she?"

"Yes. She's expecting you, Magruder."

"Ah . . . again . . ."

"No. She knows nothing. About that I'm quite certain. I wonder what that lady looks like," McKitrick speculated disdainfully. From a folder he held up a large photo of Sterling Lloyd, her awful son.

What could she look like indeed? Magruder wondered.

CHAPTER 14

Sterling Lloyd's Mother
and the Sun Queen

In the car once more, speeding back toward Albany, they still cast among themselves for a scapegoat, their tones alternately whining and petulant, then brashly defensive the way they had been years before as kids when Magruder chewed them out for an infraction of the training rules. Their recall of the past was total, incredible: Every transgression, slight or imagined wrongdoing perpetrated by any one of them battered about the interior vacuum of the Cadillac. It seemed to Magruder that except for the sad night of Sterling Lloyd Kasprzak they may not have forgotten the events of a single day of the years they spent at St. Anselm's. It also occurred to him that they had lived so long together that in certain ways, in certain places of their minds, they had never outgrown an adolescence. When their reasonings for choosing a single offering to the law spilled over to the sins of adulthood, they were childishly rendered: That Adnizzio deserved punishing because his father's construction firm built the crumbly walls of McFarland and Matland's houses. Enough!

Magruder ordered them to silence. He would convince Kasprzak's mother to press charges and bring the thing to the courts. He still saw the premise of a communal guilt, though he suspected now there would be four before the docket instead of three. Both Morton and McKitrick had called his participation in the cover-up complicity: So be it. He would take his licks, too. Only in twenty-three years it was the first time he had acknowledged the word applied to himself. His real persuasion, he had always believed, had been a compassion over the ruin of three young lives (albeit tinged by a personal fear of losing his job if he defied Rowley, the old headmaster).

Sterling Lloyd's mother was a comely woman in her middle fifties, her earlier good looks unremembered because the only time Magruder had ever seen her was at her son's funeral in the chapel at St. Anselm's, and that day, dressed all in black, she had worn a veil, and Magruder presumed the familial ugliness. Now she was a widow, living in a brick town house in an unexpectedly pleasant section of Albany, a town Magruder had always abhorred. She opened the door and ushered them into a high-ceilinged hallway where she removed their coats. Then she invited them into the living room, where a fire burned in a marble fireplace, and introduced them to Sterling Lloyd's replacement, Ronnie.

Ronnie was about thirty, too good-looking, and in gold lamé top and bottom, with too many rings on his manicured fingers, some sort of eye liner and a clanking gaggle of amulets about his neck, presumedly a homosexual. Magruder and the Jersey threesome took seats across from mother and son, staring unabashedly at the sight: Ronnie truly glittered like the Sun Queen (it had to be said). His hair, fiercely blond, was done up Afro fashion and radiated outward like a peacock's tail from the orb of his head. His mother sat beside him and combed at the hair, unsnarling it, then patting it neatly into place. Magruder thought to disguise the disgust he felt. From the set of their faces, Adnizzio, McFarland and Matland evidently left off despising each other for the interim and settled on the easy target of Ronnie.

"Would you gentlemen like a drink?" he asked them. Inexplicably the male voice reminded Magruder of Carlotta McFadden of Las Vegas. "I wish you would. That way mother and I can start a little early for today."

"I don't want any alcohol," Magruder said levelly. "I don't think these gentlemen require any either."

"You said you've come about Sterling Lloyd, Coach Magruder?" Mrs. Kasprzak quizzed.

"Yes, Mrs. Kasprzak."

"Then I require some liquor, Ronnie. Make it a big fat double."

"Yes, Mummy," he responded, rising from the couch, the steel comb stuck to the back of his hair. Exactly like Carlotta McFadden, he slashed his way out of the room. Distantly, it came to Magruder that Sterling Lloyd and Ronnie could not possibly be brothers.

"Ronnie is such a lovely boy, don't you agree, Coach Magruder?"

"He's quite handsome, Mrs. Kasprzak. Yes."

"He's very sensitive, though. As a teen-ager his health was very frail, so of course we didn't send him to St. Anselm's. The sports training was always so rigorous there."

"Sterling Lloyd went there," Magruder reminded her. "He was excused from physical training and competitive sports on his doctor's advice because of his glandular condition. I'm sure some equal accommodation could have been arranged for Ronnie." It occurred privately to Magruder that if he had had the opportunity to get his hands on Ronnie, Ronnie would have gone rigorous, excuse or no excuse.

"Well there, you've caught me in the lie of my own unreasonableness, coach. The fact is, I just didn't want Ronnie to leave home. You know how a mother feels about her only son. . . ."

"I take it he went to a local high school, then?"

"No, he never left this house. We had tutors come here to prepare him for life. Ronnie's father wanted it that way also. After the debacle Sterling Lloyd turned out to be, he adored Ronnie. Ronnie's extraordinary good looks, you know. He was always photographing Ronnie or having people come in to photograph him. He just loved to dress up Ronnie in period costume and take him for walks around Albany to show him off. He had some of the loveliest costumes from the Saratoga Springs heydey when he was a little boy. Ronnie," his mother prompted as he returned with two straight-up Bourbons or scotches, "show Coach Magruder some of the pictures daddy took of you when you were a baby."

"Oh, Mother, they've come to talk about brother Sterling Lloyd. They don't want to see my baby pictures."

"Show them, darling." It was a command, pure and simple. Ronnie went exasperatedly to a sideboard, opened an album and carried it to Magruder, setting the book gently in Magruder's lap. Before his eyes, baby Ronnie, about thirteen or fourteen, lay coyly smiling and stark naked on a fur rug. He was possessed of a hard-on, or half of one at least. Magruder almost fell from his chair in shock. He smiled his best approving smile, sure his face was crimson-red and passed the book over to McFarland on the nearby divan.

"Holy shit!" McFarland judged, also reddening, sliding the book along to his cohorts. "What is it you do, Ronnie? I mean what line of work are you in?"

"I fancy that I'm a poet. But I'm afraid I haven't published too much yet."

"I think it's a conspiracy," Ronnie's mother said fiercely. "I think the literary magazines are controlled generally by very *moyen* people who contrive to keep the truly talented out of their pages. If you could just see some of the vile, sick letters of rejection Ronnie has gotten . . . ! Ronnie, darling, read Coach Magruder and these gentlemen a few of your poems. . . ."

"Oh, Mother, really . . ."

"We really have no time, Mrs. Kasprzak," Magruder said gruffly. "As I've said, we've come about Sterling Lloyd."

"I'll say one thing, Ronnie," McFarland, beet-red and asinine with embarrassment, stomped a foot in the carpeting, "you may not be making it as a poet, but you sure were a hung little kid in your day!"

"Wasn't he though?" Ronnie's mother laughed huskily, sloshing some of her drink on the carpeting. Her eyes caught fire: On the instant her mouth seemed incredibly lewd. Across from her, Magruder resisted vomiting.

"We've come to talk about Sterling Lloyd!" Magruder raged.

"Oh, what about him?" his mother asked annoyedly.

"Some new information has turned up about the matter of his death."

"He died of a heart attack in a food locker when he went to pick something up for the cook. I have a copy of the death certificate. What else could there be?"

"He died of exposure, Mrs. Kasprzak. He was locked in the freezer by some of his own classmates. They got drunk and forgot about him. When they remembered, he was already hours dead."

The news did not provoke her: She reacted to it with a level curiosity, impersonal as could possibly be. She traded a glance with Ronnie, then the two shrugged in unison and Magruder thought they would actually touch glasses.

"I'm to understand then, Coach Magruder, that these three gentlemen are the desperadoes come back to pay their dues to society?"

"Yes, Mrs. Kasprzak, they are. I want you to have the case reopened. McKitrick, the prosecutor in the next county, will agree to do it, if you'll file a petition. . . ."

She made the sign of benediction over her desperadoes: "I won't do it, Magruder. In the case of these gentlemen, to err is human, to forgive divine. Sterling Lloyd is better off dead."

The constant refrain! Tears flashed to Magruder's eyes: "Mrs. Kasprzak, Sterling was a sad, good boy. He had an incredible capacity for love, if only someone would love him back. My wife and I, it broke our hearts to see him that way . . . especially when we had no child of our own and wanted one so badly. . . ."

"If we'd known, we'd have given him to you, coach. Sterling Lloyd often spoke of yourself and Mrs. Magruder—Florence was her name, wasn't it? Yes, I remember he called her Aunt Florence—how you used to have him out to your house for Cokes and cake and how he'd stay to mow the lawn for you. . . ."

"We didn't have him out just so he'd mow the lawn, Mrs. Kasprzak. He was a lonely boy."

"Of course you didn't, coach. And Sterling Lloyd only mowed it because he enjoyed it so much. Some simple hearts find satisfaction in that sort of orderly destruction of living things like grass and clover. To look behind at the swath of your mower is at least to feel some kind of accomplishment. But I suppose in letting him cut your lawn, you gave him more love than anyone. I, alas, could not. Here, Ronnie, another drink for mummy. Make it a triple, OK?"

"Why not?" Magruder demanded. "Why couldn't you give him any love? He was your son."

"Because of his father. He wouldn't permit it. The dear daddy that adored Ronnie despised Sterling Lloyd. Despised? Abominated, I should say." They heard the clink of ice cubes returning with Ronnie as she stood and walked, staggering slightly, to a darkened wall panel in the shadow of the fireplace. She flipped a light switch to reveal a flamboyant portrait of Ronnie the Sun Queen. Beside it, niggardly in size by comparison, the black frame turned about so that the portrait face was actually to the wall, had to be Sterling Lloyd. Resignedly, sighing deeply, the mother turned Sterling Lloyd about, then reached reflexively behind her to Ronnie for her drink.

217

Ronnie turned away rather than offend his sensitivity at the sight. His mother gargled straight scotch in response. Magruder and the first-string threesome gasped in unison, then rose from their places for a better look at the portrait.

"Jesus Christ, coach!" Matland ejaculated, "Kasprzak was ugly, sure enough, but he still couldn't fly."

Phantasmagoria: a Kasprzak from Hieronymus Bosch, from a nightmare story by J. P. Lovecraft, the beast flew by moonlight over craggy Adirondak or Catskill forests, perhaps searching for the strays of sheep and cattle Brother Proteus had proposed he disembowled. Covens of bats or vultures followed after him. The eyes, appallingly, unmistakedly, were Kasprzak's own.

"Who did this thing?" Magruder begged hoarsely. "What fiend?"

"The same father I was just talking about who adored Ronnie and abominated Sterling Lloyd. He was, many people thought, a very fine painter. Not stuck in any particular stylistic rut as you can see. Both Ronnie and Sterling Lloyd posed live for those portraits, by the way. . . ."

"My God, poor Sterling Lloyd . . ." Magruder moaned. His sorrow was bottomless. Unconsciously he held Mrs. Kasprzak's glass while she turned the portrait to the wall again.

"Yes, poor Sterling Lloyd . . ." she agreed, dropping heavily to her chair as the others sat down again. "I couldn't love him, because his father, Mickey Kasprzak, who had all that money, wouldn't permit it. But I sure pitied him. Sterling Lloyd was never allowed to walk down the same side of the street with us after the ugliness became a certainty, and frequently his dear daddy would implore the universe to take notice of the creature who was attempting to dissolve into the opposite sidewalk with shame. When we went out in the car—they were always station wagons because of the third seat—Sterling Lloyd sat in the last, Ronnie and daddy were up front, and I took the middle with the dog. . . ."

"But he was your son! You gave birth to him!" The three desperadoes, all fathers, appeared incensed at the notion of rebuke. Adnizzio, who had snarled the words, was most incensed of all.

"I gave birth to no one. Sterling Lloyd and Ronnie were both adopted. With Ronnie obviously we lucked out. With Sterling Lloyd . . . well, babies all look pretty much the same when they're babies, and the bitch at the adoption agency gave us a bum steer as it turned out. . . ."

"Adopted?" Magruder was incredulous. "But wouldn't that have appeared on his records? I never knew that. No one at St. Anselm's did."

"We weren't about to put a big A on his forehead, coach. Poor Sterling Lloyd didn't know it either. He wasn't supposed to. His life was a doubly cruel affair," she sighed, taking a heavy swig on the scotch, "doubly cruel considering he was put to Mickey's use and abuse at the same time. . . ."

"What use?" Magruder asked softly, certain he knew on the instant what it had to be.

"Old Mickey despised women. He had a penis that wasn't content to stay limp at the sight of their unblemished nakedness. It actually retracted. We never had relations once in the thirty years we were married. Anyway, the provisions of Grandma Kasprzak's will were quite explicit. No dough until the first-born son, more on the second installment, etc. Thank God Grandma K. was a little daft. She never really noticed that my foam-rubber stomach collapsed inward to my backbone every time I reached for something at Sunday dinner, or that in Sterling Lloyd's case he was born five and a half months old. . . . So anyway, we got the money and Sterling Lloyd got a rather opulent funeral for an eighteen-year-old kid, I thought. I was happy for him. He needed to be dead. Thank you, gentlemen. No charges will be pressed from here."

Unbelievably, the dolt McFarland responded, "You're welcome, Mrs. Kasprzak. But tell me something if it's not too indelicate to ask. . . . I mean, if you didn't have relations with your husband what did you do for twenty years?"

"Nothing, dear. I had my hang-ups, too. It was a very convenient marriage."

Ah: The righteous quest for Sterling Lloyd's justice had come to an end apparently, like air issuing from a bellows, right in the very place, a nest of sick vipers, where he had been so despised, rejected and humiliated that his mother, given her curious capacity for humanity, had wished for his death. The culprits were no longer culpable; they were become heroes. She offered them a drink once more and the three greedily accepted, gathering closer to mother and preferred son, their talk unbelievably animated.

Magruder, for his part, sat in exile, drained and incredibly saddened at the absolute injustice of it all. Worse, perhaps, he knew it was only a matter of time before the newly exonerated threesome turned on him.

"It's all over then. . . ." Adnizzio said out loud after a time to no one in particular.

"Yes, it's over." Matland picked up the ball, began a fierce downcourt dribble: "Twenty-three years of worrying about when this old fart was going to show up to collect the debt, when he's the only one who wanted it collected anyway. . . ."

"Eric, cool it," McFarland admonished. "Coach thought he was doing the right thing. He gave us twenty years at the outset, didn't he? He could have gone to the cops right then."

"If it had been up to me, I wouldn't have prosecuted back then either," Mrs. Kasprzak spoke. "Old Mickey wouldn't have either."

"I should have," Magruder fumed. "I should have gone right to the police, and the hell with the headmaster, St. Anselm's and Florence's crying."

"What a curious turn of events," Ronnie chortled delightedly. "Look who has the only bad conscience among us now."

Wrathful, Magruder stood up, marched over to Ronnie the Sun Queen and grabbed a thick handful of the Afro, thinking he might pull some out by the roots. Nobody attempted to stop him, and everyone thought it was humorous, including Ronnie, who was into pain apparently. Surrendering, Magruder threw him hard against the back of his seat. The pliant gold lamé body moved easily, spilling not a drop of his drink. It would do no good to smash his face. It could only bring pleasure.

"Mrs. Kasprzak," Magruder panted. "I'd like to make one final request of you."

"What is it, coach?"

"I'd like the privilege of burning up that hideous portrait in the fireplace. . . . At least somehow to try to assuage the defilement of his memory."

She considered a moment: "OK. Go to it, coach. I have another of Ronnie I can put in its place."

Magruder seized the portrait, turned it about for a final nauseous look, then shoved it into the flames that licked immediately across the frame, racing onto the old canvas, devouring blessedly the terrible eyes.

The others toasted the burning with their drinks while Magruder patted his eyes on the sleeve of his jacket.

"To life!" Matland proclaimed. "To life!" as the others drank in unison. But Magruder heard only the howls of anguish from that wandering soul way out in Eternity.

CHAPTER 15

The Killington Affair

"They were nice people," McFarland opined.

"Yes," Matland agreed. "Intelligent people."

They stood outside the Kasprzak town house in the full darkness, wisps of snow that confirmed a blizzard predicted for later that night already descending. Mrs. Kasprzak or Ronnie had turned on the winking wreath of lights surrounding the door and a speaker system began chiming out "God Rest Ye Merry, Gentlemen."

Magruder was fitfully discouraged. The season crashed in on him as well. It was days away from Christmas now and he felt a tremendous rush of loneliness and recalled that he had not yet phoned his sister in Queens to inquire if he might spend Christmas and New Year's with her, for he had nowhere else to go. Then he snapped back: The three before him, exonerated everywhere they had touched down today for their crime against Sterling Lloyd, regarded him from an analytical place. Perhaps they meant to abandon him there on that very sidewalk, before the house where the one whose justice he had championed once lived.

"Now what?" Magruder heard himself asking. "Where to now?"

"I'm not going back to Jersey!" Adnizzio proclaimed fiercely. "I may be a free man now in New York state, but if I get near Angelina, I'll be in jail for sure back in Monmouth County."

"You may be a dead man also, Vinnie, if her old man and her brothers, uncle and the greaser sweetheart with the *garrotta* are somewhere in the vicinity," McFarland said mockingly. But then he seemed to recall: "I'm not going back to that cunt Rita, either. Rita will come to me on her goddamn knees after all the years of humping my ass and conniving I put into business and my marriage and children. . . . She's going to nail up public notice of ecstasy if I can get it up next year one twelfth as often as old Gennaro, huh?" he suddenly mimicked in rage. "The hell she is! She's going to nail up public notice of repentance on the church doors before she ever gets into bed with me again!"

"Ditto!" Matland hurled. "I won't go back to Judy either! She'll come to me. Let's go to Killington and ski the rest of the week. There's nothing to bring me back to Jersey anyhow. I was anticipating spending at least the next few days in a jail cell."

"What about me?" Magruder asked. "Shall I come along or take a bus back to New Jersey?" He sighed heavily: He was a forgotten man again. About him, the sea change had been instantaneous. The collective remembrance of their wives' perfidy had stolen the fire of their real wrath toward him. For now certainly, perhaps for good and all, though he guessed the collective courage that scorned their wives would remain buoyant for about two days hence, on Friday. And after that, if their women got to them, there was absolutely no way of telling what might happen. . . .

McFarland, as ever, led with his soul: "Sure, come on with us, coach. We've got enough equipment over there to outfit you for a little downhill racing."

"Hey, I don't know about that," Matland protested. "I mean this guy was trying to put us in jail about ten minutes ago before the truth of God came home to him."

"Aw, fuck it, Matland," McFarland urged. "Sterling Lloyd is dead and gone. After today for sure. And if he never did another thing, at least he kept us all together in camaraderie and made us good friends and true. Coach, too. And who knows but that our little society might begin dissolving? I mean we'll probably never see coach again after this. And I think I'm selling my house. I mean cripes, how long are you supposed to live next to the same two people . . . ?"

"That's what I'm doing, too," Adnizzio said. "I'm going to build a house on a hill if I can find a hill. I'm so sick of living at the bottom of that cul de sac daddy designed for us three and waiting for disaster to roll through the front door for the last umpteen years. . . . Sure, coach, come on. Let's go to Killington and let bygones be bygones."

They would not ski, Magruder thought as they headed for the Cadillac, McFarland and Adnizzio draping their arms fraternally about his shoulders. They would drink instead, bemoan the treachery of their wives that he suspected had not occurred at all, had merely been a clever women's device to shock their husbands into resistance to Magruder's purpose. Even as they climbed into the car, Adnizzio opened the trunk and pulled out the first bottle of scotch from a case. The three were swigging from it, though Magruder did not, as they headed swiftly north again out of Albany toward the Vermont line and the Killington ski complex. Predictably the three spoke of nothing all the distance except their wives. Magruder thought miserably of Kasprzak.

The blizzard grew in intensity and after Rutland, Vermont, they barely made it up the long steep climb through the Sherburne Pass of the Green Mountains. At Killington, the car slithered into a ditch from the inattention of Adnizzio's sotted ramblings, and they ended up abandoning the vehicle and carrying their suitcases the remaining mile or so to the block of condominiums where the eternal triumvirate of Red Bank, New Jersey, had three predictable identical side-by-side apartments in one of the blocks.

As in New Jersey, Adnizzio's apartment was in the center, and they stumbled inside, Magruder glad to build a fire in the fireplace while the threesome made new drinks and listened to some tapes of the Mills Brothers until Adnizzio declared he despised their optimism and opened a hidden record closet to reveal a massive tape collection of every note that Frank Sinatra had ever sung. They were off again. Magruder prepared himself a small dinner of canned beef stew, admonishing the others to eat something when he knew they would not, then resignedly covered up the three with blankets stripped from the upstairs beds after Adnizzio, McFarland and Matland passed out asleep in the shag carpeting—snoring and blubbering and side by side—almost in the same instant.

Magruder turned off Sinatra, then sat staring at their

heaving forms for about ten minutes. He had thought this in the past, and now it seemed more true to him than ever: Sterling Lloyd had had a vengeance of sorts. His memory, their fear of retaliation in his name, had kept each of them from ever becoming a whole man by himself. Their wives, he considered as he stood up to retire, would now surely be out to break up that little threesome after all those years. He wondered when they would show up. . . . Not Thursday, the next day, anyhow.

When Magruder awoke, the blizzard had ended and he made a pot of coffee and cooked a large breakfast of bacon and eggs for the troika, who woke, nauseous at the smell, and settled for bloody marys and Sinatra instead. For that day Magruder busied himself with shoveling his way out of the condominium to the road, retrieving the Cadillac that had been hauled away by the police to a nearby garage to make way for the plowing of the roads and buying additional food supplies in nearby Rutland for the weekend ahead. When he returned late that afternoon, the three were passed out on the carpeting as before.

On Friday, the next day, he skied, something he had not done in years, and was surprised and pleased at the unexpected recall of his former coaching skill. The day was bright with sun and warm to a few degrees above thawing. In the afternoon he met the sixtyish wife of an Episcopal priest from New Hampshire in the lift line and rode up with her in the chair, then skied out the day with the cleric, the wife and a spinster sister-in-law. Afterwards he joined them for cocktails and dinner in the sky-high restaurant at the upper terminus of the gondola lift.

He told them about Sterling Lloyd Kasprzak. Far below the lights of ski houses flickered in the darkness as the high wind of an impending thaw rocked the trees before them; on the slopes, the bright lights of snow cats paled in the driven whiteness. They sipped reflectively on mulled wine until the cleric broke the long silence: "It's out of your hands now, Egil. It's in God's hands. That's all that can be said."

"Perhaps," Magruder agreed vacuously. He had not had recourse to God in ages. Perhaps now, flat up against this wall, it was time to go back. . . .

Later they descended the mountain in the wildly swinging gondola. Magruder took their addresses, promised because of the startling intensity of her request to write the spinster lady, then bade them good-by on their return to New Hampshire. When he arrived at the condominium, they drank still, Sinatra still sang, and McFarland and Adnizzio were both on a crying jag. Incredibly, they were all identically dressed in their St. Anselm's varsity sweaters, ancient knits that appeared to be systematically unraveling under the pressure of age and girth. Matland, the only one with a thought toward inevitably recovering from his bender, sat in the kitchen, ashen-faced, eating tiny nibbles of a can of cold beans, resolutely trying to keep from vomiting it back.

Magruder cooked a simple stew from the supplies he had purchased the day before and forced the three to try to eat some of it about ten o'clock. Just as they began, more pathetic in their nausea and strewn about the floor before the fireplace, wrapped in their blankets, Angelina Adnizzio, clad in tight shiny ski wear, pushed through the door and stood, legs apart and hands on her hips, glaring at them. Happily, she carried no whip.

"Go to your wives!" she glowered at them. "Phew! When's the last time anybody in here had a goddamn bath?"

She walked to the large front window and began winding out two of the sections simultaneously to air the place as McFarland and Matland clawed and jostled each other at the door for the privilege of first escape toward their wives. Magruder watched, fascinated, a little frightened even, as she stomped past, ignoring her husband still wrapped in his blanket, who gazed at her petulantly, pouty-lipped in his forties.

She entered the kitchen, seized two plastic trash baskets that were filled with discarded liquor and mix bottles, carried them to the rear of the apartment, slid back a glass door that opened onto a snow-covered deck and hurled the lot over the railing into the snow below. She returned to the kitchen, looked about for a moment for more debris to hurl perhaps, then lifted the lid of the stew pot simmering atop one of the burners to peer in at Magruder's effort. She tasted it with a wooden spoon.

"This stew isn't bad, Vincente," she called out to her husband. "But it needs more salt and a little garlic. You never put in enough salt. How much did you use?"

"I didn't make it, Angelina. Coach made it."

At that she said nothing, merely picked up the pot, carried it to the rear deck and hurled it over the railing into the snow after the bottles. Magruder winced at the hatred it implied.

"Why did you come, Angelina?" her husband whined.

The wind whistled through the apartment now, the window curtains billowing out into the room. Magruder drew his chair closer to the fireplace for warmth.

"To make certain you were all right, *caro mio*. I worried so." She moved beside him, reaching a tentative hand into the mop of his hair, greasy now from sweating out the alcohol of two and one half days. His head fell instantly to the familiar comfort of her knee.

"I'm so dirty, Angelina," he whimpered. "I haven't had a bath in three whole days."

"I'll clean you, *caro mio*. You feel so weak now. I can understand with all of this terrible pressure on you. I'll bathe you and give you a nice clean shave."

"No. I can't have you see me like this. . . ."

"Yes, *caro mio*. And I have seen you like this before. Remember that time on our vacation in Palermo when you caught the terrible fever and were in bed for five days? Who washed you and fed you, emptied the bedpans? It was your Angelina, remember?"

He sobbed now, throwing two arms so fiercely about her knee that he almost toppled her. "I remember, Angelina. You didn't get sick. . . ."

"I never get sick. I can't afford to. . . ." Magruder, growing more disgusted by the moment at the spectacle of mothering, almost finished her sentence out loud for her: One of us has to be strong, after all. He lifted a log and dumped it into the fireplace atop the coals with a loud clunk! sound. She glared at him for the interruption: "What about Kasprzak?"

"Nothing," Adnizzio sniveled. "We're free men. Nobody wanted to get involved. Nobody wanted to prosecute. Not even his own mother when she heard how he died. There's nothing anybody can do."

"*Basta!* I was right all along!" she triumphed, hopping about a little while her husband still gripped her knees, snarling at Magruder. "But, *dio mio*," she suddenly feigned, "what troubles we wives have caused! We didn't have to use that silly ruse at all about having relations with papa Gennaro to provoke anger in our husbands against Magruder. Especially," she sighed, "since it backfired and all the anger came right back at us. . . ."

"A ruse . . . ? It was all a ruse, Angelina?" Adnizzio begged. Magruder actually sniggered out loud.

"Of course, Vincente," she crooned. "He was a wonderful man, your father, but he had his principles the way I have mine. Do you think he'd actually consent to an affair with his own daughter-in-law? Ask your sisters-in-law, your brothers' wives. Do you think they'd be any less faithful? Their husbands would kill them if they even suspected. . . ."

"But what about Rita McFarland and Judy Matland?"

"Vincente! They're my best friends! They drink and get a little obnoxious at times . . . but infidelity? Vincente, I can practically reach out and touch both their houses, and I'd know for sure if one of them was sneaking off for an affair with somebody. God knows their husbands are no prizes . . . not doctors like you," she whispered confidentially now, caressing her own husband's face, jerking her head toward the walls of the condominiums to either side of her, "but no, it's not possible. It would all have been out in the open ages ago. And Vincente, one last thing . . . you're the boss now. It's time to lay the old myths to rest and create some new ones. Papa Gennaro was almost seventy-five, after all. Magruder over there is about sixty-eight or so. Ask him when was the last time he got laid. . . ."

She sneered at him and Vincent Adnizzio, grown bolder now and questioning, turned away from his mother's knee: "Well, coach?"

"As Angelina seeks to imply, Vincent, it has been quite some years."

Adnizzio stared up at his wife: "Angelina, so you think it was all . . . ?"

"Myth, Vincent. If anything, you revered your father too much. He was an old man. That's it. If he was out raising hell like everybody said after your mamma died, he would have kicked off in some doll baby's bed long ago. Come on, *caro mio,* we'll go upstairs now and I'll run you a tub. We'll get you cleaned up and I'll make you a nice supper so you'll get your strength back."

She pulled him to his feet and threw one of his arms about her shoulder. He leaned on her heavily for support like a man bleeding to death instead of someone who had been on a sleeping drunk for two days. They began the ascent up the stairs and Angelina suddenly turned to address Magruder: "You sleep down here tonight, Magruder. In the guest room."

"Do you mind then if I close the windows and doors, Angelina? Before I freeze to death?"

"Permission granted, Magruder. I'd welcome your death in imitation of Kasprzak, but the pipes would burst also, and that would be expensive."

She struggled with her burden up the last of the steps

to the bedroom and Magruder went to close the deck door and the windows. He returned to his seat, idly poking at the fireplace logs, listening to the soft placating of her voice from above. In another moment, having succeeded in undressing him, she wheeled her stark-naked husband out of the bedroom to the bath, where she began filling a tub.

"Sit in, Vincente, while it fills and I'll go down and heat up some nice minestrone I brought up with me. That's it, sit in easy. Here, darling, make some bubbles. . . ."

Magruder, disgusted at listening to her prepare the bath of a child, poured himself a drink. She came out of the bathroom, closed the door behind her and marched down the steps toward him. She still had not removed her ski jacket.

"You forgot his rubber duckie, Angelina," Magruder sneered at her.

"Have you got any more plans for my husband, Magruder?"

"It remains to be seen, Angelina, dear. Justice has hardly been served, after all. Sterling Lloyd's shade is still wandering restless through the universe out there. . . ."

"Fuck your poetry!" she hissed. She was on top of him in an instant, her left hand seizing the collar of his turtleneck and twisting it so that he gasped for breath, her right snatching up the bread knife from the table beside his chair that held the remnants of his abortive stew dinner. She kneed him squarely in the crotch, nearly causing him to vomit. Magruder, fearing, was astounded at such strength in a woman. He reached out, instinctively, desperately grasping her neck with two hands in a choking motion to fend her off. She touched the point of the bread knife hard to the artery on the left side of his neck.

"You're not going to take my husband away from me!" she rattled hoarsely, though quietly enough so that Adnizzio might not hear over the running of his bath. "You are not going to destroy my home and family!" She jabbed her knee hard another time into his crotch, shoved the knife harder so that he knew she had drawn blood. "Take your hands from my neck, you prick! Take them away or I'm going to slash your throat! Right here!"

He did as he was told, fearing her inordinately now, touching his hand to his neck as she withdrew the blade, feeling the blood she had drawn. She stayed on top of him, still holding the turtleneck, whispering fiercely to his face, "It's over, Magruder! If no one will help you and no one will prosecute, then it's over. You stay the weekend and ski, leave with us on Christmas Eve for Jersey, get your fucking car out of my driveway before my daughter and her husband come back from their honeymoon, and I never want to see you or hear of you again!"

She stood up, wiped the tracing of blood on his turtleneck, then threw the knife expertly through the kitchen door where it landed with a metallic clunk! sound in the sink.

"You're the strongest woman I've ever encountered, Angelina."

"Too bad you weren't a younger man, Magruder. You must have had a hell of a body in your early forties. Nice and hard like a football coach should. . . ."

"I could take my story to the newspapers, Angelina,"

he said defiantly, enraged despite himself, that she dared seduce anywhere.

"Would you, Magruder?"

"I might. . . ."

"We'll see. . . ."

She stared down at him reflectively, as if from a great distance. This woman is going to try to kill me, it came to Magruder from an equally distant place.

"Angelina . . . ?"

"Coming, Vincente, darling. In a minute. I just want to make sure the soup doesn't boil over."

Then she went to the kitchen, opened a can of soup from the cupboard, threw it into a pot and turned the flame beneath it up high: "Make sure that shit doesn't boil over, Magruder. Earn your keep for the weekend," she said as she marched upstairs to bathe her husband.

In half an hour or so, his fear and anger had subsided. Then he grew embarrassed at the weepings and tear-coated recriminations that came from everywhere within the three conjoined condominiums after Adnizzio, McFarland and Matland were presumedly bathed and shaved by their wives. He decided to take a long walk in the Killington moonlight.

The wind had died. Above, on the mountains, the snow cats still crisscrossed the slopes that were clearly seen now, grooming and dragging the snow-making guns after them. The night was becoming cold again, and crisp, but exhilarating and beautiful, and Magruder declined the rides offered him twice by young people in Volkswagens, preferring to walk instead. He stopped for a single drink in the first bar he came to, thought it sad that the place was filled with young people only, that the elderly might even be made to feel uncomfortable or embarrassed in going out to such a place.

In more time, taking a second drink he had not really intended, he was doubly saddened: When the annoying rock band stopped for a break, Christmas music from a Montreal FM station came on, recalling to Magruder that Florence had preferred the French stations for the holidays, the soft lilt of French carols, the boys' chorus from Notre Dame in Quebec. He had not listened closely enough with her, he thought, had not cared enough to understand more than a few words of the French she understood. It came to him shockingly, sweeping aside the debris of the Kasprzak affair that had so engrossed his energies, that this would be the first Christmas in forty-one years he would not spend with her. How he missed her now! How awful to be alone without her this holiday. How true all the clichés of guilt and depression and loneliness that funerals and the festive seasons meant for others produced. . . .

Forty-one years: Was it possible he had been married to the same woman for so long? There had been passion, he thought. At least in the beginning. But it was not the kind the right man might have known with the likes of Angelina Adnizzio. He took another drink, thinking of how it might have been with Angelina, then pushed aside the drink, considering there would never have been enough time for St. Anselm's, football and Angelina in one lifetime. Besides, she was Italian. That sort of marriage, at least when he had married Florence, was absolutely frowned upon. Florence had not been so beautiful, as exciting as an Angelina Adnizzio, but she had been proper. Acceptable. Yes, that was it. To Magruder's pride, Rowley, the old headmaster, had called her exactly that one day, seeing her pouring at a tea.

He left that bar and went on to the next, savoring the cold on the walk, trying to figure out how long the reconciliations back at the three condominiums might take so he could return to sleep. He paid a cover charge, stepped into the din of continuous rock music, appraised that it was filled completely with young people, that the blinking strobe lights hurt his eyes, took a single drink and left.

At the next bar, a quiet piano lounge whose maudlin repertoire depressed him inordinately, he drank too much, thinking of dead Florence, unapproachable Angelina and poor Sterling Lloyd. The crowd at least was somewhat older and mostly married and less noisy, and when the piano player, a soft-voiced, middle-aged lady who insisted she knew the lyrics of every American song ever written extended a microphone on the end of a boom from her piano to Magruder at the bar to ask for a request, he replied boozily, "I'll never achieve my expiation now."

The piano lady professed to a guffawing audience to be absolutely stumped for the first time ever. The bartender, a kindly person, got two ski instructors to take Magruder home.

"Worthless . . . worthless old fool . . ." he described himself to everyone there as they led him from the lounge. The patrons were silent from wonderment.

In the morning, when he awoke, uncertain at first where he was, the newly reconciled six were evidently having breakfast in McFarland's apartment. He heard them through the wall, laughing and even singing, doubtless enjoying their new lease on life. He rose, washed and shaved blearily, then thought first of some coffee and breakfast as Angelina Adnizzio walked in the door, bearing a covered dish of flapjacks, eggs, hash-brown potatoes and sausage and a pitcher of bloody marys.

"Egil, darling, how do you feel this morning?" She placed the food and the eyeopener on the table and came forward, pecking him a kiss on his neck on the cut where she had drawn blood with her bread knife the night before.

"Awful. I must say that you're kind of chipper though, Angelina."

"Who wouldn't be? Vincente started acting like a man, picked up where his father left off and fucked my brains out for the first time in twenty-some years."

"Something achieved by all this, at last it would seem."

"Yes," she said levelly. "It seems with the final Christmas Eve departure of old Egil Magruder, we three wives are about to have red-blooded studs for husbands for the second start in life. . . ." She considered a moment longer, then spoke detachedly as she prepared his coffee:

"I do have one thing to thank you for, Egil. When Vincente's dick went limp over the years, I didn't have to theorize about latent homo tendencies like the other wives. I knew for sure what the problem was. . . . Eat up now, Egil. We'll leave for the slopes in about forty-five minutes."

They piled into McFarland's station wagon, drove through brilliant sunshine to the Killington main lodge and skied a series of intermediate trails for about an hour to warm up for the run down the expert trail beneath the main chair lift that Adnizzio, McFarland and Matland were going to try for the first time ever in honor of their emancipation from Sterling Lloyd. The three women would stick to the intermediate trails and meet them at the lodge for lunch.

Not long before noon, halfway up for their first time on the main lift, at the time when the line was calculated to be sparest, Matland, who shared the chair with Magruder, complained of a painful left-leg cramp and asked Magruder to raise the safety bar so he might stretch the muscle. Magruder complied and when he half turned about to drop the bar behind them, Matland shoved him fiercely from his seat. In desperation Magruder clung two handedly to the arm rest while begging Matland, "Eric, no! No! Please, Eric!" Then, his horror intensified at the realization that Adnizzio and McFarland in the chair behind them exhorted Matland to kick him off. Matland did, laying the middle of his left ski violently across Magruder's forehead as Magruder lost his grip. He gave up the ghost and fell, dropping his poles, plummeting the long distance down toward the jumbled range of snows that must contain rock ledges beneath them. On the way down he saw for certain the great winged beast that was Sterling Lloyd soaring franti-

239

cally toward him to save him. Also on a cross trail he glimpsed for an instant the figures of the three women of New Jersey cheering the advent of his death among the other horrified skiers who screamed for another reason as Magruder thudded into the snows.

CHAPTER 16

Limbo

He awoke early the following morning, a sunless Christmas Eve, in the Central Vermont Broken Skiers' Hospice on the outskirts of Rutland, his head spinning from the drugs they had given him, the pain in both legs excruciating despite the painkillers. It surprised him after perhaps a minute of consideration that he was not being fed intravenously. He could not remember having taken food.

His left leg was in traction, broken evidently; the right one, when he probed beneath the covers to test for the hurt, was heavily bandaged about fifteen inches or so along the outside of his thigh. He remembered then that he had fallen right onto the upended tip of his ski pole, and that a girl skier, one of the first on the scene to help dig him out of the deep pocket into which he had miraculously fallen, had begun screaming hysterically about the fact that he was bleeding to death. Then at that moment, looking upward at the terror of her eyes, he was resigned to his dying. Wished for it, in fact: Their betrayal had been incredible, worse than anything he could have imagined. He cried helplessly as two members of the ski patrol applied a tourniquet to his leg to stop the bleeding, eased him gingerly onto their sled and hauled him off down the mountain.

Now he looked through the blinds beside him, seeing the chill gray, first light of the dawn, recalling that it was Christmas Eve, that tomorrow, Christmas Day, was sure to be the loneliest of his life so far. If a nurse came by he would ask for a priest, make his confession and take communion on Christmas morning. . . .

His eyes traveled to the end of the room, barely discerning objects, coming to rest on the apparition of a man sitting beneath a goose-neck lamp, apparently writing on a sheaf of papers. A bolt of terror shot through Magruder: "Who . . . ? Who are you?" He had difficulty speaking, as if his mouth and tongue and teeth had become velveteen, traveled raspily over one another. He did not think the man had heard him.

The man rose as Magruder pulled the covers close up about him for protection, made his way out of the shadows, assumed a definitive shape as he switched on another lamp nearer the bed: It was the Vermont trooper he had begged to accompany him to the hospital the day before. The remembrance returned with a brilliant clarity: When the ski patrol got him off the mountain, the trooper and a volunteer ambulance were already waiting. So were Adnizzio, McFarland and Matland. As they slid him inside the ambulance Magruder looked through the etched panes of glass on his right at the three, who stared at him somehow speculatively, Magruder considered, as if they wondered at the chances for his death before he reached a doctor in Rutland. With the last strength left to him, Magruder had swung himself into a sitting position, grabbed at the arm of the trooper standing before the rear door, pulled the man over on top of him, begged him to protect him from the three: "He's a doctor," Magruder said, pointing to Adnizzio. "He'll try to get into the hospital." Then he passed out, the curious drone, the waves of white light ebbing and flowing all about him as it had when he went under the dentist's ether as a child. The last spoken words penetrating the drone were those of Adnizzio: "I'm a doctor, officer. He's almost seventy. He had a fainting spell and fell out of the chair lift up there."

"Are you all right, Mr. Magruder? Do you want me to ring for the nurse?"

"No, I'm all right, thank you. It's dawn, isn't it?"

"Yes, about seven-thirty."

"Have you been here all night?"

"No . . . just about an hour this time. I was doing a little paper work. I have to go on duty about eight o'clock. I know a couple of the nurses and they let me in. I was here from about one-thirty to three this morning, though. Unofficially, you know. A little insomnia. One of the kids was up with a cough, so I couldn't sleep anyhow."

"I'm sorry to put you to so much trouble," Magruder told him. He thought now of ringing for the nurse, asking for a sedative.

"They came by about two-fifteen."

"Who?"

"The doctor and the other two guys and three women in a big Caddy with Jersey plates."

"Jesus . . ." Magruder ejaculated softly, terrified at the strength of their wish to see him dead, wondering dimly whether it was worth fighting on against them.

"They stopped the car and the doctor was just going in to the nurses' desk when he saw me. He went back to the car and they took off."

"Thank you. I think maybe you saved my life last night, for all it's worth."

The cop stood up, moved to the blinds and opened them some more so that Magruder could see the first real light behind the dark silhouettes of the mountains to the east of them. He sensed the cold, saw the rising trails of vapor in the air coming from fireplaces or chimney stacks round about. The trooper tapped on his teeth with the end of his pen: "You know, Mr. Magruder, it just doesn't make sense. I took those guys' names yesterday since they were all witnesses, and ran a check on them. They're all family men, they're all pretty well off, kids in the right schools, pillars of the community and all the rest of it. The doctor even plays poker with the chief of police down there. What could they possibly gain by seeing you dead?"

Magruder shook his head in response. He was too weak. It would be hopeless, inane, to begin the incredible tale of Kasprzak here.

"Was it the truth then? I mean about the guy shoving you off the lift chair?"

"No, of course not. I must have been in shock. Did you ever hear tell of anyone doing that?"

"No, sir. But then I don't ski. I can't afford it. It sounds improbable, but maybe every sport has its private method of execution. Look at stock-car racing, or snow mobiling for instance. . . ."

"Don't be such a romantic." Magruder laughed at him despite the pain. "I had a fainting spell."

"I thought you told me I'd saved your life last night."

"I had a fainting spell."

But the trooper was not satisfied. He paced about a bit, tapping his teeth again, repeatedly checking his wrist watch, then walked back to the bed: "You know, Mr. Magruder, there's no real legal means to ensure that Dr. Adnizzio won't get in here if you don't press charges. We can't post a full-time guard and I can't go to the hospital director with hunches when the good doctor hasn't broken any laws we know of. . . ."

"It's nothing, officer. I was very upset at the time," Magruder said, feeling tired, as if he needed to sleep again.

"All right, Magruder, have it your way. Anyhow, if he gets in here, he won't be alone. We're pretty tight with the nurses. They'll put a call into the barracks as soon as he hits the floor, and one or two of them will be here with him at all times. If he tells the nurse to leave, you request that she stay."

"Why are you doing this . . . ?" His name, by his lapel badge, was Drapeau. "Why are you doing this, Drapeau?"

"Part curiosity, Magruder. And part to ensure my good conscience. If anything ever happened to you when I at least had a suggestion it might happen . . . well, you know. . . ."

"Yes, thank you, Drapeau." Unexpectedly the cop shook his hand then left for his shift as an elderly nurse came in to test his pulse and temperature.

"You're a tough old bird, Magruder," she affirmed.

"Temperature and pulse pretty near normal and we must have put a gallon of antitetanus into you yesterday."

"A testimony to a life spent on the playing fields," Magruder said ruefully, remembering the words of Morton the headmaster.

Her tasks done, she came to his right side, rigged his call button in a certain way so that just the tip of it protruded from between the double thickness of mattress: "If that doctor from Jersey or any of his friends get in here without us knowing, you hit three short blasts on that thing and everybody from the head nurse to the dishwasher will be here in ten seconds."

"It isn't as bad as it seems, nurse. Officer Drapeau is being very kind, but I doubt Dr. Adnizzio or anyone will be back again. I'm embarrassed that it turned into all this."

"Ernie Drapeau isn't being particularly kind, coach. He's being very curious like a good cop should. Ernie went right into surgery with you, and he wants to know about somebody who was bumped off in New York state named Sterling Lloyd. . . ."

"Ah, Sterling Lloyd," Magruder sighed. "Poor Sterling Lloyd. He was a very obese boy who died of a heart attack in a deep freeze twenty-three years ago."

"That's not the way you told it yesterday, coach, when they were putting you back together." She winked at him. "Hungry? . . . *No?* Well I'll have your breakfast sent in anyhow. You can pick at it."

Then she was gone, and Magruder had absolutely no idea any longer how anything was going to end.

Unbelievably, they came that afternoon, five minutes after the beginning of visiting hours, the hysteria they felt barely concealed as they offered him a Christmas–get-well basket of fruit: Vincent and Angelina, Justin and Rita, Judy Matland but not Eric.

"Where's Eric?" Magruder asked calmly. "Parking the car?" There was a young nurse doing inconsequential things about the room, and when he asked the question she shot him a too-knowing look.

"Eric has the flu," his wife lied in an octave-high voice like Eleanor Roosevelt's. Her hands, the birdlike ones he remembered from the time she had threatened him at the Adnizzio–Modesti wedding, fluttered before her face. She tried to light a cigarette, but the nurse told her no.

"Let's hope Eric doesn't die of the flu. He's a young man, after all. Lots to live for now."

"Yes . . . a ha ha, yes, yes . . .": Somehow they got it out in perfect unison, then stared at him all together with identical plastic smiles, the only twit in their midst being Judith Matland, who drew greedy puffs on her cigarette without being able to light it.

The stalemate was a monster. Magruder understood that they also had no idea where it was going except for his certainty that they would like to kill him then and there, take advantage of his vulnerability in traction, assuage their remaining conscience with the fact of his age and impending senility. In his mind's eye he saw them advancing ritualistically on his bed, smothering him to death with five identical and uniformly antiseptic-smelling pillows . . . except for the young nurse who, done puttering now, wearily sat down in a corner chair and began working a crossword puzzle.

"What's a five-letter word for snake?" she called out in the stillness.

"Nurse, if you've got nothing else to do here, it's quite all right to leave," Adnizzio told her. "I'm a doctor. We'd like to talk privately with Coach Magruder since we have to leave soon for New Jersey."

She silenced him with an annoyed wave of her hand: "It can't be viper. That doesn't fit. Think of something else."

"Cobra, darling. My husband is a doctor, dear, and I used to be a nurse, and when any doctor gave me an order or, in this case, a polite request, I knew just what to do."

Magruder saw the hesitance in the young nurse's eyes and hit three short blasts on the call button. In moments, it seemed, four people erupted into the room: two more nurses, a maintenance man certainly—since he held a pipe wrench in one hand—and a severe gray-haired lady who introduced herself as the hospital dietician. Magruder apologized to them for his inattention in rolling over on the call button. They withdrew and Magruder smiled a kind of triumph at his five visitors: Their hatred was an open glare now, and he knew with certainty that they knew. . . .

"Sooo . . ." Angelina judged, the word issuing from her like a sighing of winds.

"Yes," Magruder assured her. "Screw yourself."

Matland's wife, manic now, began talking about his unfortunate dizzy spell and fall and how lucky he was to have survived. Absurdly, she asked how his forehead came to be bandaged. The question provoked a sharp intake of breath by Adnizzio and McFarland, an attempt to silence her and Magruder thought to tell her simply that her husband had kicked him there with the flat of his ski, but he remembered the nurse, the friend of Drapeau, opted for discretion and told her he could not remember.

The nurse left abruptly, provoking a hope that was dashed some thirty seconds later with the entry of a cleaning lady who set to work wiping meticulously at the slats of the blinds until Adnizzio, who identified himself as a doctor, suggested the dust might be harmful to the patient. She agreed that it might, and that's why she was removing it.

A repairman who said he had come about the broken TV set was next, and he proceeded to remove the back piece and probe the innards of the thing for about ten distracting minutes, visibly straining the visitors' nerves with the din of football crowds and half-time drums until he declared the picture as good as he could get it and left.

There was no longer any reason for them to doubt. The warning was being clearly signaled. In the wake of the repairman's departure, the kitchen sent up his second lunch, even after the five had seen the first one being removed on their entry. The nurse who set up the tray warned him emphatically that he would have to eat for strength and got Adnizzio, whom she knew already was a doctor, to agree just as emphatically with her. After lunch, a nurse's aid in a candy-striped dress came to trim his hair, her constant chatter delighting Magruder, restoring his spirits, since it so obviously disconcerted his visitors. When she left, came the longest interval they were alone with him.

"You're a never-ending surprise, coach," McFarland finally spoke after about two whole minutes of a tense silence. "Looks like that old senility's been confounded yet once again. . . ."

He sang or lilted the last of the words, but there was a new respect in his eyes. Magruder basked in that gaze, watched bemused as the three women, tittering with nervousness again, actually lit their cigarettes this time, drawing in lungfuls of comfort. Judy Matland overindulged evidently: In another moment, when Ernie Drapeau, the trooper, walked in the door and nodded politely to the assemblage, she fainted dead out of her chair onto the floor.

Nicholas the Tedesco showed up the next day, Christmas, with a box of sausages and cheese and fruitcake and a jug of his wine for Magruder. Magruder convinced the head nurse that it was safe for the two to be alone by themselves, and when she left, the Tedesco kissed him gravely on the forehead, opened the wine and poured them two full glasses. He drew up a chair beside the bed and sat down, neglecting to remove his great coat or fedora.

"Not much of a way to spend Christmas, Egil."

"I wasn't exactly planning on it, Nicholas. Thank you for coming up. Did you drive the Buick?"

"No, I came on the Vermont Transit. If I took the car, there would be no way to stop the Celestiale Quartet and my gentlewoman friend, Theresa Bugalli, from coming along. They are all very concerned about you. It was Theresa who prepared the sausages and cheese and fruit-cake. The Celestiale Quartet send you their first recording of various Vivaldi concerti . . . but I digress. I didn't want them along because I wanted to talk with you alone."

"How did you know I was hospitalized?"

"Our friend Angelina. She called home to give the good word about poor Sterling Lloyd to her brothers-in-law. She actually told them Matland shoved you from the ski chair. They called me pointedly to give me the cheering news. Vincent's brother, Rocco, had about forty people over last night to celebrate. You're very lucky, I think, to be still alive."

"Triply lucky, I'd say. Angelina almost did me in with a bread knife, and Vincent tried to get in here the night before last, God knows what to do. . . ."

The Tedesco shook his head sadly, took another gulp of his wine: "Who would think it could have come to this?"

"They're getting even now for all those years of worrying. Years that it seems now were all for nothing. Anyhow, Sterling Lloyd's justice, for what it's worth, is pretty much kaput."

"Perhaps, Egil, but yours is not." Nicholas the Tedesco looked for a long minute through the blinds at the grim Christmas Day outside, shuddered perhaps at a quality of light that could so deaden the spirit, then turned to Magruder: "I did something you might not like, Egil. I found that list in your glove compartment of the other boys you stopped to see when you came across the country to New Jersey. I called them all and told them what happened. They'll all be here on Wednesday when Vincent and his two friends return to Vermont to pay you a little visit. They're mad as hell. That colored guy from Chicago, Vauchon, he's bringing a bunch of niggers with him to help out in case Vincent's brothers show up and try to get nasty. I have a feeling Vincent and friends are in for some real trouble."

"It still doesn't help the cause of Sterling Lloyd Kasprzak," Magruder sighed.

"I know. A travesty for certain. When I return to Jersey, I'll have to put the finishing touches on the epic of Sterling Lloyd."

"What will you say?"

"That his soul was condemned to travel fitfully about the universe for all Eternity."

"That's exactly what has happened," Magruder judged softly, reaching for a refill of his wine. As ever, the Tedesco's vintage was potent. Combined with his sedative, the pain and itching in his legs swam far off, became only a distant twitching so that a certain pleasurableness returned. The Tedesco peeled a tangerine from the fruit basket, began eating the slices and spitting the seeds with audible plink! sounds into a metal wastebasket.

"I am thinking of asking for the hand of Theresa Bugalli in marriage," the Tedesco said after a time.

"Isn't this rather sudden?" Magruder kidded him. "You hardly know her. You only met her last week at your grandniece's wedding."

"It was love at first sight," the poet said earnestly. "Both of us concede it to be so. And we're quite compatible, Egil. We both enjoy the master, Vivaldi, and dancing

and fine wines and haute cuisine. And poetry! I read to
her at length from Sterling Lloyd's epic, and would you
believe, she wept openly, couldn't stop herself from crying. What sensitivity!" he enthused, standing up and
walking swiftly about the room, his face almost childlike
with the delight of having a woman companion again
years after the death of his first wife. His delirium nearly
convulsed Magruder with tears, sent the awful realization
of his own loneliness—even so short a time after
Florence's death—thudding into his heart like a spear.
Magruder downed his wine in one gulp, felt his jealousy
of the Tedesco rage up inside him like a volcano: "Isn't
she rather a heavy-set woman for a man like you,
Nicholas?"

"She's going to diet, Egil. She'll lose one hundred
pounds at least. I've seen pictures of her not long in the
past. She was slim and quite small-boned like my first
wife, God rest her soul. It's just that the specialties she
makes particularly well—veal *piccante,* mussels *leopardo,*
chicken Sorrento and others—cannot be made in small
single portions, so alas, living alone, she's forced to eat the
entirety herself. But Egil," he waxed delirious, filling their
wine glasses again, "you should taste her veal *piccante!*
The merest hint of capers, a tiny breath of anchovy . . .
indeed the night this last week she served it to me I for-
sook my own wine and raced out before the entrée course
and bought two of the finest bottles of French wine
available. Egil"—he grasped Magruder's two hands in his
own—"Egil, she could come with us to Florida. Think
how wonderfully we'd eat. . . ."

"Are we going to Florida together, Nicholas?" He

asked the question lamely, knowing it had lain in the back of his mind since he first met the crazy Morelli.

"Who else will you go with?"

"I met an unmarried lady skiing this week at Killington. . . ."

"Bring her along! We'll get a big house and all live together to save money. What's she like?"

Curiously Magruder had thought of her often that morning, had even considered phoning New Hampshire to wish her a Merry Christmas.

"She's sixty-three. She's very intelligent. We spoke for a time about Sartre and Ionesco. She's the sister-in-law of an Episcopal minister from New Hampshire."

"Ah, a Protestant. . . . Still, if she signs the papers that the children should be raised Catholic, then it's all right. You might even get her to convert."

The notion cracked Magruder up immeasurably. He laughed hilariously, spilling his wine all over the bedclothes, restoring the joy of Christmas to his sad room in the central Vermont Broken Skiers' Hospice, for the most inanely wrong reason: How he loved the sweet madness of Nicholas Morelli!

He laughed so hard that he could not even protest when the nurse walked in, spied the illicit wine jug and ordered Morelli out of the place and into the snow.

CHAPTER 17

The Trial

Justice for Magruder was decided upon in a far shorter time than twenty-three years. It took all of about fifteen minutes he reckoned, if even it took that long. Swift retribution for someone at last.

All the participants in the trial of Adnizzio, McFarland and Matland had evidently assembled and conferred in Rutland, Vermont, the night before the scheduled return visit of the three from New Jersey that Wednesday after Christmas. Martin McFadden, Jack Welsh, Albert Deutsch, his daughter, Ingrid, and future son-in-law, Emmett Carruthers (Carruthers had apparently enjoyed an amicable Christmas with the Deutsches in Nebraska), Matthew Vauchon and his man Brighton were all waiting about Magruder's bed when the culprits entered the room shortly after visiting hours began. At the sight of the others, the three gentlemen of Red Bank barely resisted the collective urge to flee again.

"Nice try, gentlemen," McFadden of Las Vegas glowered at them.

"Coach had a fainting spell in a lift chair," McFarland blurted. "He fell out! We're lucky he's not dead!"

"Look, he's out of traction," Adnizzio enthused, his

smile frantic, woefully unable to conceal his fearing. "How's that old leg feel now, coach?"

"Which one, Vincent?" Magruder asked wryly. "The broken one or the scarred one?"

"The broken one," Adnizzio answered meekly, seeing the defeat. In response Magruder lifted his casted leg about a foot in the air, then dropped it heavily back to the mattress: "I'd like to oblige you by high-kicking the other one, Vincent, but my Vermont doctor tells me it might pull out my stitches for me."

"Coach," Matland began gravely, "coach, a man of your age shouldn't be skiing at all. It's a hell of a strenuous sport, you know. But look, before I forget, here's a little something we rounded up down in Jersey to help out with the medical bills and such. . . ."

Mindless of the universal sniggering, he thrust the envelope at Magruder. But Vauchon snatched it neatly from his hand and actually slit it open with a single manicured extra-long nail. He fingered the bills inside briefly, the corners of his mouth turned downward in contempt.

"As your attorney, coach, I'd advise you not to accept this money."

"Can I at least know how much it is, Matthew?"

"Ten one hundred dollar bills. A measly thousand dollars. Not nearly enough to even think of settling for. We're talking about attempted manslaughter, after all. . . ."

"That's wrong, Matthew," McFarland pleaded. "Coach had a fainting spell. He's old. He was raving when they brought him down here. He must have told the doctors and nurses crazy things."

"Bullshit!" Vauchon hurled. "Matland pushed him out of the chair! Adnizzio's wife even called her brother-in-law to brag about it. We have a gentleman named Nicholas Morelli who will attest to that fact."

"Nobody wanted to do anything about Kasprzak!" Matland nearly screamed. "Do you know what this old fart has put us through for the last twenty-three years? Then to find out that it had been for nothing! I'd still like to kill him!"

"If you do that, you'll be in worse trouble than you were over Kasprzak," Welsh said stonily. "There's a trooper here in Vermont who's snooping around on this now. He has your names. If anything happens to coach, that cop is going to do the logical. . . ."

"We might simply circumvent that or any other possibility and have coach file charges against you gentlemen today," Vauchon spoke. Then he snorted, threw the conscience money back to Matland.

"Is coach going to press charges?" The question came from Matland after a silence of perhaps half a minute.

"Coach?" Vauchon asked.

"We've kept Kasprzak in the family this long, gentlemen, and I think we should deal with this new problem among ourselves also."

"Whew, thank God. . . ." the expected sigh of relief from the New Jersey three.

"Coach's consideration is laudatory. However, a punishment is necessary. Demanded, I would say." Unexpectedly, it was Carruthers, with a forcefulness that astounded them: In little more than a week, eighteen-year-old Ingrid had evidently brought him down off the booze. His hands no longer shook. The previous awful splotchiness of his skin had receded to a uniform redness that even looked healthy. His soon-to-be father-in-law agreed emphatically, slapped Carruthers approvingly on the back: "What Emmett says is right. If they get away with this one, there's no law of God or man they wouldn't spit at for the rest of their lives."

"Let's just call it even and forget everything, fellows," McFarland suggested. "Kasprzak is over and done with, and coach's little accident was a mistake. . . ." He laughed, glowing with feigned pleasure, placing a friendly hand on the expensive cashmere of Vauchon's shoulder. Brighton removed the hand, returned it conclusively to McFarland's side. His laughter trickled off to nothing.

"You guys haven't got the right to decide any kind of a punishment for us!" Adnizzio said furiously. "If the law didn't want anything to do with Kasprzak and coach isn't going to press charges against Matland, then . . ."

Matland interrupted, "Why me? We were all in on it together."

"You shoved him out of the chair, Eric," McFarland said.

"Only because you can't get four people in one chair, shit brains! If we're really going to lay the blame in the right place, let's start with Vincent's wife. The whole thing was Angelina's idea anyhow."

"You leave my wife out of this, Matland! If she hears you're talking against her, she'll have that family of hers do a number on you when you get back to Jersey."

"Fuck off, wop! After all these years of living next to

258

you, I'm damn sick and tired of hearing everybody being threatened by that protective greaser underground you're supposed to be a part of. Fuck off!"

"Shut up, Matland!" Martin McFadden ordered. "Ingrid here doesn't need vocabulary lessons at her age, and the nurses'll be in here to kick us out if the din gets any louder."

"Let's cut the recriminations," Carruthers spoke again, "and talk about the collective punishment we're going to impose. And make no mistake, gentlemen, we are going to impose it."

"What sort of punishment were you thinkin', Emmett?" Albert Deutsch asked. Then for no apparent reason he told something that everyone already knew: "Emmett's most qualified to talk about this. He's a professor of moral theology at Notre Dame."

Everyone nodded gravely, afraid, Magruder thought, of the massiveness of Deutsch. Still they looked to Carruthers none the less.

"There really isn't much precedent for this, you know," Carruthers extemporized. "I mean, hopefully, not in our time. We've got to presume that civilization is enough advanced so that punishment usually isn't customarily meted out beyond the law. So it behooves us, civilized, educated Christian gentlemen, to find a humane, equitable solution. We might fine them, for example, attach their earnings for a certain amount to be applied to a charity of the coach's choosing. . . ."

"We're talking about a physical punishment, Emmett," Jack Welsh said annoyedly. "Something to make up for the civilized, educated, Christian and gentlemanly fact of coach's two bum legs. These guys haven't got any conscience left that could be affected by anything less than pain. Seek your precedent there, brother."

"Well then, seafarers have always employed keelhauling. The American Indians used the gauntlet as a means of punishment, and"—he began guffawing, seeing some absurdity in it all—"we might stretch them out on an ant hill, or lynch them, or crucify them. . . ."

"Why don't we just whip 'em and get it the hell over with?"

The words, from Vauchon's Brighton, came from without the ring of concentration about Magruder's bed. They were startling words: The pleasant lilt of his islander's accent was harsh with disgust now.

"Brighton, be silent," Vauchon growled at him.

"No, I mean it, boss. It's time for some nigger bluntness. These people are going to stand around here for the rest of the day trying to figure out the halfway point between physical punishment and the wants of civilization. Whip 'em, I say. It's the only logical thing to do. What else is there? Tying them to a car bumper and dragging them bare-ass naked in the cold for a time? Flog 'em, I say, and we'll go home to Chicago and forget St. Anselm's School for Boys and the burden of your eighteenth year forever. Besides, this tiny little lily-white state makes me nervous."

"Brighton's right," Ingrid spoke quietly now. "Do it and get it over with so you can finally go on to being grown men in your own minds. . . ."

"Ingrid," her father warned, "I don't think we need that kind of opinion from an eighteen-year-old."

"Yes you do, daddy. Brighton and I are the only out-siders and we're the only ones that can see the atrophied part of you. It's sad, in the same way that the story about the crabs is sad. Right now is your chance to redeem the past. Just do it, and don't let these three guys negotiate their own punishment. Kasprzak didn't choose death by exposure, and coach didn't ask to be pushed from a chair lift."

"Nobody's going to whip me!" Matland declared. "None of you have the right to do that. Jesus Christ, it's medieval!"

"Pushing a seventy-year-old guy from a ski lift seems pretty medieval to me, friend," Brighton spoke fiercely now.

"End of discussion, nigger!" Matland thundered. "I'm getting out of this crazy house!"

He made for the door, but Albert Deutsch seized him abruptly by the collar, whirled him powerfully about: "You stay, Matland. We aren't through deciding on you yet."

Then Magruder spoke for the first time: "If they all agree that you're to be whipped, Eric, then you'll be whipped, or flayed, or pummeled or whatever." He sighed with weariness or exasperation, the pain in the stitched leg having become more excruciating at that minute than ever before. "It's lamentable that we have recourse to taking directions from Ingrid and Brighton, but what they say is true. We've lived so long with our guilt over Kasprzak that we've become ineffectual in dealing with that problem or anything that flows from it. There's no objectivity any longer. Yes, let them be whipped. Otherwise I will go to the police. Decide quickly though, because that trooper Jack was talking about will be here in a while after the nurses get the word to him that I've got a full house of visitors."

"I'm to be whipped, huh? Well, which of you is going to do it?" Matland spat. A caged animal, his back to the wall, he made a slow turn, hands on his hips, searching out the hesitancy in every face: "Will you, Jack?" He demanded of Welsh. "How about you, Matty Vauchon? You, Carruthers? Yes, from what I remember of you, you might be my best bet . . . come on, brothers, as the Bible tells it, let the most righteous among you step forward."

Brighton stepped forward. "When, where and how many lashes are required?"

"Brighton . . ." Predictably it was Vauchon. But not in reprimand now, more like a despairing moan completely out of character with Vauchon's normal hauteur. "Brighton, why are you doing this?"

"Boss, it's fifteen years now that I've worked for you. You're a fine employer, but you think like a white man. A Catholic white man. Nothing but moral quandaries and man's imperfectibility. I don't know how you had any time to make so much money. Sometimes when I'd drive you and Mrs. V in the car and you'd start talking about Sterling Lloyd's justice, I used to think of crashing into a brick wall somewhere just to get it over with. Boss, if some outsider like me doesn't interfere, then nothing is going to happen to these guys. Anybody can see that. You already let Kasprzak get away from you. If we don't tend to the justice of Magruder right here and now, then they'll get off a second time, and you'll all be moralizing for the next twenty-three years."

"Listen to what he says," Ingrid the other outsider prompted. "Give them their punishment now and you won't be blaming each other until your dying day for not having done it."

"Why are you so damn interested in punishing me, young lady?" Matland demanded furiously.

"Because, from all accounts, Mr. Matland, you're a despicable prick who needs it."

"Ingrid!" her father and husband-to-be admonished in the same breath.

"He is a prick," her friend Brighton supported her. "She knows exactly what she's saying. Now, how many lashes?"

"It should be a symbolic number," Carruthers suggested. "Perhaps ten, for instance, for the Ten Commandments. . . ."

"How about twenty-three for the twenty-three years of Sterling Lloyd Kasprzak?" Brighton said.

"Twenty-three!" McFarland exploded. "That's not right! That's inhumane!"

"How many feet would you estimate you fell, Coach Magruder, when they shoved you out of that lift chair?" Brighton demanded, surging on.

"All right, twenty-three," Adnizzio agreed quickly. There was a stifling silence, perhaps half a minute long, that was broken by a suddenly dazed-looking Matland, who said simply, "It's actually going to happen. They're actually going to do it to us." He blinked a few times, as if erasing spots from before his eyes: "What a perfect entrapment. We can't even go to the police." He began laughing a little like a classic scenario of someone descending into madness, then blubbered a little also, as if he really meant to cry, "Will it happen today?"

"No," Magruder said, "I want to be there. The doctor will release me in two days, on Friday. It will happen on Friday."

"Two days from now?" Adnizzio asked. "What's to prevent us from leaving for Europe in the next two days?"

"Six burly black gentlemen seated in a car out there in the parking lot," Vauchon said levelly.

"I see."

"Yes."

"Where does it happen, coach?" McFarland begged hoarsely. On the instant Magruder felt sorry for him, might have relented, seeing the anguished perplexity of his face: Not excessively bright, as everyone noted, he had doubtless trailed along after the other two through both capers, even though years apart.

"Back up the mountain at Killington will do fine, I suppose. We can go up into that forest behind your condominiums. It should be private enough."

"Will you use a belt, Brighton?" Matland whined. "You won't use the buckle end on us, would you? My father did that to me when I was a kid. I still have the scars to show for it. . . ."

"No, I'll use a bull whip. I won't even draw blood."

"Where will you get a bull whip, Brighton?" Vauchon asked. "They're illegal most places, I believe."

"I brought it with me from Chicago, boss, when I heard what the problem in Vermont was all about."

"How thoughtful of you," Vauchon judged ruefully.

"Yes."

Then there was nothing more to say: They began leaving in twos and threes after saying good-by to Magruder. When they were all gone, Magruder stared out the window for a time at the grimness of the day. Then he began to cry a little realizing the enormity of what the business of Kasprzak had become.

CHAPTER 18

The Punishment

On Friday, before the flogging, there was an almost comradely, festive air about the whole thing: perhaps a great lightening of the collective mind after all.

Magruder was released from the hospital about 10:30 A.M. and driven back up the mountain to Killington by Welsh and Vauchon. Around noon, when Adnizzio, McFarland and Matland were pretty much drunk and everyone else a few strengthening drinks to the good, they left the bar of Adnizzio's condominium and lurched through the knee-deep snows into the nearby woods and over a ridge of hemlocks into a wide, tree-filled ravine that was out of sight of anyone at the ski area, and presumedly out of hearing as well. An embarrassed Magruder was carried there on a stretcher by four of Vauchon's six black henchmen who muttered and cursed as they lunged through the deep whiteness in business suits and overcoats. It somehow amused Magruder that each of the major participants, excepting Carruthers, but including Ingrid Deutsch and the three who were to be flogged, had carried a bottle away from the bar with them. For courage, evidently.

In the ravine, Brighton ordered Adnizzio, McFarland

and Matland to remove their jackets and strip to the waist, until they were barebacked and shivering, then positioned each of them facing against the trunk of an appropriate tree, thoughtfully offering to handcuff them about its girth lest they faint away from the pain and have to be revived again to stand up under their own power to more lashings. Only Matland accepted the cuffs; Adnizzio and McFarland clung to their trees as if the wood were a lover. Lastly, Brighton offered them a chock of rubber to wedge between their teeth to keep from crying out. The chock of rubber was universally accepted. Then Vauchon's man began to flail them. Notwithstanding the Vermont doctor's orders, Magruder required a gulp of liquor as the body of Adnizzio, the first struck, contorted against the tree bark in agony.

Magruder marveled at the expertise of Brighton with a whip. Vauchon's lackey, dressed in newly purchased ski clothes, fur boots and comic Santa Claus hat with a jingle of bells at its peak, set gravely to his task, flogging them alternately in turn through twenty-three full sets, either laying the leather full across them with a fierce smack! sound or stinging them violently with the thong at the whip's end. Not a drop of blood was drawn on any of the three. Halfway through, Matland apparently passed out and slumped down at the knees, the cuffs, as they were intended, holding him flush against the tree bark. Adnizzio spat out his rubber chock and sobbed audibly, stiffening and yelping each time the snake crossed his flesh; the two great tires of fat that overflowed his belt line on either side of McFarland's girth quivered violently all the while. Grimacing and wincing, everyone drank a little except for Carruthers, who professed to want no alcohol at all. When he was done, Brighton rolled up his whip and laid great handfuls of snow on the backs of the three, all of whom were uniformly sobbing now. Over and over again the whip master assured them that his task was ended; the three turned away from their trees after Brighton unlocked the cuffs from Matland, and absurdly, though somehow perfectly, everyone congratulated them on their splendid courage.

McFarland took a long bite on a scotch bottle and whimpered to know if the whipping would leave scars. Adnizzio and Matland drank also, both wiping at their rheumy eyes with handkerchiefs.

"Not scars, Justin," Brighton told him bemusedly, his eyes twinkling, addressing any one of them familiarly now for the first time. "There were no cuts, so there'll be no scars. Some welts, black and blue marks for a time, but they'll go away. Nothing to remember your little humiliation like this, if I may show you. . . ."

They watched perplexed as Brighton pulled off the ski jacket, then yanked a turtleneck sweater over his head so that he was stripped to the waist like the three he had whipped. When he turned about and offered his back to the assemblage, the collective gasp was appalled. McFadden and Welsh even whistled out loud: The black flesh of Brighton's back was an infinite crisscross of long and short scars. They could have been made only by the lashings of a whip. Ingrid Deutsch actually placed a finger on the back, began tracing the high ridges of the more prominent scars.

"Didn't I ever show you these, boss?" he inquired of

Vauchon. When he turned to face them, there were actual tears in his eyes. Reflexively perhaps, McFarland the wounded handed the other his scotch bottle.

"No you didn't, Brighton. How did it happen?"

"It was a cliché, boss. It happened in Georgia after an altercation with a white man. The very first year I had arrived in the United States. A grave and unexpected injustice let me tell you."

"Do you feel better after what you've done today, Brighton?" Magruder asked distantly, seeing the elaborate deception, yet somehow totally unoffended by it.

"Distinctly better, Coach Magruder."

"Congratulations then. A little something seems to have been appeased in everyone's case today, I'd say. We should go now, gentlemen. Our business is finished."

Adnizzio, McFarland, Matland and Brighton dressed once more and they started out of the ravine up over the ridge again, heading for the condominium, Magruder being carried as before, though this time, with a trail broken, the way was not so difficult for his bearers. At the top of the ridge, previously unseen, Ernie Drapeau, the trooper, leaned against a tree.

"What was that business all about, coach?" he asked. It was not a police interrogator's voice. He seemed affected with a mild curiosity. Nothing more.

"A little tribal justice, Officer Drapeau. All in the family, you know."

"Tribal justice, huh? Well, I guess it doesn't cost the poor beleaguered taxpayer anything."

"You're quite right, it doesn't."

"I'm to assume then that your accident on the ski lift

and Sterling Lloyd Kasprzak's untimely heart attack so many years ago are now ancient history, huh?"

"Yes, all gone and forgotten, officer."

The cop shrugged: "Have it your way, Magruder. Only one thing. I want all of you people . . ."

Magruder interrupted him: "We are. We're leaving Vermont this very afternoon."

The procession filed past Drapeau and headed down toward the condominiums. In another half hour, when Magruder was helped into Adnizzio's Cadillac for the return to New Jersey, he supposed that it was for good and all.

PART II

STERLING LLOYD'S JUSTICE

CHAPTER 19

First Crack
in the Wall

The real justice of Sterling Lloyd Kasprzak began nearly a month after the flogging of Adnizzio, McFarland and Matland at Killington. In the interim, Magruder went to his sister's house in Queens to mend. It was not unpleasant. They sat for hours of every day in her kitchen drinking endless cups of tea on the oilcloth over her table, perusing the boxes of faded old photographs of the Magruder past, their parents, aunts and uncles, cousins forgotten or dead, photos of Florence.

She had been truly beautiful in a special way, Magruder thought. Demure and shy (invariably she always cast down her eyes when she spoke, after the first few moments of contact), it was her fragility that had attracted him to her in the beginning. In the end she had proved too fragile indeed: She had borne him no sons, died gasping for air because of her asthmatic condition. Once, about ten years after their wedding, his passion to have children became a bitter frustration he could no longer conceal; he had considered trying to have the marriage annulled. It was Rosalind, his sister, who drank tea with him daily now, who had talked him out of it almost thirty years before.

There were pictures of her husband. Magruder had never liked him. A Jew, a produce wholesaler who dressed too flashily and drove big expensive cars when Magruder had not even owned a car during the first eight years of his marriage, he had always managed to unnerve Magruder, making him feel uncomfortable with his munificence in restaurants or at the theater or at films, the certainty that he had gobs of money to hurl around when Magruder had, if anything, too little. By degrees, too, Feldman had taken Rosalind away from him, made her into Rosalind Feldman so that ties with old friends (even with her brother) had gradually weakened, then seemed completely to dissolve. The change in her was appreciable: She spoke differently, dressed differently, became almost Jewish herself, it seemed to Magruder, in the way she thought and acted. She stopped going to Mass, viewed the rhythms of Magruder's Catholicism with a faint bemusement as if his persuasion were very childlike. He grew cautious of the easy reference to seasons like Lent and Advent, the impending holy days when he was around her. After a time, when she entered her house, she automatically touched a kiss to the mezuzah on the door post. Then, all her friends were Jewish and Magruder felt like a complete outsider. During an interval of five years until her husband's death, he had not laid eyes on her once.

"Sam was a good man, Egil," she said to him, reading his thought perhaps. "He was always kind to me."

"He made me uncomfortable with all the money he threw around when I didn't have any."

"He was compensating. He was afraid of you because

you were a football coach and he was lousy at sports."
She laughed. "Whenever you came to visit he'd spend
the week beforehand memorizing statistics. When we decided to marry, he forced himself to read the sports page
every day even though he'd never read it before. He always wanted you to find him interesting. He wanted you
to approve of him."

Magruder smiled whimsically, thinking that it all might
have been otherwise: "Curious. He knew so much about
the game I always thought he was being superior. Conde-
scending perhaps, as if I should have been coaching the
Jets or somebody like that. . . ."

"Before he died he asked me never to tell you about
memorizing the statistic books."

"He was a proud man," Magruder offered helpfully.
Still he did not like Sam Feldman.

Nicholas the Tedesco and his betrothed, Theresa
Bugalli, came by at least twice a week for dinner. The
first time Rosalind prepared the meal and everyone ate
politely. Each time after that, by tacit agreement, Theresa
Bugalli cooked and everyone ate immoderately. With
their meals they drank wine, ate by candlelight at
Nicholas the Tedesco's request, listened to Vivaldi and
Bach cantatas. They made plans for the move to Florida
and Magruder saw the absolute wisdom of having
Theresa Bugalli along for his second retirement as resi-
dent cook. They planned to leave for Naples in late February after Theresa and Nicholas' marriage, the day after
the doctor (who confirmed that Magruder would walk
the rest of his days with a limp and a cane) decided it was
appropriate to remove his leg cast. They spoke no more of

Sterling Lloyd, Adnizzio, McFarland or Matland: There was nothing more to say.

On the third Sunday of January, the Tedesco drove the Buick, which was kept now in his driveway in Jersey City, across the Hudson and East River to Queens to take Magruder to Secaucus for Mass and the first reading of the bans announcing the impending marriage of Nicholas Amadeus Morelli and Theresa Fruschetta Bugalli. They enjoyed a champagne brunch with the Celestiale Quartet after the Mass.

On the twenty-seventh of January, a Tuesday morning, the first date of three that Magruder would circle in black pencil on the calendar of Rosalind's kitchen, the Tedesco called breathlessly at 9:00 A.M. Magruder stood up to answer the phone.

"Egil, this is Nicholas. Are you sitting or standing?"

"Standing."

"You'd better sit. Are you sitting?"

"Yes." Magruder laughed. "I am now. What's the matter? Did someone leave you money? Is something wrong with Theresa?"

"It's McFarland. He's dead."

"What? Jesus Christ, are you serious?" Magruder stood bolt upright at the news, hobbled little steps. Rosalind hurried to the living-room phone.

"I'm not kidding you, Egil. It happened yesterday afternoon down in the pine barrens near Manahawkin. Our three friends went down for a little target practice and only two came home. McFarland dropped a loaded shotgun and it went off. Vincent said it blew off half his face. He was dead before they even got him out of the woods to the car. His funeral is two days from now, closed coffin. They took his wife off to the looney bin last night. Vincent said it was awful. He's a doctor and thought he'd seen it all, but he can't keep any food in his stomach."

"Were they skeet shooting? Were they on a target range?" An absurd thought occurred to Magruder. But it could not be: There was simply no reason for it.

"I don't think so. There's nothing but woods down there. No, in fact, Vincent said they were shooting at beer cans."

"With a shotgun?"

"Don't ask me, Egil. I don't know anything about guns. I don't want to know either. Poor McFarland. Are you going to the funeral?"

"Yes, of course. I'll phone the others. They may be able to come East for it. Where's it to be held?"

"Same church as Aurelia Modesti's wedding. Do you want me to come across to Queens for you?"

"No, that's all right. I'll get Rosalind to drive me over. Good Lord, I just don't know what to say."

In two days they drove to Red Bank, New Jersey, in the last car of Sam Feldman's life, a huge boxcar of a black Lincoln that Rosalind always joked she kept around only because it looked so good at funerals. And she went to many funerals these days, apparently.

Justin McFarland was buried in a closed coffin by his children while Rita, his wife, lay sedated at a private psychiatric clinic near Princeton. Adnizzio and Matland, both ashen-faced, with Adnizzio visibly twitching, sat with their wives in the same pew as the McFarland children. McFadden, Welsh, Vauchon and Brighton, Albert Deutsch and the newlyweds, Emmett and Ingrid Carruthers, sat all together in a single pew looking decidedly bewildered about McFarland's dying. Magruder and Rosalind sat with Nicholas the Tedesco and Theresa Bugalli and the four members of the Celestiale Quartet. From the altar, the celebrant—the same nervous, acne-covered priest who had married the Modestis not long before—spoke unconvincingly of the capriciousness of Fate, neatly extracting his God from responsibility for the thing. Afterward, the hundred or so mourners filed out the side doors and into the snow-covered churchyard, where they lowered McFarland into the earth. Eric and Judith Matland cried copiously at the graveside over the loss of their cohort. In a distant corner of the graveyard, Vincent Adnizzio leaned against a fence, supported, as ever, by the strong Angelina, and retched and vomited bottomlessly all through the graveside ceremony and afterward as well. When the celebrant was done with his praying, everyone threw a handful of earth onto the lid of Justin McFarland's coffin, and began filing quietly off toward their cars.

The St. Anselm's first stringers, Brighton and Ingrid, the Bugalli-Morellis, and the Celestiale foursome gathered about Magruder and Rosalind as Magruder hobbled with a cane to the side of the old Lincoln for the return trip to Queens. The smoke of their breathing in the cold congealed to an actual cloud above their heads. Even over the general noise of cars starting and moving off, they heard Adnizzio heaving his bilge in the distance. The Matlands walked tearfully by them, vaguely acknowledging them, shepherding McFarland's children home.

"Poor Justin," McFadden spoke quietly after a time. "What a way to go."

"Vincent's really taking it to heart," Albert Deutsch said, jerking his head back toward the graveyard. "He sounds like he's just about to kick off himself."

"Vincent felt so impotent," Nicholas the Tedesco said tearfully. "Here he was a doctor and could do absolutely nothing for Justin. He didn't even have his bag in the car with him. His friend died in his arms and all he could do was cry. Such a tragedy . . ."

They all shook their heads sadly at the notion, then stood shuffling about in the cold for a time.

"Well, somebody say something," Jack Welsh urged.

"One down and two to go," Vauchon's Brighton said unexpectedly. They all studied him closely, Vauchon more speculatively than anyone. Since the trial and punishment in Vermont, Vauchon seemed to hold him somewhat in awe: The day of the automatic reprimand was evidently over for good.

"Really, Brighton? Do you think so?" Magruder asked him. Brighton had a seer's contemplative look about him. Magruder addressed the oracle from a long way off.

"Uh huh. The rot in the root is twenty-three years old, coach. The tree has got to die."

After that, for sure, nobody said anything else.

Rosalind drove Magruder back to Queens and they spoke not a single word all the way home.

CHAPTER 20

Second Crack
in the Wall

Alas, Brighton, the oracle, gave faultless prophecy.

Some three weeks later, on the eighteenth of February, the second day circled in black on the wall calendar of Rosalind's kitchen, Magruder heard the news that Vincent and Angelina Adnizzio were both dead.

The word came to him at 1:30 in the afternoon, just after lunch, as he and Rosalind played casino at the kitchen table amid the clutter of their lunch dishes. He was totally unprepared for it: Curiously, the bizarre reality of McFarland's death had swiftly receded, become replaced by his preoccupation with courting the minister's sister-in-law from New Hampshire. They had exchanged letters several times, then Magruder had phoned her and asked her to New York for a few days of dinners and plays and visits to museums like the Guggenheim and the Whitney that Magruder had never had the opportunity to visit in the past. To his delight she accepted, though she declined to stay at Rosalind's house. She would stay at the apartment of friends in Manhattan instead.

On their second night together, in a small French restaurant, she had asked him, "What is it you want of me, Egil?"

"Nothing yet. My wife is too soon dead."

"I understand."

They lay the groundwork, however, talking of Naples, Florida, laughing at the notion of a senior citizens' commune. He described, with his limited capacity for rapture, how Theresa Bugalli cooked. She categorized herself as a meticulous housekeeper, spoke of her obsession with cleanliness. It would do: He decided then and there he would ask for her hand when six months had elapsed from the day of Florence's burial.

That afternoon, over their hand of casino, Rosalind spoke pleasurably of Patience Windham of Laconia, New Hampshire, when the telephone rang. Magruder reached to the wall for the receiver. It was Theresa Bugalli.

"Egil! Egil, this is Theresa! You won't believe what happened, Egil!" Her fear, the edge of her hysteria raced at him over the wire. He lurched to his feet yet another time and Rosalind hurried to the living-room extension. Behind Theresa's staccato blubberings he could hear the incredible wail of a man's crying that could only be the Tedesco.

"What's wrong, Theresa? Did something happen to Nicholas?"

"Egil, it's the Adnizzios! Vincent and Angelina are both dead!"

"No! No! No! No! No!" He was braying now, the moan of disbelief come from a bottomless place inside him. "Theresa . . . it's not possible!"

"Egil, come to Secaucus right away! Please! Make

Rosalind drive you over. Nicholas is out of his mind! I'm afraid he'll do something terrible! I called the doctor, Egil. I'm going to make him give Nicholas something to sleep. Please come now!"

Magruder had no words: Some cruel god had spawned a nightmare. He stared through a kitchen window at the stubby lawn of a neighbor's backyard where wisps of dry snow blew about, his own thoughts like those very wisps now, considering vaguely that there was only Matland left, Matland vulnerable and naked as a lone archery target before the wrath of that god with an infinite supply of arrows, a casualness of time. He must warn Matland! But warn him against what? Perhaps that out there, beyond life and through the narrow funnel that led to the universe of souls, the hobgoblin that was Kasprzak had finally made a friend . . . ?

"Egil! Egil, can you hear me?" It was Theresa again. He was about to answer, but Rosalind cut in: "Theresa, this is Rosalind. Stay calm. We'll leave now. We'll be there as soon as possible."

His sister replaced the receiver at the same time as Magruder simply let his own fall against the wall and, like a maddened automaton, began pounding the kitchen table top with his cane, scattering the cards and smashing the leftover luncheon dishes and cups, slashing so intensely against the unknown that he actually broke the cane in two. His sister hung back, fearing, until Magruder sat down again, sobbing into his arms: "Rosalind, what's happening? What's going on? They're all dying! Sterling Lloyd wouldn't have wanted it this way."

She patted his shoulder consolingly: "We should go to

New Jersey, Egil. Theresa sounds like she has her hands full over there. Let's go now."

At Secaucus, in Theresa Bugalli's house, heavy with a past of uneradicable smells, old furniture and wallpaper, framed photographs and lights flickering before numerous saints and a plenitude of the Virgin, Nicholas the Tedesco was already cried out, sat calmly now at the dining-room table drinking tea that he laced with his wine. Theresa Bugalli worked a rosary through her fingers. Aunt Olympia watched a soap opera on the television in the living room. They had not bothered to turn on the sound for her.

"When did it happen, Nicholas?" Magruder asked as he sat down heavily across the table from the Tedesco.

"This morning at the house in Red Bank. About eight-thirty, before Vincent was scheduled to leave for the hospital."

"How?"

"They had a shoot-out with the police right on the front lawn. One cop dead, two wounded. Vincent took a single bullet through the heart. Angelina had about ten slugs in her."

"But why? How could it happen?" The poet had begun crying again, choking, as if he could not put the words in sequence to tell the terrible story.

"Egil, it was Matland! It was all Matland's fault! Egil, he's awful! The worst person in the whole world."

"What did he do, Nicholas? Tell me everything. Begin at the beginning."

He spoke calmly now, grimly amused, despite every-

thing, that he had frantically considered warning
Matland of a danger when Matland had been the real
danger all along. Something he had always known about
Matland, some seed of corruption or cowardice lodged
within him, some rift in his character, something unmanly
and self-serving, untrustworthy, sneaking and yellow had
just flowered to perfection evidently.

"Matland fingered Vincent to the police for killing
McFarland. It's like you thought, Egil. It wasn't an accident," the Tedesco gasped. "Vincent shot Justin
McFarland right in the head. No wonder he was sick at
the funeral."

"Oh, my good God!" The words came from Rosalind.
She had begun crying now for the first time, shoving the
end of her scarf in her mouth.

"But why?" Magruder begged. "McFarland was dumb.
He was the least effectual of the three. For what reason
would Vincent kill him?"

"He kept a diary about Sterling Lloyd and the twenty-
three years. He'd been thinking about getting it edited
and taking it to a publisher, but he never did anything
about it until they came back from Vermont and everything seemed over and done with. He figured to make a
killing on it like those Watergate crooks who stand to get
rich from their crimes by publishing. But you're right, he
was dumb. He told everything, and Vincent and Matland
warned him they weren't going to have that stuff printed
about themselves. They tried to get him to burn the manuscript, but he wouldn't do it, so he's dead. Vincent and

Matland flipped a coin to see who was going to pull the trigger down there in the pine barrens and Vincent lost. . . ."

"They were doubtless using a two-headed coin provided by our friend Matland," Magruder said levelly. "I take it he was prepared to turn state's evidence and testify against Vincent?"

"Yes. He would've gotten off with very little. Vincent's lawyer got the whole story from the police this morning and told Vincent's brothers. Nobody knows where that manuscript is, so Matland must have it. Egil, it must have been terrible . . . terrible to die that way. When the police came to the house to arrest Vincent this morning, Angelina went berserk. She ran out the back door with Vincent's shotgun to get Matland. But Matland and his family had already cleared out and she ran back and started blasting at the cops. They said she kept screaming that nobody was taking her husband to jail. She died first. That's when Vincent started shooting with a handgun. He's the one who actually killed the cop before he got it himself. Oh, Egil . . . Egil, what a tragedy! It's an American tragedy in a little suburb in New Jersey. Who could have foreseen that anything like this might happen?"

Magruder had no answer. He thought of Angelina Adnizzio, her passion for living. He had an instant vision of her throbbing that morning on the Red Bank lawn in final agony, vital and raging against the interloper Death. For a moment he felt physical pain, intensely suffering as she must have suffered: It came to him then that perhaps he had even loved her a little. . . .

"Where's Matland now?" Magruder demanded savagely. "Where is that cowardly betrayer?"

"Nobody knows. The police must have him in protective custody. I went to a family council this morning at Rocco Adnizzio's place. I implored them to kill Matland. They can't. They're helpless. For once, with all their *garrottas* and guns, they're flat against the wall. If anything happens to Matland, the police would be on them in a minute. Matland is safe."

"No, he isn't," Magruder said stonily. He looked into the other room. Tears ran down the furrows of old Olympia's cheeks. On the TV screen before her, someone had died and was evidently being buried.

"What are you going to do, Egil?" the Tedesco asked, sniffling now, his voice coated with phlegm.

"I know what I have to do. But like Vincent's brothers, I just don't know how to do it."

In two days more the lovers Adnizzio were buried from the same church as McFarland was buried, the church in which their daughter was married. As before, Magruder sat with Rosalind, McFadden, Welsh, Vauchon and Brighton, Albert Deutsch, Emmett and Ingrid Carruthers, Nicholas the Tedesco, Theresa Bugalli and the four members of the Celestiale String Quartet. The coffins of the lovers lay side by side before the altar, Vincent's a dark and rich-looking mahogany, Angelina's snowy white like the coffin of a child. The young priest, grown more courageous by virtue of repetition evidently, spoke movingly on the theme proposed by Nicholas the Tedesco: that the affair was indeed an American tragedy, visited capriciously on this little town of New Jersey. There were perhaps four hundred mourners at the funeral. Matland was not in attendance, nor was any member of his family. But Magruder guessed he dwelt prominently in the minds of many there.

Afterward, when they lowered the twin coffins into the earth, the young Modestis had to be carried away from the graveside. Outside the churchyard, as before, the St. Anselm's stringers, Brighton and Ingrid, the Bugalli-Morellis and the Celestiale foursome gathered about Magruder and Rosalind as Magruder hobbled with a new cane to the door of Rosalind's black Lincoln.

"Well, Brighton, you were right," Magruder told him. "Where's Matland?"

"Not far from here, coach. He may even be watching us at this very moment."

They looked all about, suspecting his presence everywhere, Magruder certain however that he was holed up in some more distant place surrounded by police for protection.

"What are you going to do, coach?" Welsh asked the question after a time.

"I know what I have to do. I just can't do it until he surfaces."

"Could he be at Killington?"

"No. Vincent's brothers have already checked it out."

"He'll surface soon enough," Brighton prophesied again. "He's got McFarland's manuscript and he's itching to see a publisher with it. You'll hear from him in a while."

"I'm going to kill him when I find him," Magruder said distantly. "It has to be."

"Yes," Brighton agreed. There was a general garbled concensus about that, then nothing as they all quietly left for their cars.

CHAPTER 21

All Fall Down

With no news of Matland's whereabouts, they put off the move to Florida almost daily after the cast came off during the third week following the death of the Adnizzios. Magruder checked off the calendar every morning, began to despair of ever hearing from the betrayer, looked instead to the date in May when six months would have elapsed since Florence's burial.

Five weeks after the Adnizzio funeral he surfaced. Hearing Matland's voice in his sister's kitchen, Magruder resisted the urge to hurl imprecations at him, accuse him of the treachery he had committed. Rosalind was on the phone in the living room. Through a series of doors Magruder could see her hand signaling, admonishing him to remain calm.

It was a terrible thing you did, Eric, Magruder wanted to tell him. Worse than anything. You betrayed a trust that was hallowed by twenty-three years.

"We missed you at Vincent and Angelina's funeral, Eric," he told the traitor instead.

"I couldn't go, coach," Matland said with a fake earnestness. "I was so sick I couldn't get out of bed. Judy and I and the kids went to a motel after the shoot-out with the cops and just camped there for about a week."

Magruder did not snort at the lie, did not tell Matland that Angelina would have killed him if he had actually been in the house at the time of the shoot-out.

"Why did you phone, Eric?"

"Well, coach, there's a small problem I need to take care of."

"What is it?"

"Well, I've written a book, coach. . . ."

"Oh?"

"Yes. A book about us. You know, about Kasprzak and all the years we worried, and about how it turned out in the end. I mean, I thought the story should be told, coach."

"Am I in the story, Eric?"

"Yes, coach, of course."

"I'm quite flattered. By name?"

"Yes, coach."

"Well, it sounds enterprising. Have you got a publisher for it?"

"Yes, coach, I do. That's why I called you. I'd like you to sign a form the publisher has prepared releasing us from the possibility of a libel action."

"That seems presumptive, Eric. I haven't read the book after all."

"It treats you well, coach. It makes you a hero. There's nothing pejorative or demeaning at all."

"I'm flattered twice over, then."

"Will you meet with me, coach, to sign the release?"

"Yes, I suppose so. It doesn't seem the proper time to be obstinate with the lone survivor after everything that's happened." It came to him then that he knew how to do what he had to do.

"I'm scheduled to be in New York the day after tomorrow, coach, for lunch with my editor. Perhaps we could meet somewhere for a drink."

"I get too little exercise these days, Eric. I need to walk to get my legs back in some kind of shape. Why don't you oblige me and meet me for a stroll in Central Park?"

"In the park?" The voice seemed annoyed. "I thought a final drink in a quiet bar somewhere would be more like it."

"I've never enjoyed bars, Eric. You know that. Look for me on a bench on the downtown side of the West Seventy-second Street entry. I shouldn't be hard to find. I doubt there are many people in the park without a dog in early March."

"Well, OK, coach, we'll do it your way. I'll bring a pocket flask and we can have that drink anyhow. Is scotch OK?"

"Yes, that will be fine, Eric. What time will your lunch be over with?"

"About two-thirty, I think."

"Let's meet at three-thirty, then."

"All right, coach, see you then."

"Yes."

After Matland rang off, Magruder began calling the others, summoning them to New York.

It snowed that day, certainly the last snowfall of the year, large flakes of heavy wet stuff that barely stuck at all to the streets.

By three-thirty all the props were in place. Magruder waited on a bench, perhaps two hundred yards or so into the park from Central Park West. Out on the sidewalk, barely seen through the trees and over a low wall, the Celestiale Quartet played a street concert. Matland walked into the park right on schedule, looking surprisingly fit and very tanned. Magruder guessed he had been hiding out somewhere down in the islands.

"Coach . . . hello!"

"Hello, Eric, you look quite healthy."

"I spent some time in the islands. Down in the Grenadines. I took time off from work. Vincent and Angelina's deaths upset me very much."

"Yes, I can imagine. You'd known them so long. It was a terrible thing."

Matland took out a pint of scotch: "That quartet out there isn't bad." He nodded toward the Celestiale, evidently not remembering that they had played at the wedding of the young Modestis. "Strange that they're playing here just like that in the snow. It's kind of beautiful and sad."

Dimly through the trees, Magruder could see that perhaps twenty people were gathered about the musicians. Two cops on horses watched from the opposite curb. The Celestiale played the "Pavane for a Dead Infanta" that they had described to Magruder that morning. It was funereal music they agreed just perfect for the occasion of Matland's death.

Magruder set about the business of killing the traitor. He removed two plastic cups from a paper bag he carried, set them between himself and Matland on the bench.

"Thoughtful of you to remember to bring something to drink from, coach." Matland laughed. "If we sit here long enough in this snow we can have a little water with our scotch."

"Yes, I suppose we can." Magruder smiled at him. Matland poured both glasses half full of the straight scotch. Magruder took out the envelope the brothers Scanella had gotten that morning from their cousin the pharmacist in Newark, poured the white powder into the drink closest to Matland.

"What's that stuff, coach? Is it sugar or something?"

"It's potassium cyanide, Eric. It's a very powerful poison."

"What . . . ?" The fear leapt into his eyes that were very blue and defined in the middle of a deeply tanned face. Magruder picked up the glass and handed it to him: "The choice is yours, Eric. You don't have to drink this if you don't want to. I can't force you."

"Are you out of your fucking mind? You're damn right you can't force me. Nothing in the world is going to get me to lift that glass. . . ."

Magruder removed his hat: It was the prearranged signal. Before them, not twenty-five yards off, the others ascended the small hillock behind which they had waited, began fanning out in a half circle to cut off his escape. Matland looked desperately toward the street. The two mounted policemen moved slowly off uptown. Directly before them Myra Vauchon and Carlotta McFadden stood side by side, severe and beautiful in nearly identical fur coats. Matthew Vauchon, Brighton, Martin McFadden and Jack and Astrid Welsh formed the arc to the right. To the left were the Carrutherses and Albert and Marta Deutsch. Matland swung about, searching for an escape. Four of Vauchon's blacks from Chicago were there. A black nurse they brought with them supported a heavily sedated Rita McFarland.

"Why, coach . . . ?" The plea was a hoarse whisper. He grabbed Magruder's arm, began crying furiously, buried his head against the shoulder of Magruder's overcoat. "Coach . . . why?"

"You betrayed a sacred trust, Eric. You committed the worst crime of all. They were your teammates. You had a pact with them. If nothing else after twenty-three years, at least they trusted you."

"Vincent killed Justin, coach," he sobbed openly now. "It was Vincent, not me."

"You used a two-headed coin, Eric, when you flipped to see who would do it."

He looked at Magruder, broke into an absurd smile despite his crying that signaled the real beginning of his defeat.

"How did you know that, coach?"

"I know you, Eric. I've always understood many things about you. There are parts of you you're not even responsible for, sad as that seems. Like the way you were a yellow football player."

He sobbed bottomlessly, pleading with a two-handed grip on Magruder's arm. The snow was heavier now; Magruder watched it settle on Carlotta McFadden's bare head, wondered what havoc it might wreak on the perfection of her hair-do.

"What about Judy and the kids, coach? What will they do if I'm gone?"

"The same thing that Rita McFarland and her kids are doing, Eric. Trying to survive, I expect."

He alternately laughed and cried now. He was becoming quite mad. Magruder picked up the laced drink, handed it to him pointedly: "There's more of that white powder, Eric, so don't think about chucking this drink."

Matland took the plastic cup; surprisingly his hand was quite steady.

"It's ironic, coach. Here I was going to make all this money on the book. I mean, Cripes Almighty, who has a story like ours to tell? It's unique as hell when you think about it. Now, with all the unfinished sections, it'll probably never be published. . . ."

"Matthew Vauchon has already started a proceeding to make sure of that, Eric. This is the last day of the affair of Sterling Lloyd Kasprzak."

They sat quietly for a time now, listening to the melancholy notes of the funereal "Pavane" coming from the sidewalk.

"Will it hurt, coach?"

"What, Eric?"

"The poison. Is it very painful?"

"Yes, it will hurt. But it acts very quickly."

"I hate pain, coach."

"I want you to be brave, Eric. For once I want you to act like a man and put your cowardice behind you. The others are all here. Let them say of you that you died with dignity."

Magruder picked up his own drink. Reflexively, perfectly, they touched glasses. Matland seemed quite calm now, a genuinely sardonic look on his face. He turned swiftly and planted a kiss on Magruder's cheek: "That wasn't a Judas kiss, coach. That was for love."

"Thank you, Eric." Magruder felt an awful tightness in his throat that was completely unexpected. Matland smiled around at the half circle before him: "I'll say good-by to you now, everyone."

"Good-by, Eric . . . good-by . . . good-by . . ." Everyone's eyes were moist. Marta Deutsch collapsed sobbing on her husband's shoulder.

"I'll be heroic, coach. They'll never be able to say again that I was yellow or anything. . . ."

"It all depends on you, Eric."

"To the justice of Sterling Lloyd Kasprzak," Matland proposed a toast. Then he drained the glass in a single gulp as Magruder sipped at his own drink. Matland dropped the glass to the snow and took a grip on Magruder's arm with his two hands, squeezing forcefully on the arm as he fought the terrible pain, shuddering and gasping in his agony but never once crying out. In about two minutes he was dead. His hands gave up the grip and fell heavily onto Magruder's shoulder.

They stretched him out on the bench and covered him over with newspapers as they had planned, left the scotch bottle to give some veracity to the suggestion that he was a bum sleeping off a drunk. He grew cold already, perhaps: Thin wisps of snow began collecting on his head.

Then they disbanded, heading off in multiple directions, Magruder to the sidewalk to hear the Celestiale play the last strains of the very sad "Pavane." He waited only a minute until Nicholas the Tedesco and Theresa his wife pulled up in the Buick that was loaded down for the trip to Florida. They departed, Nicholas making a U-turn, then heading south as the quartet began packing their instruments for the return to New Jersey. They stopped for a moment at a mailbox just a bit above Columbus Circle where Magruder deposited two letters that dealt with unfinished business: the one to Patience Windham of Laconia, New Hampshire, and the other to Ernie Drapeau, the trooper of Rutland, Vermont.

R8